THE RINGS OF GRISSOM

TALES OF A FORMER SPACE JANITOR

JULIA HUNI

IPH MEDIA

Editing by Paula Lester of
Polaris Writing and Editing.
Cover designed by Les of German Creative.

Julia Huni
Visit my website at http://www.juliahuni.com

First Printing: Jan 2021

IPH Media

BOOKS BY JULIA HUNI

Colonial Explorer Corps Series:
The Earth Concurrence
The Grissom Contention
The Saha Declination

Recycled World Series:
Recycled World
Reduced World

Space Janitor Series:
The Vacuum of Space
The Dust of Kaku
The Trouble with Tinsel
Orbital Operations
Glitter in the Stars
Sweeping S'Ride
Triana Moore, Space Janitor (the complete series)

Tales of a Former Space Janitor
The Rings of Grissom

Planetary Spin Cycle

Krimson Empire (with Craig Martelle):
Krimson Run
Krimson Spark
Krimson Surge
Krimson Flare

If you enjoy this story, sign up for my newsletter, at juliahuni.com and you'll get free prequels and short stories, plus get notifications when the next book is ready.

For my friends Jim and Nancy,
who knew a thing or two about marriage.
We miss you, Jim.

ONE

THE BARISTA IS in a foul mood. Her nametag, labeling her Sunshine, hangs at an odd angle from the top of her apron. Her hair sticks out crazily, as if she combed it with the micro-whisk she's using to foam a venti mocha-cherry skinny-fat mud-pi-chito.

She slams the huge mug and saucer onto the counter and bellows, "Train!"

Ty O'Neill and I look around the coffee shop. We're the only occupants. "Is that Triana?" he asks with his shiny smile as he approaches the counter.

"Who else would it be?" she snarls. "Here's your plain coffee, too." She drops a mug a few centimeters above the faux granite. It lands with a crack, the steaming beverage splashing out.

"Is something wrong?" He's too nice to just take the coffee and run.

"Whatever gave you that idea?" Sunshine spits out. "Everything is peachy!"

O'Neill nods uncertainly, takes the cups, and drips across the room to our table. "I'm not sure how this is going to taste."

"The machine dispenses the ingredients." I blow on the foam. "Hard to mess that up."

He sits across from me and smiles. As always, it sends a flutter of

1

warmth through my chest. His eyes lock onto mine, and I'm lost in their chocolate beauty.

After a few seconds, it feels a little weird. "Are you just going to stare at me all morning?"

He laughs. "Sorry. I'm just happy to be here with you."

The door swings open, and two women in Peacekeeper uniforms enter the cafe. Sunshine looks up with another scowl, but the officers ignore her. "Are you Annabelle Morgan?" the shorter one asks.

O'Neill goes still and turns to face them. "What's this about?"

"Sera Morgan, you need to come with us." The taller one—her nametag reads Watson—flicks her holo-ring, and a message pings me. "You don't have a visa."

"She just arrived on the *CSS Vesteralen*," Ty says. "The cruise ticket includes a tourism visa."

"Sera Morgan, your visa expired when the ship departed." The women ignore O'Neill.

I pull up the message on my holo-ring. It's from the Peacekeepers, detailing a list of infractions I've committed by being on the planet and a list of fines and penalties for each infraction.

"The ship only left twenty minutes ago," O'Neill says.

"And she wasn't on it." Watson pins a glare on O'Neill. "Who are you, her lawyer?"

"I'm her security detail," O'Neill says, flicking his identification to the peacekeeper.

"This says you work for SK2, not Sera Morgan." The midget—Kato—eyes him speculatively.

"Sera Morgan is the daughter of the chair of the SK2 board." O'Neill stands, staring down at Kato.

"And on the planet illegally." Watson straightens her spine, bringing her eyes level with O'Neill's hairline. She gives him an icy once-over that would impress my mother and turns to me. "Sera Morgan, come with us. Now."

It's odd that they're immune to O'Neill's charm. Most women find him irresistible. Most men, too, for that matter. Maybe they're a new breed of android. I get to my feet and put a hand on O'Neill's arm. "I'm sure we can fix this. Let's go with them and work it out."

O'Neill's gaze softens when he looks at me. "I can take care of this."

"No, you can't." Kato's hand moves to her side. She's carrying a weapon, but her fingers reach toward the handcuffs clipped to a ring on the belt. "Sera Morgan must come with us."

I pick up my mud-pi-chito. "Can we get these to go?" I ask Sunshine.

She growls. I take that as a yes and carry the mugs to the counter. She dumps the coffee into plastek cups and slaps a pair of lids on the counter next to them. "Make sure you recycle 'em. That'll be two more credits."

Before O'Neill can move, I flick the credits from my holo-ring and snap the lids onto the cups. "Thanks for your help." I add a huge tip, hoping to brighten her day. And that she'll remember me if I disappear into the Grissom legal system, never to be seen again.

Not that I'm worried about that. Grissom is a civilized planet. As far as I know.

Coffee in hand, we step into the sunny street. It's more crowded than when we arrived—the *Vesteralen* departed shortly after dawn, and I got off just before it left. The two peacekeepers flank us, and civilians on the street give us a wide berth.

We arrive in front of a marble building with tall columns and wide steps. The words "Grissom Justice Department" are engraved in weird, spiky-looking letters across the top. Inside, O'Neill is directed to a waiting area.

"I'm her security detail," he protests. "I need—"

"You need to take a seat, Ser." Watson smiles—an expression that doesn't reach her eyes. "Surely, you aren't inferring the Grissom Justice Department would do anything to endanger your client."

O'Neill holds up his hands. "Of course not." He leans in to give me a quick kiss. "I'll be right over there."

"Security, huh?" Kato mutters as she opens a door. "That's not what we call it."

Watson chuckles and herds me through the door. It closes behind us with a strange feeling of finality.

IT TURNS out leaving a cruise ship before your ticketed departure station causes problems. Who knew? When I left the *CSS Vesteralen* at Station Cristoforetti, I didn't worry about my luggage. Or my pre-paid ticket to SK2. Or my entrance fee to the Dancing in the Stars competition.

Actually, I didn't know anything about that last one until I got the bill this morning. It came in a few minutes after we arrived at the coffee shop. Someone must have signed me up—probably Joan. She's on the *CSS Caledonia,* but she appears to have friends throughout Pleiades StarCruises.

I had abandoned my cabin on the ship because I couldn't let O'Neill think I didn't care about him. He'd taken leave to visit his family here on Grissom while I returned to SK2. After all the misunderstandings between us, I knew it was more about getting away from me than seeing them. Vanti, his old partner and another SK2 security agent, was returning to SK2 with me and R'ger Chaturvedi.

"You took the shuttle from Cristo at oh-six-twenty?" James Shu-Arya, an immigration agent assigned to my case, sits across the metal table from me. He makes a note on his tablet and sighs. He wears a threadbare suit, and his bad comb-over and the deep grooves by his eyes and mouth show he hasn't had any rejuv. I hope his apparent destitution is not an indication of his professional abilities.

"Yeah." I shove a hand through my own messy hair. "I needed to see Ty —Ser O'Neill—and the ship was scheduled to leave at six-thirty."

"You had no intention of returning to the ship?" He sighs again and yawns.

"What makes you say that?" I'm not sure admitting to anything is a good idea.

"You packed a bag." He points to the small tote bag laying by the door. "And you left the station ten minutes before the ship sailed." He raises his eyebrows but doesn't make eye contact.

"I didn't realize it was a big deal." My fingers tap the table. I shove my hands in my lap. "I can pay the fines."

"Are you trying to bribe me?" His head pops forward, and he fixes his bloodshot eyes on me. "Because I'd be okay with that."

"No, I'm trying to do what's right." I indicate my holo-ring. "I can flick the credits over right now if that helps."

"Aw," he moans. I'm not sure if he was hoping for a payout or that he'd be able to shake me down for attempted bribery. "I'll take you to the desk sergeant." He pushes the chair back and stands. "This way."

He leads me through the barren hallway to a barred window at the end. "Sergeant Nenge will take your payment."

"Name?" Nenge asks.

"Triana Moore," I say automatically. Then I shake my head. "Or Annabelle Morgan."

Nenge's eyes flicker with interest. "Which is it?"

"Both. Annabelle Morgan is my birth name, but I use Triana Moore—for privacy." My mother is one of the wealthiest people on Station Kelly-Kornienko, which means she could buy most of the galaxy if she thought it would turn a profit. I ran away when I was eighteen, changed my name, and attended the Techno-Inst. Then, in a move that would make my therapist—if I had one—a star on the vid circuits, I took a job as a maintenance worker on SK2. I lived under the radar for a few years until I met Ty—and came to my mother's attention once again.

I flick my holo-ring to bring up the PayNow app, and Nenge sends me the bill. It's an astronomical amount—or would be for a maintenance worker. Fortunately, Annabelle Morgan's account holds more than enough credits to cover it.

"Thank you for visiting Grissom," Nenge says, his voice devoid of sarcasm.

"My pleasure." I glance at the door. "Can I go now?"

"Please." His hand moves, and the door clicks open, accompanied by an ear-splitting buzz. "It'll stop once you go through."

"Thanks." I hike my bag onto my shoulder and hurry out.

TWO

THE DOOR SNAPS SHUT, and the buzz stops. I'm standing in a large, echoing room. A couple of bubbles with the word "Peacekeeper" emblazoned across them hang from cables on the far side. I seem to be in the garage.

"Hello?" I call. No one answers.

I turn and pound on the door, but nothing happens.

"Ah, the fugitive."

I spin around to face Watson and Kato. "Can you tell me how to get back to Agent O'Neill? He's waiting for me."

"It'll be a long wait." Watson takes my arm and hurries me toward the first bubble. "You are going back to the *Vesteralen*."

"But I don't want to go back to the ship!" I try to dig in my heels, but she pushes harder. The woman is like a tank. "O'Neill is staying here!"

"He's a resident." Kato opens the bubble door, still fingering her handcuffs. "He can come and go as he pleases. But you're an illegal alien, and you're being deported."

"I paid the fines!" I protest as they shove me into the back of the bubble. Automated security restraints wrap around my body and pin my arms to the armrests.

"Those fines were for breaking the law," Watson says. "You still don't have a visa, so you need to leave." The two women take seats at the front of the bubble, and a purple haze snaps across the space between us. A force shield—probably intended to keep violent offenders away from the arresting officers.

"I can get a visa!" I cry. My words bounce back to me. Watson and Kato speak, but I can't hear what they're saying. The force shield has an audio damper built in. If I could access my holo-ring, I might be able to circumvent it, but my hands are immobilized.

The bubble pops off its charging cable, and we shoot out of the garage. A wailing siren blares as we streak into the street. The bubble lifts off the ground, travelling a couple of meters above the road to avoid traffic. In minutes, we've reached the shuttle port.

Watson releases the restraints. Before I can flick my holo-ring, Kato has her cuffs on my wrist. She yanks me out of the seat by one arm and twists it around behind me as she shoves me out of the bubble. Watson grabs my right arm and pulls it around for Kato to lock the cuffs. Then they push me across the tarmac.

An unmarked shuttle, small and sleek, stands on the apron. As I stumble across the plascrete, I try to send a message to O'Neill. It's hard to do with my arms behind my back, but I manage to send something. At this point, I'm not sure who it went to or if it was gibberish, but at least someone will know something is wrong. Or they'll think they got drunk-dialed.

The women hand me off to another peacekeeper and shut the shuttle hatch in my face. I turn to the black-clad officer, but he's wearing a mirrored helmet and has no nametag. "What's your name?" I ask.

"You can call me Bill," he says, his voice deep and clear. "Get yourself strapped in. We have a launch slot in three minutes."

"Are you really going to chase after the *Vesteralen* and dump me?" If I move slowly and keep him distracted, maybe we'll miss our launch window.

"Not going to work, sweetheart," Bill says. He's already strapped into the single seat in the front of the cabin and is swiping icons on his control holos. "I've never missed a launch, and I'm not going to ruin my record for you. If you don't want to get splatted across the back of the cabin, you'd best get strapped in."

"But what about my cuffs?" I turn so he can see my hands. He flicks a finger, and the cuffs fall away from my wrists.

"Fancy." I kick them across the cabin and move toward the three seats in the rear.

"You might want to pick those up," Bill calls over his shoulder. "Loose items become projectiles in high-velocity situations."

It sounds like a quote, but I can't place it. I stomp across the tiny cabin and snag the cuffs, shoving them into my bag. Then I strap into a seat and activate the messaging app on my holo-ring.

The first message is a non-deliverable with a string of gibberish in the subject line. So much for my behind-the-back message sending. I swipe it away and write a quick text to O'Neill. When I flick send, nothing happens.

A yellow icon pops up near Bill's head, and he swipes it away. "Sorry, external messages are quarantined. You'll have to wait until we reach the *Vesteralen* to send."

I grind my teeth and start digging into their security system.

WHEN WE DOCK with the *CSS Vesteralen*, I still haven't cracked the message quarantine. I consider leaving a couple of my favorite trouble-making viruses behind then decide burning my bridges might not be my best action. I may want to return to Grissom someday—especially since I'm planning on a long-term relationship with O'Neill.

"Airlock is sealed." Bill releases his seat straps and turns to face me, drifting away from the floor. "You're free to go, Sera Morgan."

"Gee, thanks, Bill." I spit the words out one at a time. "Tell Watson and Kato I had a great time."

Bill's mirrored visor clears. Brown eyes stare at me from a face that's familiar but subtly wrong.

"Are you Ty's… brother?"

His lips press together. "Cousin. You aren't welcome on Grissom."

The hatch pops open, and Bill pushes me toward it. Without gravity to hold me to the floor, I can't stop. I swing at the seat restraint and miss, sending myself into a spin. "What? Why not?"

Bill grabs my shoulder, stopping my rotation. "He always was too soft when it comes to pretty girls."

The words sting. What other pretty girls is he talking about? "Please, just let me talk to him before you deport me. Take me back down."

"Not happening. Goodbye, Sera Morgan." He shoves me out of the ship.

I grab for a handle, but I'm already in the inflatable airlock. The hatch slams shut behind me, and another opens a few meters away.

A face looks out. "Welcome back to the *CSS Vesteralen*, Sera Morgan. Ser Chaturvedi has been asking about you. Please push yourself this direction. Or do you require assistance in free-fall?"

"I'm fine," I grumble. I could refuse to move—the shuttle can't leave until the inflatable airlock is empty and resealed. Bill might want to space me, but the *Vesteralen* officer isn't going to let that happen. He might use a grapple to drag me inside, though, and that will be embarrassing. Besides, I need to send that message to O'Neill, and I need to be inside the ship to do that.

I push my feet against the shuttle hatch and sail through the airlock. A quick flip puts me beside the officer, my knees flexing as the ship's gravity pulls me to the floor.

"Nicely done, Sera Morgan."

What a brown-noser. "I prefer Triana." I settle my bag on my shoulder and flick my holo-ring. The message has already gone through, and there's a response from O'Neill. "Sera Moore, if you insist on formality. I need to get back to my stateroom."

"Let me take your bag, Sera." The officer leaves the name off altogether. I can't really blame him. My mother, Dame Imogen Morgan, is a major stockholder in the Pleiades StarCruise Line. They're much more concerned about upsetting her than me.

"I'm good," I holler over my shoulder as I bolt for the stairway.

The door to my suite whooshes open at my arrival. I hurry in, slinging my bag onto the plush sofa.

"Back so soon?" Lindsay "Vanti" Fioravanti lounges in the doorway of the second bedroom.

"Not now, Vanti." I hurry past her and into the larger cabin. A huge bed takes up half the room. Floor-to-ceiling windows provide a spectacular view of the stars. This cabin is on the dark side of the ship—the starboard side is facing the sun. If I wanted to see that view, I could, of course, since the windows operate as a viewscreen.

Ignoring the incredible view of the ringed Grissom, I flick my holo-ring to lock the door. Then I pull up Ty's message. We're far enough from the planet already that real-time communication is impossible without specialized equipment.

His head and shoulders appear in my palm. "What the zark happened?" He takes a turn around the small room—it looks like the waiting area of the Peacekeeper station. I thought Watson said comms didn't work there? "That peacekeeper—Kato—said you went back to the ship. Call me. You owe me an explanation. Tell me why you changed your mind." He cuts off without another word.

Changed my mind? Those peacekeepers deported me and then lied about it! Something is not right.

I pull up my message app and explain what happened. I send the message through normal channels. Then I encrypt a copy of it and send it to O'Neill's secure SK2 message account. If the peacekeepers lied to him about me, they might be censoring his messages as well. But SK2 employs the best security credits can purchase.

Now I just have to hope he's dedicated enough to check his work messages, even when he's on vacation. I drop onto the bed, covering my eyes with my arm. *Ty, check your work mail. Ty, check your work mail.*

THREE

POUNDING on the door wakes me. I didn't sleep well last night, and my early morning departure from the ship didn't help. I check my messages, but nothing new has arrived.

Why would the Grissom Peacekeepers lie to O'Neill about my motives? Time to dig deeper into that mystery.

"Triana, open the door." Vanti pounds again.

I flick my holo-ring, and the door slides open. "What?"

"Did you hear about the shuttle?"

"What shuttle?" I roll over.

"The one you came up on." She crosses the room and plops down on the bed.

"What about it?" I hope Bill dinged a satellite and has to pay a fine.

"It exploded."

I sit upright, my heart pounding. My stomach lurches and churns. "Is Bill—what happened?"

Vanti shakes her head. "The pilot is alive. Those passenger shuttles are built with a safety capsule—the personnel section gets blasted away if anything happens to the engine. He had a rough re-entry, but the capsule landed intact."

Relief floods through me and a little guilt. I didn't want Bill hurt, just fined. That'll teach me to wish evil on others. Karma, right?

"R'ger is asking about you," she goes on. "And it's time for dinner. I've been tasked to remind you that you're representing the SK'Corp board of directors on this voyage and are expected to behave accordingly." The last part comes out like she's memorized it. Her lip quirks before I can ask, and she flicks a message up on the window-screen.

I stare at it. "The Ice Dame doesn't leave anything to chance, does she?" The message tells Vanti it is her responsibility to "ensure Sera Morgan understands she is representing the SK'Corp board…"

Vanti curtseys then grasps an imaginary something and pulls it down in front of her face. "And, scene. All those acting lessons are finally paying off."

"You took acting?" I roll off the bed and to my feet.

"Only in the academy." She leans a shoulder against the door jamb. "Required courses in the undercover prep track."

I snort a laugh. Vanti is a never-ending series of surprises. "Aren't they afraid they'll lose you to the entertainment industry? I think vid stars make more credits than security agents."

"And give up all this fame and adulation?" Vanti rolls her eyes. "If a cadet decides entertainment is a better fit, we probably don't want them in the agency, anyway. Come talk to R'ger."

I wave her off. "I need to get showered and changed first. What time is it?" Ship time is usually based on the time zone of the station most recently departed, but I have no idea how long I slept.

"Dinner in two hours," she says, straightening. "It's formal." The door slides shut behind her.

AN HOUR LATER, I step out of my cabin. I'm dressed in one of the many outfits my mother's personal secretary, Hy-Mi, procured and coordinated for my visit to Sally Ride. He's updated the app database, so all I had to do was flick the date and occasion. The long, green gown clings to my hips and legs, making me wish I'd gotten a butt contour like Gloria Huatang.

"You look lovely, my dear," R'ger says as I emerge. He's a sweet older man, and as I recently discovered, my father. He's dressed in his traditional Armstrong garb: a long robe of rough brown silk with a cowl neck.

"I see you opted for pants today." I nod at the black fabric peeking out from the bottom of his robe.

He laughs. "It's a bit chillier on the ship. Don't want my giblets freezing."

I close my eyes, trying to block out that image. "Just what a girl wants to hear from her dad."

"Dad jokes are my specialty." He raises his glass in a toast. It's half-full of a virulent green slush. "Now that I can acknowledge you as my daughter, I plan to use them abundantly."

I chuckle. "Perfect." I wander across the room to order a sparkling water from the AutoKich'n. Then I change my mind and dial up a whiskey. "Did Vanti tell you what happened?"

"She said she'd let you fill me in." He pats the couch next to him. "I gathered you left the ship to tell Ser O'Neill how you feel about him. Didn't go well?"

I plop down next to him. "No. It went great! He met me at the shuttle port—Vanti warned him I was coming. And we got it all hashed out in record time. Then it got weird." I explain about the coffee shop and the peacekeepers. "They said they were notified when the ship left, and I wasn't on board."

"Is that possible?" R'ger turns his glass in his hand, admiring the color, I guess.

"Possible? Yes." I swallow a gulp of whiskey and let it burn down my throat. A deep breath settles the warmth in my stomach. "Likely? Not very. I doubt the Grissom Peacekeepers are worried about wealthy cruisers overstaying their welcome. I mean, I have plenty of credits. They should love having me spend them on their planet, right?"

"I've heard the Grissomites are a bit—they're careful who they let stay. Immigrating to Grissom is impossible unless you have a proven source of income. And they prosecute tourists who outstay their visas. You're lucky they didn't fine you."

"Oh, they did." I pull up the list of fines and their astronomical total.

"But are they that fast? I mean, I didn't spend a credit until after they grabbed me. We only got coffee and O'Neill paid for that. Then there's the fact that the peacekeepers told him I left of my own accord."

"Do you know anyone in the Grissom Peacekeepers? Maybe someone who has a grudge against you?"

I shake my head. "No one I know. But I'm sure there are legions of people Mother has pissed off."

"You can't blame everything on her."

"Sure I can. That's what mothers are for." I sip the whiskey again. "Here's a weird thing—the pilot who brought me to the ship was O'Neill's cousin. He said I'm not welcome on Grissom."

"Ah ha! Now we're getting somewhere. The family is trying to keep you away."

"No, he works for immigration." But did he? He wasn't wearing a uniform. "Are you saying his family set this up?"

"How powerful is his family?" R'ger picks up a pitcher and tops off his glass. "Could they influence peacekeepers? What did the arrest report say?"

"Arrest report? There wasn't one." I finish my whiskey and eye his pitcher. R'ger has exotic tastes in beverages—and they aren't always appealing. "What are you drinking?"

"TereshTini. Not quite the same as the ones I had on Tereshkova but damn good." He sips and swallows. "If you were deported, there should have been an arrest report. And interstellar law requires you sign it when you're booked."

"Maybe they didn't want to upset the Ice Dame?" I start to pour some TereshTini into my glass, but R'ger puts a hand on my arm.

"Use this." He hands me a clean glass. "You don't want to pollute the palate. And I don't think they give a flying fig for your mother."

I set the glass on the table and start a search on Grissom law. R'ger is correct—they should have insisted on me signing the arrest report. I connect to the local copy of the Grissom database—updated while the ship was in port—and start a search on Kato and Watson. Then I run another on O'Neill's extended family. Bill might not have been his real name, but I'll find that cousin.

Within seconds, I get a hit on William Hillis y Mendoza bin Tariq e Reynolds. "Bill Hillis—Ty's mother's brother's son. CEO and shuttle pilot for Mendoza Enterprises. And guess what?"

R'ger raises an eyebrow.

"Katheryn 'Kate' Kato is his wife."

FOUR

R'GER GETS TO HIS FEET. "It's the family. They don't like you—maybe because of your connections." He holds up a hand when I open my mouth to agree. "Or maybe because they think you're bad for him. He was pretty upset with you when he left the ship. If he told them, then you show up, and he comes running back to you?" He holds up both hands. "If he was my cousin, I'd be worried too. People don't always make good choices when they're in love."

I look away. The last few weeks have been pretty rough. When O'Neill told me he loved me, I ran away. And then I did it again. And again. No wonder he'd sworn off me. And yet, when Vanti told him I'd followed him to the planet, he'd come right back to me. If I was his cousin, I'd be pretty pissed at me, too.

"This is personal?" I stand and nearly fall over as the volume of alcohol in my system overwhelms my sense of balance. R'ger grabs my arm and holds me up. "I'm screwed. They've stopped my messages." I fling my message queue onto the window screen to show him. The list of blocked outgoing messages fills the screen with red text.

"Let's get you some BuzzKill," R'ger says.

I shake my head. The alcohol has kicked in and everything swims pleasantly. "I prefer a little buzz right now."

"Food, then, is the next thing on the agenda." He takes my arm and guides me toward the door. "If Kato is Bill's wife, why didn't Ty recognize her?"

I shrug. The room sways around me. "Looks like they met after Ty moved to SK2."

Vanti appears from nowhere and steps in front of us. "Passageway is clear, but let me go first."

"Is this security stuff really nessess—nessessess—importan'?" I stumble over nothing. "A cruise ship should be safe."

"If you recall, they were stuffing people into freezers on your last cruise." Vanti darts into the hall then gestures for us to follow.

"Yeah, but that was mos'ly crew. And we caught 'em." I mime catching a ball and spin around. R'ger catches me before I land on my butt.

"And there's only one evil gang in the universe." Vanti gives me a mocking thumbs-up.

I float along behind her, R'ger keeping tethered to the floor. At the end of the passageway, we step through an audio shield. The noise of hundreds of chattering passengers assaults my ears.

"I wonder why we don't have those in the Control Center?" I ask the room in general.

"What, full-service dining rooms?" R'ger guides me to a large table near the center of the room.

"No, audio shields. Was jus' thinkin' about how everyone could hear Rash when I reported the murder." The last word comes out louder and several heads swivel to look at us in alarm.

R'ger smiles and murmurs charming nothings at them. When they've returned to their meals, he pulls out my chair. A human waiter appears to shake out my napkin, and R'ger takes the seat opposite me. "Probably because they're very expensive."

I nod, astounded by his wisdom. "You are the smartest man I know, Dad."

He chuckles and hands me a roll. "I think you need some food."

THE WAITER BRINGS our pre-ordered meals. Mine includes a large crustacean tail, a thick steak, and some fried potato strips. R'ger has soup and a selection of sushi. Vanti has disappeared into the background.

"Why doesn't she just eat with us?" I ask. The food has counteracted most of the booze, and I miss my buzz a little. "I mean, one of those waiters could stab me with a steak knife before she got here."

Vanti materializes behind R'ger. "I have a military-grade ScanNSeal. And a quick-acting tranq dart. You'd be fine."

I look her up and down. She's wearing her usual form-fitting black. "Where are you hiding all this gear?"

She smiles without showing her teeth. "That's my little secret. By the way, I got through to Griz for you."

Griz is her nickname for O'Neill. Neither of them has explained what it means, but I guess it dates back to their academy days. It used to bother me, but I've gotten over it. Mostly. "What did you say?"

"I told him that you were deported against your will, and your messages have been blocked."

"What did he say?" I demanded.

"Thanks."

"That's all?" I stare at her, my heart in my stomach. "Is he—is he coming back to SK2?"

"He has to." Vanti shrugs and steps behind a potted plant. "He still works for the company."

And she's gone. I peer through the fronds, but there's nothing. How does she do that?

"That young woman is frighteningly competent." R'ger pats his lips with his napkin and leans back. A waiter appears as efficiently as Vanti and whisks the plate away.

"Maybe she trained in hospitality," I mutter.

THE SIX-DAY FLIGHT to SK2 seems to take forever. I send a message to O'Neill every few hours, but every single one bounces back. As a distraction, I throw myself into the cruise ship activities. After four days of playing cards, doing yoga, sitting by the pool, and drinking too much, I'm exhausted. On day five, I book a spa day for myself then, on a whim, add Vanti to the reservation.

We arrive at the spa, and they show us to a pair of changing rooms. I start pulling off my shoes when I hear Vanti swear. At least I think she's swearing—it's too low to understand but violent in nature.

"What's wrong?" I poke my head out the door.

"I'm supposed to wear this?" She stands outside my changing room holding a thick white robe.

"Yeah. You leave your clothes in the locker and wear the robe."

"With nothing underneath?" She stares at the offending item in disgust.

"Haven't you been to a spa before?" There are several on SK2, including an affordable one on Level 9.

"Why?" She crosses her arms over her chest, the robe flung over her shoulder.

"To relax? Seems like you could use that."

"It's my job to never relax." She looks around the hallway as if she's sure a pack of ninjas will appear out of thin air any second with throwing stars and Katanas.

I probably shouldn't have watched that vid on *Ancient Tēvē* last night.

"Look, you've checked out the whole ship, right?" I pause after each question, waiting for her grudging nod. "You've vetted the entire crew—I saw you working on that before we left S'Ride. You checked the spa again last night and did another walkthrough this morning. What else?"

Her eyes narrow, and she ticks items off on her fingers. "Upgraded facial recognition systems at all doors. Biometric detectors integrated into your holo-ring. Tested all creams, lotions, oils, beverages, and snacks."

"Seriously? If someone wants to kill me that badly, I don't have a chance."

She laughs. "I was kidding about the snacks. Those are tested when they're brought on board." She turns away. "I'm not comfortable leaving my weapons in the locker, though."

"You can take out a whole army with just your hands," I remind her. "I'm not worried at all."

I return to my changing room and slip out of my clothes. The ability to have a spa day without worrying about the cost is one of the perks of being a top-lev. But the crazy security is a definite down-side. I pull on the robe and step into the hall.

Vanti is waiting in a matching white robe. She's got fluffy slippers on her feet and a small black bag clutched in her hand. I don't remember her carrying it earlier.

"What's that?" I scuff my slippers against the carpet to build up a static charge.

"There are some items I won't work without." She doesn't elaborate.

I tap her hair with one finger, and the static charge zings. *Ouch!* She doesn't even blink. Vanti is part superhero. I'm convinced.

The rest of the day passes in a relaxed haze. We get massages. Vanti only threatens the massage therapist once, right at the beginning. Then we use the steam room, the aroma therapy studio, the relaxation chamber, and finally, the aestheticians. At the end of the day, we return to our changing cubicles relaxed and refreshed.

Vanti stands in the hallway when I come out. She's wearing her severe black uniform. The small bag is gone. Her hair is its usual perfect copper curtain. "That wasn't too bad."

"Would you like to do it again sometime?"

Her lips quirk in a tiny smile. "Nah, once is enough."

FIVE

WHEN I ARRIVE ON SK2, my holo-ring pings with a message that has been waiting for me. It's from O'Neill! I hurry off the ship and step into one of the convenient comm suites located along the transit arm that connects the ship to the SK2 customs terminal. I set the system to "private" and flick the message.

O'Neill's head and torso appear before me in all his shiny glory. But he looks tired. Dark circles shadow his eyes, and his skin is pale and dry. He grimaces at me, as if smiling is too much effort.

"Triana, I don't know what's going on." He runs a hand through his hair, and it doesn't fall back into place. Something is really wrong in the universe. "The peacekeepers said you decided to return to the ship."

"I was deported!" I yell, even though I know he can't hear me.

"Vanti says the peacekeepers are lying, and you were deported. I don't know who to believe anymore."

"Believe Vanti!" I yell again. "She's telling the truth!"

"Please, call me when you get this message. I don't know why you haven't responded." The holo dissolves.

"Because they've blocked me!" I holler.

I record a short message and route it through the SK2 business system. Now that I'm back on home turf, I can make use of my hacking skills—

and, of course, my top-lev full-access status. I send the message to O'Neill's work account and cross my fingers.

Vanti waits outside the comm suite.

"Aren't you off duty?" I grumble as she falls in beside me. "If I'm not safe on SK2, I may as well lock myself in a titanium bubble for the rest of my life."

"Technically, I'm off duty." She shrugs. "I just wanted—do you want me to send any more messages to Griz before I head dirtside?"

I stop in the middle of the wide passageway. The trickle of passengers still leaving the *Vesteralen* flow around us. "I gotta know. Why do you call him Griz?"

Vanti smirks. "Top secret." She glances at the time. "My shuttle leaves in twenty. Do you want me to send any more messages?"

"Tell him to check his SK2 account." I turn, and she turns with me. "Whoever's behind this has blocked my incoming messages to his personal account."

She nods and flicks her holo-ring. The red "recording" light blinks once, and she murmurs something under her breath. Then the ring switches to green and goes dark. "It's gone. He'll get that one, for sure. I told him he should come back on the next ship."

"No!" Heads swivel in our direction. I smile and wave, as if I'm posing for a tabloid. I lower my voice. "I don't want to give his family any more reason to hate me. He needs to take his full vacation then come home. I'll be here."

"Got it." Vanti gives me a snappy salute. "I'll send that as soon as I check in to the shuttle. See you next time."

Before she can turn away, I throw my arms around her. She tenses then her face relaxes into surprise. "You might want to warn a girl. Hugs can be misinterpreted as attacks."

I laugh. "If I warned you, you'd run away. Everyone needs a hug once in a while."

She gives me a quick squeeze then slithers out of my embrace.

With Vanti, I'll call that a win. "Be careful out there."

She winks over her shoulder and disappears into the thin crowd. How she becomes impossible to spot so quickly is another mystery. The woman is a master.

I heave a sigh and head home.

A MESSAGE PINGS my ring as I exit the float tube on Level 6. It's Hy-Mi, my mother's personal assistant. It can wait until I'm home.

I saunter through the concourse and along the radial to A Ring. Kara and I share a one-bedroom compartment on the outer-most ring on Level 6. It's enormously expensive—at least for a maintenance worker and an aesthetician—but the view is worth every credit. Plus, my top-lev allowance gives me plenty of wiggle room financially. I don't like to take credits from Mother, but if she's going to keep pulling me into the family business, I'll earn every micro-credit.

I wave at the access panel, and the door slides open. The compartment is dark, so I flick on a single lamp and drop into a chair. The cargo handlers will deliver my luggage as soon as it's unloaded, so I can't even unpack. Nothing to distract me from Hy-Mi's message.

The window dims when I flick the icon, and the little man's avatar pops up. It bows, as Hy-Mi always does, and speaks. "Dame Morgan requests the pleasure of your company at four this afternoon." The holo dissolves, and my view of the stars returns.

I glance at the time—I have twenty minutes. *Thanks, Mother.* I consider ignoring the summons—which is exactly what it is. No one on SK2 would dare to decline an invitation from the Ice Dame. Not even me.

At least not if I want her to keep paying for my compartment. See, this is why I ran away in the first place! The credits come with a whole web of strings.

I push myself out of the chair and head for the float tubes.

"THAT'S WHAT YOU'RE WEARING?" she asks as I step into her office promptly at four.

"I didn't realize there was a dress code," I mutter. "Besides, this is one of the outfits Hy-Mi coordinated for my trip." I feel bad throwing the old man under the shuttle, but it's true, and I'm too tired to come up with a better excuse.

"Those were for the cruise." Mother sniffs and smooths her severely tailored business suit. "Your daily attire is in your closet."

"I don't live here, Mother," I remind her. "And I'm not working today, so I can wear what I want."

"As a top-lev, you're always working." She shakes her head. "All those years of training, gone. You always scored so well in deportment."

"I scored well in everything. I didn't have a life outside of studying, remember?" I roll my eyes. "What did you want, Mother?"

She gestures regally to a high-backed armchair by the faux fireplace. I take a seat and hold my fingers toward the simulated flames. The variations in appearance and temperature are masterful—and just short of convincing to anyone who's seen a real fire. Still, it's an attractive focal piece to the room.

She sits across from me and crosses one leg over the other. She looks like a twenty-something model posing as a business consultant for an expensive advertisement. Unlimited access to rejuvenation treatments will do that. Her long blonde hair—sporting a rebellious purple streak at one temple—flows over her shoulder in perfect waves. Her blue eyes blink at me. "Tell me about the Family Meeting."

I heave a sigh. She attended the meeting virtually, but I knew a full-debrief would be on the schedule as soon as I returned. I cast my mind back to the event and try to think of something I haven't already reported. "Uh, R'ger seemed to get along with everyone."

"Of course he did." She waves that away. "R'ger is charming. How did the others react to the revelation of his Family connections?"

"How did you react?" I retort. According to R'ger, no one, not even my mother, knew he was a senior member of the Kindujas Family until just before the meeting. The Kindujas hadn't been seen at a Families Meeting in decades, so having Imogen Morgan's country-bumpkin lover show up as their representative had been a bit of a shocker. "Everyone pretended it was old news."

"But did they accept him?" She throws the question out as if it's unimportant, but her eyes bore into mine.

"I told you, he got along fine. Once they were sure he was legit, everyone treated him like any other Family rep."

"That's not helpful—I could see that much from the holo."

She rambles on about wanting a feet-on-the-ground report, but I've lost interest. Mother had attended those meetings in real-time through the eye-wateringly expensive communications system available only to top-levs. Everyone else has to send recorded messages outside the system. But if you have the credits—and access to the equipment—you can have a real-time conversation.

"I need to talk to O'Neill," I say, interrupting her lecture.

Her eyes widen, and her mouth freezes wide open in shock. No one interrupts the Ice Dame. Milliseconds later, her teeth snap closed. "What did you say?"

"I need to talk to O'Neill. He's on Grissom, and the recorded messages just aren't cutting it. I need real-time access."

She crosses her arms over her chest. "Why?"

Throwing caution to the solar wind, I pour out the whole story. "Someone is interfering in our relationship," I conclude. "I need to put things straight."

She leans back in her chair, her eyes focused on something—or nothing—behind me. Finally, they snap back to mine. "This one time."

My breath catches in my throat. "Really?" I squeak.

"I remember what it's like to be young and in love with someone inappropriate." She wrinkles her nose. "Or apparently inappropriate. But this is a onetime offer. Are you sure he's the one you want to spend it on?"

There's no question. "Yes. I need to talk to him. Now, if possible."

She rolls her eyes—or gives the suggestion of eye-rolling without stooping to that level of crass expression. "Hy-Mi will set up the comms." She rises smoothly from her chair. "And when you're done, we will finish this conversation."

"Of course!" Although I'm not sure what she really wants to hear. "Thank you so much."

She flicks her fingers—the sophisticated gesture encompassing a dramatic wave-off in a tiny movement—and returns to her massive desk.

I resist the urge to jump over the desk and fling my arms around her—and not only because such an athletic feat is beyond me in normal gravity. She wouldn't appreciate a hug any more than Vanti had.

The door slides open, and Hy-Mi bows from the threshold. "This way, Sera."

SIX

THE INTERSTELLAR COMMUNICATIONS booth is located behind the float tubes in the center of the Level 83 lobby. This equipment is so expensive and so rarely used that even top-levs share.

Hy-Mi shows me how to dial the connection and engage the system. "It's best to set an appointment. You wouldn't want to waste connection time arguing over availability." If Hy-Mi is worried about the cost, you know this thing is expensive.

I drum my fingers on the console. "Maybe I'd better do that." Part of me wants to throw caution to the wind and just call. It would be the kind of dramatic, romantic gesture an *Ancient Tēvē* heroine would make. But the idea of my call coming through when O'Neill is talking to his parents or using the loo makes me hesitate. Besides, I'm not sure I could manage to hack into this system for a second call if I blow the first one. This thing is crazy complex. "How about I set it up for later tonight? Say, nine-thirty?"

"Very good." Hy-Mi nods in that regal way that almost appears to be a bow. "Let me know if that time needs to change. Sometimes these things are difficult to schedule."

He secures the booth with his handprint, and we cross the lobby to

Mother's massive compartment. A few steps from the door, he stops me. "She needs to hear Ser Chaturvedi was accepted by the Families."

"I'm not sure I can tell her any more than she already knows." I rub my temple. "Besides, she doesn't care what anyone thinks. Why is this so important?"

Hy-Mi smiles sadly. "She *says* she doesn't care what anyone thinks. But she's considering a long-term commitment to Ser Chaturvedi. That's not just a personal decision. She wants to know the rest of the board still respects her business sense."

"They've never cared about her previous contracts," I protest. "Or maybe they did, but *she* didn't care what they thought. Why is this different?"

"Ser Chaturvedi is the great love of her life." His quiet tone doesn't hide the feeling behind his words. Hy-Mi has experienced great love, so he's quite dramatic about it—in an understated, totally Hy-Mi way. "She feels for him as you feel for Ser O'Neill. But she's also responsible for this station. She can't make decisions solely on her personal feelings, but she can't let Ser Chaturvedi go. It's a dilemma. Just reassure her."

He waves the door open and gestures for me to precede him inside.

The idea of my mother experiencing the same feelings I'm going through is mind boggling. The Ice Dame got her name for a reason. She's ruthless. Cold. Calculating. Her being in love doesn't compute. Besides, no one wants to think about their parent being in love. It's too weird.

I send a text to O'Neill then spend twenty minutes assuring my mother that everyone at the Families Meeting loved R'ger.

"Even if they didn't, he's a tried and tested member of the Kindujas." As soon as the words are out of my mouth, I realize they're probably a mistake. Like every top-lev, she knows no one will admit to disliking any of us.

She smiles—a genuine smile. "Of course." It seems I underestimated her confidence in the social system. She doesn't really care if the other top-levs like him—only if they behave as if they like him.

"They liked him well enough before they knew who he was," I add, but she's stopped listening.

"Thank you for your report," she says. "I'll see you at dinner. Make sure you're appropriately attired."

Recognizing a dismissal when I hear it, I nod and retreat.

———

DINNER IS WITH ME, Mother, and R'ger. The two of them eat at one end of the long dining room table, giggling and cooing at each other. I sit at the other. Luckily, my stomach is already in knots, anticipating my upcoming discussion with O'Neill, so their display can't put me off my dinner. I sip my sparkling water and zone out,

"Did you decide where you're going to live?" R'ger's question snaps me out of my reverie.

"I live on Level 6." I set my glass on the table with a loud crack. This is another conversation I'd prefer to avoid. "I don't mind coming up here to help out when necessary, but I live and work down there."

"You know your identity has been exposed, don't you?" Mother raises an eyebrow.

"By whom?" I demand, staring her down.

She shrugs one elegant shoulder. "Not me. Someone down there—" she says the words as if they smell "—must have leaked it. It's been on the news."

"What?"

R'ger flicks his holo-ring and throws a vid on the table-top projection. It shows me entering the MCC in my station coverall. The words, "Top-lev slumming in the bowels of the station," scroll across the base of the hologram.

"I can't believe anyone cares enough to put this on the news." I *can* believe it, but I don't want to. This probably explains why there weren't any messages from Rash waiting in my queue when I returned. I'd planned on reporting to the ops center first thing in the morning—one more thing to worry about. I groan.

"Now that you're exposed, it's time to come home." Mother pats her lips with a napkin. "No one on the station is going to hire you—that's against corporate policy. We have to avoid the perception of nepotism."

I laugh. "You can't hire family because it looks bad, but you can dele-gate all kinds of decision-making to us? Makes perfect sense." I toss my own napkin on the table and stand. "I'm going to bed."

"You haven't exactly provided any scintillating conversation tonight." Mother waves me away. "You're excused."

I walk to the other end of the table and kiss R'ger's cheek then stalk out the door.

My room looks like it hasn't changed since I ran away almost seven years ago. The blank walls hide the meters of closet space, packed with the latest fashions in my current size. The pale blue bed cover looks identical to the one I picked—from a limited catalog of "appropriate" furnishings—as a teen. I fling myself down on the bed, set an alarm for my discussion with O'Neill, and fall into an exhausted doze.

Hy-Mi meets me at the comm booth at nine-fifteen. He lets me in—for some reason my all-access ring doesn't open this door. I file that away for later. Between my MCC credentials and my top-lev access, I should be able to go anywhere on the station.

"The call is set for nine-thirty and will ring through to Ser O'Neill's holo-ring. Do you have any questions?" Hy-Mi gives me a narrow-eyed look.

"I'm good. You didn't need to stay late to help me with this."

"Actually, I did. Your mother insisted." He bows. "But now, I shall retire. I wish you the best."

"Thanks." I sit on the plush bench and lean against the hard wall of the booth. Although it was made for top-levs, it's surprisingly utilitarian. My heart beats in overtime, and my breathing ratchets up. The glass of the booth fogs. I increase the airflow, and the glass clears. I feel like a teen waiting for her first date. I close my eyes and breathe, slow and deep.

"Triana." O'Neill's voice startles me, and my eyes pop open. He stands there in all his shininess, and I have to remind myself he's not really here.

"You look better." I blink, my eyes stinging a little. "I wish you were here."

"Tell me what's happening." He crosses his arms over his chest.

"Someone doesn't want us together," I say. After talking with Vanti on the ship, I know blaming his family for this situation is just going to back-fire. "But it isn't me."

"I'm looking into it," he says. "There's no reason you should have been deported. It doesn't matter—I can come back to SK2 immediately."

"No." I hold up a hand. "Stay and spend some time with your family. Then come back here. For me."

Finally, he smiles. "You'd better be there when I get back."

"Don't worry, I'm not going anywhere."

SEVEN

Kara twists a lock of sparkling green hair between her fingers. She's been doing it all evening, and her usually perfect do is looking a bit frazzled.

"What's going on?" I reach over and pull the innocent strand from her hand.

"I—I don't know how to tell you this…" She trails off, looking away.

"You and Erco are signing a procreational contract, and you're moving dirtside to raise a pack of tiny Ercos."

She gapes at me. "How did you know?"

"What?" I gape right back. "I was kidding! You hardly know the guy!"

"We've been together for months," she says. "Besides, you just know when it's the right one."

This relationship *has* lasted longer than all her previous ones combined. But that's no reason to jump into having kids. "So do a short-term contract first."

She smiles, and this time, her face lights up. "We're ready to have children. We've been talking about it since you left for S'Ride. And I have enough credits saved up to start a salon in Pacifica City. Near my family."

Her family is awesome—I'd move to Pacifica City if they'd adopt me. "When's the big day?"

"Tomorrow."

I stare at her, speechless.

"Hah! Got you!" She giggles and gives my shoulder a friendly push. "Next month. We want Ty to be there, since he kind of introduced us. Plus, the lease on this compartment—I can't leave you high and dry. I have a friend who might want to move in if you need a roommate."

"Yeah, about that—"

Her eyes narrow. "You're moving, too."

I nod. "I can't work on the station anymore—Mother's seen to that. I could pay the rent easily, but if I'm not working down here, what's the point? Although, it's kind of nice having a bolt-hole away from the Ice Dame."

She puts her arm around me. "You'll be fine. I'm sure someone will want to hire a former space janitor."

"As long as that someone isn't my mother, it's all golden."

THREE WEEKS LATER, O'Neill finally returns to SK2. I'm waiting in the arrivals lounge on Level 40, dancing from foot to foot. When the doors open and he steps inside, I throw myself at him. He tumbles back, breaking the plane of the virtual security barrier.

"Halt!" A voice commands.

"Sorry." I grab O'Neill's hand and pull him forward. "Sorry!"

"Oh, Sera Morgan! I didn't realize it was you." The security guard smiles, but it doesn't reach his eyes.

"You were just doing your job," I say with a smile I hope looks more real than his. "We'll get out of your way." I hurry O'Neill toward the float tubes.

"Where are we going?" he asks as we drop.

"Your place," I say.

He shakes his head. "We can't. I don't live there anymore."

"What do you mean?" We step out on Level 27, and I turn toward Radial 10.

"I transferred off station when we were on S'Ride." His eyes meet mine briefly then slide away. "Remember? I said I couldn't work for you anymore. I requested a transfer. They packed up my stuff and put it into storage."

I stop in the middle of the corridor. "Oh. I didn't think that—do you still have a job here?"

"I'm currently on leave without pay." His lips twitch. "I was hoping my wealthy girlfriend could help me out."

I don't laugh. "Are you back for good or just back for now?"

He runs a hand through his hair. It doesn't look any longer, but in the few weeks he's been gone, it's morphed from wavy to curly. As usual, it effortlessly falls back into his casual style. "I don't know. That depends on you."

I thought we'd gotten this all hashed out on Grissom. Why is it coming up now? I hate these kinds of conversations. "I want to be with you. Wherever you want to be. Pick a place, and I'm there."

"What about her?" He glances at the overhead.

"She doesn't need me." I wrinkle my nose. "At least, she doesn't need me right now. She's only fifty-ish. She'll be running this place for decades. She doesn't need me mucking things up for her. I can come back in twenty years and learn everything I need to know then."

"See, this is the problem." O'Neill crosses his arms over his chest. "In my mind, in twenty years, we're still living happily ever after. Not splitting up so you can come home to learn the family business."

"But you could come, too." The warmth that flooded through me at "happily ever after" drains away at his stoic look. "What do you want me to do? Renounce my heritage? Fake my own death?"

He takes my arm and guides me back toward the float tubes. "Let's find somewhere to stay before we make any decisions, okay?"

"I'm stuck on 83." I sigh. "Mother decided the station can't hire top-lev offspring—it doesn't look good. And to be fair, can you imagine Nicolai Bezos working in Ops? He'd be useless. But now that they know who I am, I'm out of a job. They've hired my replacement already—some guy named Wilco."

"He's got some big shoes to fill," O'Neill says. "I'm not saying your feet are big."

"He's definitely got a lot to learn." I hold his gaze. "Come upstairs. Mother has a gazillion guest rooms if you don't mind being that close to the Ice Dame."

"I guess I'll survive." He slides his arm around my waist, and we step into the float tube.

"I NEED TO GET OUT," O'Neill says when we meet for breakfast a few weeks later. He's been living in one of the guest suites on Level 82. They're permanently reserved for guests of the top-levs. "Gloria Huatang just moved in next door."

"What?!" Gloria is my nemesis. We grew up on Level 83 together, and she's always been the mean girl to my nerd. She's had her hooks out for O'Neill since before he and I met but knowing he's with me makes the chase even sweeter, I'm sure.

"She said she's trying to be more independent, like you." He bites his lip, trying not to smile.

"Independent? By living in her grandfather's guest suite instead of his penthouse?" My skin crawls as I imagine her knocking on O'Neill's door late at night in her sleazy lingerie, claiming there's a problem with the plumbing. "Call maintenance," I mutter under my breath. "We'll help you."

"What's that?" O'Neill looks up from his ultra-healthy shreds and crumbles and snitches a piece of my bacon.

I mock-slap his fingers. "Order your own, granola boy."

He smiles and eats the bacon. I know he wouldn't steal food from any other top-lev, and my heart turns to warm goo. *Take your lingerie and shove it, Gloria.*

"I got a message from Grissom last night." He says it casually, as if it's no big deal.

My ears perk up, and my eyes narrow. I force them open with a faux-confident smile. "What's up back home?"

"My cousin Bill got fined for the shuttle crash," he says. "Did you know my cousin was the one who took you back to the *Vesteralen*? Funny coincidence. If only you'd known each other, he could have stopped the whole deportation. Anyway, as I'm sure you've heard, the shuttle exploded after he dropped you off. Now they're saying it was pilot error. He says he did everything exactly by the book. He's asking if I can come home and help him sort it out."

"Pilot error?" My heart squeezes in my chest. I want to tell him Bill is a lying back-stabber, but I remember what Vanti told me—how close his family is. I don't want to make him choose between me and them. "Did they check into the sabotage aspect? I mean, top-lev." I smile modestly and point to myself.

"Of course. They checked that first." He nods. "If they hadn't, I would have harassed them until they did. After all, protecting top-levs is my job."

He's been kind of miserable and aimless the last few weeks, trying to figure out what to do with his time while not pressuring me. He obviously wants to go investigate this situation and trying to stop him will only damage our relationship.

"Let's go clear Bill's record." I lift my mug in a toast.

He does a double take. "You want to come, too?"

"Of course—I wanted to come last time. As soon as I got back, I had Hy-Mi arrange a visa for my next visit. Let's go."

"What about her?" He asks the same question he asked three weeks ago.

I give him the same answer. "She doesn't need me."

EIGHT

WE TAKE a shuttle dirtside to witness Kara and Erco's contract. As we enter the vehicle, I stop to look at the airlock. Like the shuttle on Grissom, this one appears to have a detachable passenger compartment. This looks like it would be expensive, but the shuttle company must be highly risk averse.

"Satisfied with the technical specs?" O'Neill asks as he straps into the plush, reclining seat with heater, private holo-screen, and nighttime mode. This is the station board of directors' private shuttle, accessed through the private waiting room and spotless airlock atop the station.

The pilot's cockpit is hidden behind a huge screen that shows the stars outside. This shuttle will seat eight, with room for a pickup grav-ball game to spare. Additional seats can be installed but never are. There's a full bedroom suite in the back, even though this shuttle is only used for the twenty-minute drop to the surface. The board gets the best, whether they need it or not.

I snicker. "I have no idea what the tech specs are on this thing. But after your cousin's wild ride, I was curious."

"This is the board's private shuttle," he says. "Vetting pilots and mainte-nance personnel was part of my job. Unless they've snuck in someone new in the last few weeks, we're safe." He tosses the words off, but sweat sparkles on his upper lip.

"You're nervous." I jab a finger at his chest. "Why?"

"I hate flying," he says. "So much...space out there."

"You didn't seem to mind the cruise."

"Oh, big ships are fine—they don't feel like this." His hands tighten on the armrests. "And after Bill's accident, this feels—I can't explain it."

I put my hand over his. "You don't have to."

After a textbook flight and flawless landing, the shuttle rolls to a halt outside the Pacifica City Station. The pilot's voice comes over the speakers. "Welcome to Kaku. Please be careful when opening the overhead compartment."

I giggle. "There are no overhead compartments. The pilot must watch *Ancient Tēvē*."

O'Neill reaches up and presses a panel in the wall above his seat. It pops open, revealing an empty compartment. He smirks and points to his chest. "The hired help loads these. You top-levs never see them."

We're only here for the day, so we have no luggage to collect. A high-end bubble pulls up to the ramp as we step out of the shuttle. The door pops open as we approach, and we climb inside. Although I've taken this shuttle before—before my escape to the Techno Inst—I'm suddenly aware how isolated top-levs can be. We haven't spoken to another human since we left Level 83. The entire trip could be automated—like this bubble—and we'd never know.

O'Neill settles beside me and tells the bubble where we're going. "Réalta Contract Center."

"Estimated time of arrival, ten forty-three," an androgynous voice says. "Would you like refreshments?" A menu pops up in front of the seats.

O'Neill raises an eyebrow at me.

I shake my head with a laugh. "Ah'm not sure I'll make it all the way to the Centah without sustenance," I say in a thick Kakuvian drawl, fanning myself with my hand.

"We have a full selection—" the voice starts.

"Cancel," O'Neill cuts in.

Réalta is the neighborhood of Pacifica City that Kara's family lives in.

The Contract Center is housed in a building that looks like it's made of ancient stone. We exit the bubble, and it slides away. The shallow steps rise to a wide veranda. Tall, fluted columns hold the roof high above our heads. Three sets of huge double doors open into a vast entry hall.

The invitation contained a code slip with a virtual guide. The vibration in my ring urges my hand to the left. We cross the polished tiles and continue into a hallway. The ceiling here is only three meters high instead of five, and it feels almost cozy by comparison. The guide brings us to the third door on the left, which opens as we approach.

Inside, Kara and Erco wait with two other young couples. We exchange greetings and hugs, as if we haven't seen each other in weeks. Kara left SK2 only two days ago.

"Are they here for contracts, too?" I whisper to Kara, nodding at the other two couples.

"No, those are cousins." She drags me across the room to meet them. "Mine and Erco's. It's traditional here. One recently contracted couple from each side. They're supposed to give us guidance or something. This is Aloff and Verina."

I nod and bump Aloff's fist. "We met before."

"At Christmas. Years ago," Aloff says. "You got me out of the family dinner. I still owe you."

I laugh and turn to Verina. "Hi, I'm Triana."

She stares at me, her eyes wide. "You're Annabelle Morgan."

I grimace at Kara. "Yeah, but call me Triana."

"You're Annabelle Morgan," she says again.

Kara pulls me away. "She's a bit star struck."

"You think?"

She laughs and drags me to the other couple. "This is Stervo and Ariel. Ariel is Erco's cousin."

I bump fists with them. "I knew a Stervo at the Techno-Inst. Actually, we never met in person—he was part of my—"

"—software club," Stervo cuts in. "That was me. This is Ariel." He nods at his partner.

"No way!" I say, knocking knuckles with Ariel.

"Way," they say together.

"Do you watch *Ancient Tēvē*?" I ask. I'm always happy to meet another aficionado.

"Is that where you got that line?" Stervo shakes his head. "I've been saying it ever since I heard it from you, but I never knew it was a quote."

"I'll send you a link to the vid if you want." I give him a once-over. "You clean up pretty good. No green skin or horns." Stervo had been a member of my online hacking club back at the Techno-Inst. We all used avatars rather than our real images—which meant we could look like anything. One of the members looked like a pink blob for a time. "Have you met any of the others?"

"No," Stervo says. "I've stayed in touch with Portia, but we've never met in person. You?"

I shake my head.

Ariel's eyes flick over my shoulder, and she straightens up. "Who is *that*?"

I glance behind me and grin. "That's Ty O'Neill. He's with me." After all this time, we still haven't defined our relationship, but if her expression is any indication, laying claim is a good idea.

"You still got six months with me." Stervo shoots a glare at O'Neill. "Are you shopping already?"

"Honey, I never stop looking at the merchandise." Ariel fluffs her hair and crosses the room.

"Should I be worried?" Stervo's lips compress.

"I don't think so," I say, watching O'Neill fist bump the other woman.

"You got him tied up?" Stervo asks.

My eyes just about pop out of my head. "Uh, you and I aren't close enough to discuss bondage."

He laughs. "I meant a contract. Gotta ward off the predators. She might be on the prowl, but I got a signed contract that says she can't touch for another half year."

My stomach churns. My mother has had contracts with various "suitable" men over the years. Now she's in a "free form" relationship with R'ger. I've avoided committing to anyone in the past, but O'Neill has made it clear his ultimate goal is marriage. Not just a five or ten-year contract but life with no escape clause.

I've seen plenty of vids on *Ancient Teve* where people got "married" but most of those relationships ended within a few years or even months. The whole concept of a lifetime commitment makes me squirm. But the idea of O'Neill shopping for a new partner as we reach the end of a contract makes me want to vomit. *You can't have it both ways, Triana.*

The contracting takes about five minutes. A clerk comes in, reads a brief overview of the contract—ten-year, procreational contract with exit clauses if there are no children at the three and six-year points. He throws the long form of the document on a large holo projection in case we want to read it. Then Erco and Kara wave their hands through the accept icon, register a palm print on the clerk's tablet, and they're done.

"Ten years, signed away like that." Ariel snaps her fingers. "I prefer the short ones. Two years, tops." She leans around me to eye O'Neill. "Unless something really special comes along."

O'Neill takes a step away, as if hiding behind me. "That was very... clinical." His chin juts at the tablet.

"You haven't witnessed one of these before?" I step forward to add my acknowledgement to the document and gesture for him to do the same.

"Nope, they aren't as common on Grissom." He flicks the icon and presses a thumb on the tablet.

After everyone present has registered a thumbprint, the clerk flicks a copy of the document to each of us and hurries away. I swipe mine into my long-term storage and smile at Kara. "Congratulations. Now what?"

"Now we party!"

NINE

A FEW DAYS LATER, we take a fast transport to Grissom. The ship, Pleiades Transport TL-245, isn't as plush as the cruisers, but it's a lot faster. The smaller vessel has more powerful engines, so it can reach the jump point in half the time a cruiser takes. Plus, it jumps directly to the Grissom system instead of swinging out to Sally Ride first like the cruise ships.

Each passenger on the transport has a small berth—just big enough to sleep in. It's about a meter square and two-and-a-half meters long, with full entertainment package and top-of-the-line privacy screens. They're nicer than my employee berth on the CSS Morningstar, and the food is better than the Techno-Inst's dining hall. Which isn't saying much, but we only have to eat a couple of meals on board.

Hy-Mi packed a "suitable wardrobe" for me, but it departed by freighter two weeks ago—the transports only have room for a small bag each. I brought my favorite leggings and tops, underwear, and a sweater. I figure I can always buy something nicer before we meet Ty's family.

The trip is completely uneventful. We dock at Cristoforetti Station and leave the ship.

"I'm surprised Mother didn't require security for me." I hike my bag up on my shoulder.

"Oh, she did." O'Neill nods at the couple behind us. "They're with the agency."

"Why didn't you tell me?" I glance over my shoulder. The pair are older —probably in their mid-forties. Or at least they appear that way. Kara made me look ancient for Halloween one year. Rejuv and modern aesthetics make age-guessing nearly impossible.

"She preferred it this way," he says.

"What about what I prefer?"

He smiles uncomfortably. "You don't really care as long as they don't get in your way, right?"

I stop in the center of the corridor and cross my arms over my chest. "Yeah, but I'm the one who's being protected. I have the right to know who's doing it. I thought they were just nosy."

He chuckles. "You didn't even notice them until now."

I let out an angry huff. "Yeah, but if I had, I would have been worried."

"You're right—it's your life. You should make the decisions." He stops and waits for the couple to catch up to us. "Triana, this is Ferrigi and Andron. They work for SK2 security." He turns to the men. "Sera Morgan wants a run-down on the security plan."

Ferrigi's eyes dart around the transportation hub. "Let's get to a secure location." He gestures for us to continue. "The terminal has communications rooms."

We crowd into one of the booths. Andron stands outside the glass door, his wide back a barrier between us and the outside world. I stare up at Ferrigi. "What's the plan?"

As he explains their procedure in excruciating detail, my brain glazes over. I really don't care as long as they stay out of my way, but the idea that my mother set them on me as watchdogs burns. And O'Neill was in on it?

"Thanks, that's enough." I cut him off like a top-lev and wince internally. I hate when people do that, but sometimes it's so easy to slip into the mold. "Could you please wait outside while I speak with Ser O'Neill?"

Ferrigi taps on the glass, and his partner moves out of the way. Once the door closes behind him, I turn on O'Neill. "You are not my security anymore. If this relationship," my hands gesture between the two of us, "is going to work, we need to be partners. Not a kid and her babysitter."

He flushes. "If you cared about your safety at all, that would make sense. If you recall, I brought it up when we booked the tickets, and you said we'd talk about it later. Every time I tried, you put me off."

I start to make an angry retort, but he's right. My ears go hot as the details of those conversations replay in my head. I should have realized ignoring it wasn't the answer. Still, I'm not ready to admit I'm wrong. "Where's Vanti?"

"She's on a mission." He shoves his fingers through his hair. "You can't demand specific agents at the drop of a hat."

"You're always on call for my mother."

"Was—and actually I was on call for Don Said. His security was my full-time job. But you didn't want full-time security, so it wasn't assigned. You get whoever is available. If you're in the market, I'm sure we can get you a full-time agent. I'm not sure it would be Vanti. She hates the station."

He's mentioned their first mission on SK2 before. Something happened that made Vanti request a dirtside assignment, but he's never told me the details. I try to ignore a twinge of jealousy. "Okay, how about this? You arrange security for me—making it as minimal as possible then brief me before it changes. I promise to try to listen."

His lips quirk, but I can see he's still a little miffed. "You'll *try* to listen?"

"I don't want all the mission details. Just who, how many, and how close."

"Deal." He holds out his fist. "Two men—trained board security members from Kaku. They'll be nearby at all times but won't interact with us unless we initiate."

I bump his fist and smirk. "Yeah, I kinda got that from the hulk."

"Hulk?" He taps the glass and opens the door.

"Yeah, the big green monster? One of the original actors was named Ferrigno. Ferrigi, Ferrigno... close enough."

"I should have realized." He nods to the two men and guides me toward the dirtside shuttle.

My paperwork clears the station security as expected. Of course, it did last time, too, so I'm expecting problems when we land. But to my surprise, that goes smoothly as well. Soon, the four of us are inside a mid-class bubble, heading across Virgilton.

"You don't suppose the peacekeepers will try to pick me up again, do you?" I ask.

"I think Hy-Mi took care of that." O'Neill glances at the two agents. "What are your orders should that happen?"

"We're to escort Sera Morgan to the Kakuvian embassy," the hulk says.

"They weren't letting anyone escort me anywhere last time," I say.

The hulk's lips twitch into a cold smile. "People don't 'let' us do things. We just do them."

That's a little unsettling. The two don't appear to have any weapons—customs required any personal weapons be turned in upon arrival. Neither the hulk nor the android (my name for Andron—too easy!) handed anything over. Of course, they both looked like they could take out a whole platoon of peacekeepers with their bare hands. And if they went to the same academy as Vanti, they probably have all kinds of weapons stashed in their skivvies.

The bubble pulls to a stop, and the android steps out, scanning the area. He raises a hand and makes some finger signs faster than I can catch.

"You're clear to depart." The hulk gestures to the door. "Take your bags —I need to keep my hands free."

As we climb out, a thought occurs to me. "You don't have any bags. Where do you keep your clean underwear?"

The hulk flushes red and doesn't answer.

TEN

I BITE BACK a grin and lean close to O'Neill. "Is he embarrassed because he didn't bring any clean undies or because I mentioned them at all?"

O'Neill glances over his shoulder at the hulk. "I'd guess the latter. I'm sure they sent luggage ahead—it's standard procedure."

We're in front of a large, stone building. The front is a bare, nearly featureless wall, with a few shuttered windows on each of the three levels. A barred gate stands open at a narrow-arched doorway. Dozens of similar buildings line the street, with yellow-green plants filling the spaces between. Vines climb the corners of some buildings, and others are nearly covered in thick leaves. The sun blazes down, bright and hot.

"This way." O'Neill takes both our bags and hurries down the stone path leading to the arch. I glance at the agents, but they don't seem to mind him taking point. I guess they aren't concerned about my safety here.

"What is this place?" I ask.

"Home." O'Neill throws the word over his shoulder as he disappears into the building.

"Cozy," I mutter. Of course, I know my colonial history. Grissom was a dangerous place in the early years, and the buildings were built like fortresses. Based on this street, that style has prevailed over the years, but none of the buildings are old enough to have been built by the original settlers. "Let's go meet the 'rents. You two might want to stay here."

"The 'rents?" The android gulps. "You're meeting his family? For the first time?"

I nod.

He and the hulk exchange a look. "We'll wait here."

I step into a cool, dark tunnel. Bright light shines from the far end. O'Neill has disappeared, but the two plain doors are shut, so I keep moving ahead.

The tunnel opens into a large square courtyard. Two tall, spindly trees grow from openings in the paving stones. The wide fronds at the top provide shade. Smaller trees in pots fill the courtyard with a riot of blue-green leaves and round, multi-colored fruit. More vines—these with smaller leaves and bright blue flowers—climb the walls. The balconies line the two floors above. The air is heavy with the scent of flowers and fruit.

"Triana, over here!" O'Neill waves at me from a little structure tucked in the far corner under the larger tree. It has smooth, white half-walls on the two sides facing the courtyard and a lattice roof. More vines hang from the beams, with green flowers drooping in clusters. The little pavilion holds a bed-like structure with a thick red cushion.

Eyes wide, I cross a tiny bridge over a placid trough of water that bisects the courtyard and take O'Neill's hand.

"This is my mother, Serena O'Neill y Mendoza bin Tariq e Reynolds." He gestures to a dark-haired woman lounging on the mattress.

She jumps up and flings her arms around me. "I'm so thrilled to finally meet you, Triana! Welcome to Grissom! Welcome to our home. I hope—"

The woman won't let go. I send O'Neill a silent, wild-eyed plea for help.

"Mom," O'Neill says with a chuckle. "You're scaring Triana. They don't go in for big displays of affection in her family."

Serena's arms drop, and she steps back, her brown eyes concerned. "That's so sad. We'll just have to get you used to it. Nothing like a good hug to improve your day."

I return her smile with a weak grin and turn to the man standing behind her. He looks like an older version of O'Neill. It's uncanny how much he resembles both his parents, even though the two of them are completely different.

"I'm Ty's dad." The man holds out a fist. "You can call me Brad. Brad. Dad. See what I did there? I'm also a poet."

My lips quirk as I bump my knuckles against his. "Nice to meet you, Brad."

"Tigh-eeeeee!" A high-pitched voice echoes through the corridor. Seconds later, a tiny woman barrels across the courtyard and launches herself at O'Neill. They fall back onto the padded platform, and she rolls off him and bounces to her feet, laughing. "Excellent placement," she says with a nod.

"I've learned." He sits up and dodges as she attempts to punch him in the shoulder. "This is Aretha. My big sister." He stands, dwarfing the woman by half a meter.

She looks at me, her eyes cold and measuring. After a few seconds, she holds out her fist for the briefest of bumps. "You must be Annabelle."

"Please, call me Triana," I say.

"If you like." She turns back to O'Neill. "Did you come to help Bill?"

"We both did," he says, taking my hand and pulling me to his side.

Aretha looks me over again, her expression unreadable. "Excellent. He's coming over for dinner."

"Who are your friends outside?" Brad has a vid feed playing on his holo-ring. The two agents stand like statues at the front door. "Why didn't they come in?"

"They're security," O'Neill says. "Since Triana is Dame Morgan's heir, the board doesn't—"

"Whoever they are, they can't stand around outside like that." Brad starts across the courtyard. "I'm going to tell them to come inside. If they're worried about intruders, we can shut the gate."

"Dad—" O'Neill gives me an apologetic look and hurries after his father.

My chest squeezes in panic as I turn back to the two women. They also look very much alike. Curly brown hair, brown eyes, smooth tan skin. Serena is taller, and her age shows in the fine lines around her eyes and mouth. When she smiles, the resemblance to Ty is striking.

Aretha doesn't smile.

"Aretha, why don't you show Triana to her room?" Serena flicks her holo-ring. "We'll put your security detail in the room next to yours, so they're close by. They won't mind sharing, will they?"

"I don't think so," I stutter. "I haven't travelled with them before, so I'm not sure how this all works."

"Don't worry, we'll get it sorted. I'll make sure they have access to the security cams—we have a few of those. Ty thinks it makes the compound safer. I'll see you at dinner." She pats my shoulder then strides after the two men.

"This way." Aretha doesn't wait. By the time I figure out which of our two bags is mine, she's disappearing into the gloom of the cloister on the far side of the courtyard. I hurry after her.

The cloister runs around the sides and back of the courtyard, with white arches and wide columns supporting the balcony above. As my eyes adjust to the gloom, I notice doors leading off the cloister. A wide flight of stairs leads upward, and Aretha waits at the top, clicking her fingernails against the railing.

When I reach Aretha, she turns without a word and leads me along the balcony. More doors here, some of them open to reveal comfortable bedrooms. She takes me up another flight of stairs to the highest floor. The red tile roof covers the balcony, and the tops of the two courtyard trees sway just above. All around the square, there are more wooden doors set in white plaster. Aretha walks to the second one on the right.

"This is yours. Best room in the house." She looks me over. "Not my choice."

"What's going on here?" I decide hitting this straight on will be the best tactic. Aretha is a lawyer, so if I try to play her game, she'll dig in. "Why do you dislike me?"

"Why do you think I dislike you?" She pushes open the door and gestures for me to enter the dim room.

"I dunno, maybe the sneer on your face?" I drop my bag on the bed and turn to face her. After the courtyard, the room is dim, and light from the door behind her makes it difficult to see her face.

"I don't even know you."

"Exactly. You don't know me. I'm a nice person. And yes, I suppose you could say I broke your brother's heart, if you wanted to be dramatic. But we've patched it all up, and everything is fine. And it's not like he hasn't…" I trail off, not wanting to discuss our romantic ups and downs with his sister.

Her voice sharpens. "You admit it? He was *devastated* when he came back to Grissom. Then he gets a call from you and goes racing away, all excited. And you disappeared again. How would you feel if someone did that to your brother?"

"I'd be pissed. If I had a brother." I have a half-brother, but it's not the same. I barely know him. "But for the record, I didn't call him. That was Vanti."

"I don't care who it was—you hurt him, and when he went racing after you, you hurt him again!"

"That wasn't my fault! I was deported!" I cry in frustration.

"So you say. Grissom doesn't deport people who outstay their visas." She points to her own chest. "Lawyer, remember? I know these things."

My eyes narrow in suspicion. "I thought you were a domestic contract lawyer?"

"That doesn't mean I can't do my research," she mutters. "I have a friend in immigration. I know how it works. If someone outstays their visa, they're fined, and they have to pay for a new visa. They only get deported if they can't pay."

"That's not what happened to me. I don't know if they decided to use me as an example or if it was a personal thing, but Kato and Watson put me on Bill's shuttle faster than you can—"

"You were on Bill's shuttle?" she breaks in. "The one that blew up?"

"Yeah. I thought you knew that."

Her lips purse, and she looks me over. "No, I didn't. That's… interesting."

"Why?"

"Are you really going to help Bill?" She crosses the room and flings open the shutters. Sunlight rushes in, illuminating the colorful layered carpets, light wood furniture, and bright white walls. She turns, the light throwing her into shadow again.

57

"That's why we're here." I turn away. The room is large, and a huge, low bed fills about half of it. Piles of pillows cover the top, and gauzy fabric falls from the ceiling around the sides and end. It's looped and gathered near an ornately carved headboard. That won't be comfortable to lean against.

Near the window, a pair of pale wood chairs with thick flowery upholstered seats and backs flank a spindly table made of the same wood. A pair of bright orange flowers stand in a narrow vase.

"There's a force shield over the windows to keep insects out," Aretha says. "But the shutters help with the light. Sun rises early this time of year. Bathroom is over there." She points to a door in the corner. "We have water rationing, so there's a timer on the shower. Or you can use the sonic option, if you like that sort of thing." Her curled lip tells me how she feels about it.

She crosses the room and pauses by the door. "I don't trust you, but I'll give you the benefit of the doubt. For now." She turns and sweeps out, shutting the door behind her. The heavy wood rings loudly.

ELEVEN

O'NEILL's entire family is coming for dinner. And I mean every last one of them. All five of his siblings along with their significant others, and in Akiko's case, three children. Plus, Bill and his partner and a double handful of assorted aunts, uncles, and cousins. Several of the extended family also have offspring, and soon, the courtyard is more playground than living room.

"Come to the lounge." Serena takes my hand and pulls me away from the noise.

She leads me to the large, open room behind the lounging pavilion. The space takes up a corner of the big building, with windows on the two external sides. Light filters in through cracks between the shutters, but Serena only opens one set. "That wall faces west. It's way too hot in here with those shutters open."

The huge lounge has three separate seating areas. Unlike a similar room in my mother's estate on Kaku, this room is cozy and welcoming. Thick rugs lay scattered across a polished wood floor. Plush, comfortable furniture provides seating. Serena crosses to a cabinet and pulls it open, revealing an AutoBar. "Would you like a drink?"

"Is there a local specialty?" I ask.

"The estate produces a fabulous sparkling wine." She opens the other side of the cupboard to reveal a state-of-the-art wine storage unit. A few flicks to the interface, and a glass of chilled sparkling wine is dispensed.

"Thanks." I take the glass and sip. "Fantastic! You said, 'the estate.' What does that mean?"

"The family owns a share in the local wine estate—Apollone Vintners," Serena says. "We all help out with, well, everything, and we get paid in wine." As she dispenses another glass, more people filter into the room. She takes my arm and pulls me away from the cabinet. "Get your own drinks, folks. It's just family today."

I glance around the room. It's starting to fill up. "These are all family?"

"Everyone wanted to meet you." Serena nudges me toward a deep chair near the center of the space, next to an elegant old lady. "Have a seat next to my grandmother. Grandma, this is Ty's friend Triana. This is Lady Rylan Evangelista Mendoza bin Tariq e Reynolds y Simpson."

"Call me Angie." She holds out a bony, thin-skinned fist.

I smile, wondering if there's a social stigma against rejuvenation here. The only person I've ever met who looked as old as Angie was Don Huatang. Rumor says he's nearing 150 years, and all his rejuv has failed at once. He sleeps most of the time, waking only to demand his handlers buy or sell a particular stock.

"Do you mind if I stand?" The chair looks impossibly comfortable, but I don't want to be awkwardly gazing up everyone's noses.

Before she can answer, I am surrounded by O'Neills. Or maybe they're Mendozas. I've always had a single last name, so I'm not one hundred percent sure how the extras work together. Two men step forward. They're virtually identical, although one has a faint scar running through his left eyebrow. I wonder if he kept it so people could tell them apart.

"I'm Roberto," the unscarred one says. "Call me Ro. And that handsome devil is Yuri."

"We're Ty's brothers," Yuri says, unnecessarily. They look like slightly unfinished versions of their brother. Something about the shape of their lips or maybe the color of their hair is different from Ty, but without him standing beside them, I'm not sure what.

"I'm Triana." I hold out my fist.

Ro ignores my hand and wraps me in a bear hug. Yuri throws his arms around both of us, bouncing us up and down. "Group hug!" they yell.

"Get off her, you animals." A small woman, taller than Aretha but shorter than Serena, smacks one of the boys. "Leave the poor woman alone! I'm Akiko." She holds out her fist. "My husband Blas is out chasing children. He's the tall redhead. That's our sister Lili and her fiancé Jie." She points at a pair standing behind the twins. The woman is obviously related to Serena. The man is a shorter, bald guy with broad, muscular shoulders and a shiny head. He smiles, teeth bright in his dark face.

"Ro, get Triana another glass of wine." Akiko shoves her brothers away. "And give her some space. I'll introduce you to the rest of the tribe. You don't have to remember all their names—we only see them once a month. Usually when there's food."

"Or wine," an older man says with a grin. "I'm Ole, Brad's brother. That's my wife, Rafaella." He nods to a quiet woman in deep conversation with Serena. "Where's Ty?"

"I haven't seen him since I got here," I admit. I gulp down the last of my wine before Ro can take my half-full glass.

"He's probably playing with the kids," Akiko says. "They love their Uncle Ty. This is Servenus."

The next hour goes by in a blur as Ro and Yuri keep my wine glass full and Akiko introduces me to an ever-growing sea of unfamiliar faces. I wish I'd gotten a family tree downloaded to my holo-ring before the party. Serena said it would be a family dinner—I wasn't prepared for this much family.

The wine is delicious, and the twins seem determined to keep a full glass in my hand. It's definitely alcoholic. A warm buzz fogs my mind and relaxes my inhibitions. Soon, I'm telling stories and laughing with Akiko and the twins.

O'Neill pushes through the crowd to my side. His hair is disheveled for once, and a tiny chocolate handprint mars his perfect tunic. "Looks like you're having fun." He slides an arm around me and takes the glass from my hand. After a sip, he waves the glass at his brothers. "How many of these have you fed her?"

"You're so shiny." I lean into him as the lounge spins around us.

"Two or three," one of the twins says.

"Maybe four," the other one says with a grin.

O'Neill's eyes narrow. "Get some Buzzkill."

"She's fine. Having a great time." The boys talk on top of each other, and in my fuzzy state, they coalesce into one then split apart again.

"That's funny." I giggle. "More wine, please."

"You need to eat something," O'Neill says. "And take the edge off this buzz. Someone's been giving you the hard stuff." He clicks his tongue, and one of the boys slinks away.

"Akikikikio says you like to play hide-n-seek with the kids." I smile at O'Neill. Turning my head up to look at him upsets my balance, and I sway. His arm tightens around me.

"Akiko, why did you let them do this?"

"How was I supposed to know she's such a lightweight?" Akiko's eyes glitter. "She's not exactly tiny, so…"

He shoves the glass at her. "You let the boys spike her drink."

The missing twin returns, hands something to his older brother, then disappears into the crowd. The other one goes with him. O'Neill holds a small pill out to me. "Time for some Buzzkill. This one isn't expired." He grins, a private joke between the two of us.

I smile back and open my mouth. He drops the tablet on my tongue, where it dissolves almost instantly. The fog in my brain rolls back, slowly revealing memories of the things I said over the last hours. My face goes hot. "I can't believe—yikes." I straighten my spine and turn back to Akiko. "I hope I didn't say anything offensive to you. I seem to have blathered for quite a while."

Akiko grins. "You're funny when you're drunk. I'm sorry I didn't realize what the boys were doing. I should have noticed—they did the same thing to Blas the first time I brought him home. They didn't spike it, though, just kept refilling."

"They'll be sorry." O'Neill's voice is hard.

"Don't." I turn and put a hand on his chest. "It's not a big deal. I don't have any secrets to hide anymore."

"You did tell us about your crush on your mother's yoga teacher." Akiko grimaces.

"Ugh!" I duck my head as my face heats up again. "That was, like, fifteen years ago." Across the room, Aretha is talking to a couple who look to have just arrived. I try to divert attention from myself. "Isn't that Bill?"

Akiko and O'Neill both turn. "It is," O'Neill says. "Who's that with him?"

"That's his new partner, Kate," Akiko says. "Nice woman but a bit stern. She's a—"

"Peacekeeper." O'Neill and I say together. We exchange a glance, and he continues. "She's the one who deported Triana." He sets my spiked drink on a nearby table and urges me across the room. "I think it's time to have a chat."

TWELVE

"HI, BILL. AGENT KATO." O'Neill smiles, but his voice is cold. "Could we have a word?" He's already sweeping us into the courtyard. "Aretha, could you smooth over any—"

"No, I think Aretha needs to be in on this discussion." I raise my eyebrows at the woman. "She wanted to know what's going on."

Aretha nods regally. "We can talk in the office." She strides across the courtyard toward the opposite corner.

"Uncle Ty! Come play!" A flood of children surrounds us, calling out, grabbing O'Neill's clothing.

He disengages the grubby fingers easily. "I have to talk to the grown-ups, but I'll play after dinner, okay?"

"Awww." Disappointment washes over the eager faces, then they light up again. "Uncle Blas!" The children flow away.

I glance over my shoulder—the tall, red-haired man has appeared at the entrance to the lounge. He winks at us then calls out, "Hide and seek! Ten! Nine! Eight..."

Happily screaming children scatter and disappear.

O'Neill glances at Akiko. "Thanks."

She shrugs. "We needed a distraction." The five of us follow Aretha to an ornate door near the front of the building. Thick carvings cover the wood—vines, flowers, small creatures.

I run my fingers over a tiny lizard. "This is incredible."

"It's several hundred years old." O'Neill pauses beside me as the others pile into the room. "Grissom was less habitable in the early days—colonists spent a lot of summer days inside."

"Is this house from the colonial days?" I look around the courtyard in surprise.

"No. Our great grandfather bought the door from an estate sale." He nudges me into the room and shuts the door.

Unlike the lounge, this room is cool and formal. Heavy wood furniture with little padding fills the smaller space. A huge desk presides over several uncomfortable looking chairs. Aretha swings the shutters open. The large window looks out into a narrow, walled courtyard. Painted tiles cover the walls, but this is the northeast side of the building, so heavy shadows fill the space. A small fountain burbles in the center.

"This is the room in which official business is conducted," Aretha says. She turns and leans her hips against the desk. "What the hell is going on, Bill?"

Bill throws himself into one of the chairs. He winces. "You've met my partner, Kate." He gestures to the short woman standing by the window. She ignores us, staring out at the little fountain.

"Yes, we've met." O'Neill crosses his arms and leans against the wall.

I sink onto a nearby chair—how did they make a piece of furniture so uncomfortable? Scooting forward, I perch on the edge.

"It's my fault." Akiko steps out of the shadowed corner and holds up her hands. "I knew how hurt you were. By her." Her eyes dart toward me then back to him. "I didn't want her around, so I got rid of her."

"You coerced—encouraged? Bribed?—a peacekeeper to deport my—Triana?" O'Neill glares at his sister.

"There was no bribe! She requested assistance," Kate says, swinging away from the window. "She pointed out that the young woman technically had no legal status once the cruise ship departed. I chose to enforce that statute."

THE RINGS OF GRISSOM

"So, you *don't* routinely deport everyone who outstays their visitor's visa?" I ask.

Kate's eyes flick to me and back to O'Neill. "We don't. We can, but we don't." She steps forward and puts a hand on Bill's shoulder. "Bill is on a retainer to assist in Peacekeeper activities, so I tasked him to take you back to the ship. Where, legally, you belonged." She raises her chin defiantly.

"A word to the auditor could cause you some difficulties, I'd imagine." O'Neill's voice is calm and speculative. "I can't believe they'd let a family member administer a contract like that."

"Technically, Gwen—Agent Watson—put in the request." Kate's shoulders hunch. "We didn't do anything illegal."

"Just shady as hell." O'Neill's lips press together.

"Look, they were just trying to protect you." Aretha pushes away from the desk, coming to stand in front of us. "Akiko's your sister—it's what we do. If I'd known, I'd have helped. But that's not important now."

"It's important to me." O'Neill glares down at his sister. "You deported the woman I love."

Akiko goes still, her face blanching. After a moment, she takes a deep breath, squares her shoulders, and turns to me. "Annabelle—I mean, Triana. I apologize for all of this. It was despicable behavior, and I have no excuse. Will you forgive me?"

Her eyes bore into mine in a way that doesn't feel very contrite. In fact, I get the distinct impression she'd do it again in a heartbeat if I gave her a reason. I raise my chin without breaking eye contact, channeling my inner Ice Dame. "It is forgiven." But not forgotten.

"Good." She swivels back to O'Neill. "We need to figure out what happened to Bill's ship. The government is blaming him. Pilot error. But it wasn't."

O'Neill looks at Bill. "You're sure?"

Bill shrugs. "It went up during the reentry phase. That's all computer controlled. I laid in the standard program and pressed land. Not much room for error there."

"Did they recover the data?" O'Neill rolls his shoulders away from the wall and starts pacing. "Flight forensics is not my field."

"You must know someone," Aretha says.

"The investigator says the flight recorders were damaged in the explosion," Bill says.

"Really?" I jump up from my chair. "The passenger capsule survived intact, but the data recorders were destroyed? Doesn't that seem a bit odd?"

Kate nods. "It shouldn't be possible. That data should have been saved to the recorder stored inside the passenger capsule. But that device was damaged or malfunctioned."

"Then how did they come to the conclusion it was pilot error?" I ask.

Bill shrugs. "They couldn't find anything to blame it on, so it must be my fault—human error is more likely than a malfunction these days. They tried to pin the recorder malfunction on me, too, but it's not possible to access the device from inside the capsule."

"What about hacking?" I drum my fingers on the desk. "Could someone have hacked the system—either from inside or remotely?"

"You were the only person inside the shuttle besides me," Bill says. "Do you really want to pursue that line?"

I laugh. "Good point, but we have to look at everything. I'm not in the habit of carrying shuttle crashing loops on my holo-ring, and communications were quarantined, so there was no way for me to download anything. You could have." I raise my eyebrows at him.

"Why would I crash my own shuttle?" Bill leaps up. "You sound like the review board!"

I hold up a hand. "We're looking at everything, remember?"

"The fact that Dame Morgan's heir was on that shuttle should be considered, too," Kate says. "In fact, a failed assassination attempt makes more sense than anything else."

"The review board ruled that out. But who knew she'd be on that shuttle? Besides you." O'Neill zeroes in on Kate, his eyes burning into hers.

"Me, Gwen, and Bill." Kate faces O'Neill, ticking names off on her fingers. "And Akiko. Are you suggesting one of us wanted her dead?"

"Dead?" Akiko flings herself between Kate and O'Neill. "I wanted her out of your life but not dead. And I don't give a crap whose kid she is."

He ignores his sister, still focused on Kate. "I'm suggesting you jumped on the opportunity to deport her pretty quickly. I'm *suggesting* you might have used it as an opportunity to take care of other business."

"Now hold on a minute!" Bill pushes O'Neill's shoulder. "If you think Kate is working for a terrorist organization and used family business to —" He breaks off and stomps away. "I can't even—"

Kate runs her tongue over her teeth. "It sounds highly unlikely, if you ask me." She's calm and detached, as if talking about someone else. Of course, if it wasn't her, she *is* talking about someone else. "No one knew the Morgan girl was going to step foot onto Grissom. She didn't leave the cruise ship until it was almost ready to depart—and it was at the station for only twenty hours. That's not enough time for even the most organized terrorist cell to—we'd have to assume they'd already made contact with—that this wasn't a one-off thing. You're suggesting that I was already on the payroll, and a target of opportunity landed in my lap. Does that seem likely?"

"You tell me." O'Neill looms over her.

Kate shakes her head. "It's not. You can run a background sweep on me. I have no ties to terrorist organizations."

"What about foreign powers?" Aretha asks.

Bill spins around to glare at Aretha.

"I'm just playing devil's advocate," Aretha says. "We need to get all the possibilities out so we can decide which ones are most likely."

"I'm not working for Gagarin or Lewei," Kate says, her voice remarkably calm. "I was born and raised here on Grissom. I've only left the planet a handful of times, and those are all documented. But feel free to run a deep background. The Peacekeepers did when I enlisted."

"What about Watson?" I ask.

"What about her?" Kate says.

"Could she be the link?"

"She's as likely to be the link as I am," Kate says. "Which means, probably not. But you can run background checks on both of us. We have nothing to hide."

"Why would a foreign power do this?" Bill says. "Grissom is a peaceful world. We've had no terrorism in the last two decades. Why would anyone bother sending an agent here? It's not like they could have predicted you and Ty would get together."

I laugh. "Unless he's the agent."

THIRTEEN

DINNER, though fabulous, was uneventful. Afterwards, the adults chatted in the lounge while the kids played a game called vampire that seemed to involve a lot of shrieking. Around ten, the people with children start making noises about leaving.

"Just put the kids to bed," Serena says. "Your room is empty."

"They have school tomorrow," Akiko says. "Blas, will you get them into the carriage? I need to talk to my brother." At Blas's nod, she and O'Neill disappear into the office again.

"Do you know what that's about?" Serena whispers to Aretha. The younger woman shrugs.

A while later, Akiko emerges, wiping her eyes. She gives her mother a watery hug and disappears into the darkness.

Serena marches across the courtyard, stopping O'Neill as he exits the office. "What did you say to make your sister cry?"

"She's fine," he says. "She made herself cry." He glances at me over his mother's head. "It's all good."

Serena eyes him then takes his arm. "Come on, we're playing cards." She turns and loops her free hand through my arm. "You, too, Triana. Have you ever played Youquer?"

Hours later, Ty walks me to my room. The twins and his parents are still arguing over the last hand when we reach the third floor. We stop in front of my door, and I lean against it. "Now what?"

"My room is down on the second floor." He grins. "Right next to Mom and Dad."

I bite my lip to keep from laughing. "Nothing like being home, is there?"

He grins. "I can see why you chafe at being on Level 83." He slides his arms around me, and I lean in for a long, delicious kiss.

"You did what?" Serena's voice echoes from the courtyard, and we reflexively jump apart.

O'Neill laughs. "I think Yuri just told Mom about your drink."

"He told her? Of his own free will? Without pressure?"

"He had a little pressure." O'Neill grins. "I told him if he didn't own up, I'd spill the beans."

"Do they live here?"

He nods. "It's pretty common on Grissom. Housing is expensive, so single people live at home until they're ready to pair off. The twins have talked about getting their own place, but it wouldn't be as nice as this. Plus, free food."

I shudder. Moving back into my mother's penthouse had been uncomfortable, to say the least. I'd much rather live in a crappy one-room compartment with a roommate. But O'Neill's parents aren't like the Ice Dame. Maybe living here wouldn't be the same. I stiffen. "You aren't thinking of moving back in, are you?"

"I wasn't," he says with a chuckle. "But then you dumped me." At the look on my face, he stops. "Sorry, too soon?"

"I didn't really dump you. I just ran away." I say it in a matter-of-fact tone, as if it were the most reasonable thing to do. "You shouldn't have been surprised—you're the one who gave me the codename Runner, after all. But that's all behind me now." I tighten my arms around him, pressing my cheek against his shoulder. After a while, I loosen my grip. "What happened between you and Akiko?"

His cheek brushes against my hair. "It doesn't matter. She's not going to try anything again. We should get some sleep. Our meeting with Bill is pretty early tomorrow." He glances down at the stairs. Serena waves from the second floor. "I'll see you in the morning."

BILL AND KATE live in a standard apartment building, similar to those I've seen on every other occupied world in the galaxy. This one is ten floors. Surprisingly, given Grissom's climate, it's an above-ground building. Although, now that I think about it, I haven't seen any underground facilities here.

After they clear the building, the hulk takes up a position just outside the front door. The android stays with us as we climb the stairs to the fourth floor. O'Neill waves his holo-ring at the access panel.

"Sorry about the hike," Bill says as he lets us into their apartment. "The float tube's been out since before we moved in. No one knows what happened or why they don't fix it."

"Andron, wait here." O'Neill ushers me inside, leaving the security agent in the hall. "We've got a lot of work, Bill, so let's get down to business. What have you got?"

Bill pulls up some files on his holo-ring. "These are the communications logs from the shuttle. You want something to drink?"

While he brings coffee, O'Neill flips through the files.

"Tell me more about your company," I say. "Mendoza Enterprises. What's the story there?"

Bill raises his eyebrows at O'Neill, who raises one in return. "Tell the woman," O'Neill says. "Triana's kind of a genius at figuring this stuff out."

Bill gives me a considering look. "I started Mendoza Enterprises a few years ago. We have—had—two shuttles. Now just the one, of course. My insurance company is not happy with me, to say the least. I have a contract with the Peacekeepers to provide transportation and the occasional deportation when they need. We're basically on call with a short response time during business hours. After-hours work requires more advance notification and overtime rates. They pay a premium to have us on call. The government has several companies on retainer for various agencies."

"And Watson called you when they picked me up," I prompt when he stops talking. "Who knew you were working that day?"

"I have other clients," Bill says. "They don't pay as well, so when something like this comes up, I might try to juggle my schedule. I was supposed to do a job for Protech—just shuttling some execs out to a job site. I called Luin—she's my backup pilot. She did the Protech job, and I did this one. I didn't want her asking any questions." He shrugs uncomfortably.

"You don't say." I glance at O'Neill. "Has anyone checked out Luin?"

"She was cleared in the original investigation." O'Neill's scrolling through the reports Bill flicked to him. "Luin Montgomery Servian. Got her license three years ago. Been working for Bill and two other flight companies ever since."

"We share the part-timers," Bill says. "We can't schedule both birds full time—there simply isn't enough traffic. But she's absolutely trustworthy."

"Do you have any information on her prior to her flight license?" I ask. "Know anything about her family, where she's from—deep background, as Kate said?"

Bill holds up both hands. "She's been checked. Kate wouldn't let me work with someone she didn't think was safe. And obviously, she has connections in that field. I let her vet the pilots—and the clients."

"Who had access to the shuttle?" O'Neill asks.

"No one. We have a locked hangar at the launch field."

"No one?" I fold my arms over my chest. "You do your own maintenance?"

"Most of it," Bill says. "It's how I keep costs down. I bring in specialists for the stuff I can't handle. And the regulators insist on inspections any time you swap out anything." He groans a little. "Eats up my profits to bring them in, but I can't fly without the seal."

"Seal?" I ask.

"The regulators apply a physical seal to the ship after inspection, plus a virtual seal on our records. That way, clients can make sure everything's been inspected." He pinches the bridge of his nose. "Local law says they can do a visual inspection before signing, but most of them settle for the virtual."

"When was the last time you had this vehicle serviced?" O'Neill makes a note in a file and swipes it away.

"About a week before the crash." Bill flicks another icon and flings it across the display to O'Neill. "Here it is: engine tune-up, completed and sealed five days before."

"Who did the work?"

"I did." Bill leans back in his chair. "Everything was perfect."

"Then I guess we need to talk to this guy." O'Neill points at the screen. "Vern al-Petrosian."

"Al-Petrosian?" I choke on my coffee.

O'Neill pounds my back. "It's not him."

"Do you know this guy?" Bill grabs a towel from the kitchen to mop up the coffee I spit over the holo-projector.

"We had a run-in with a guy on Kaku," I croak. "Head of a terrorist organization—the KPC. Karhovian Peace Corps."

"Is this the same person?" Bill asks.

"Can't be." O'Neill shakes his head decisively. "Wil's in prison on S'Ride. A couple cells over from Putin." His lips quirk as he glances at me.

"Exactly where they both belong," I mutter.

"Part of his family?" Bill nods at me. "If you were involved in his arrest and incarceration, they might be out to get you."

"Let's find out." O'Neill takes my hand and pulls me to my feet. "Time to visit the regulator."

FOURTEEN

THE FIVE OF US—O'NEILL, Bill, my two bodyguards, and I—head out to the public transport station. Although we'd used the family carriage—that's what they call bubbles on Grissom—to Bill's place, Ty sent it back for his mother's use.

"The station is only a block away," Bill says as he points down the street. "Just around the corner."

The hulk nods and mutters something under his breath before loping away. Probably coordinating with the android, who is trailing behind.

"What's with the entourage?" Bill asks.

O'Neill gives him an "are you an idiot" look. "Last time Triana was here, someone tried to blow her up. Now we find that person might be connected to a terrorist gang that targeted her mother. I've already put in a request to SK'Corp to send more agents."

"More?" I groan. "This is why I ran away."

"I know." He slides an arm around my shoulders and gives me a quick squeeze before letting go. He doesn't even look at me as his head constantly swivels, eyes evaluating and cataloging each pedestrian and carriage along our route. He's in full protective agent mode.

"Is Vanti coming?" I'm not sure how I feel about that. While we were on S'Ride, Vanti and I formed a sort of friendship. But she's not the warm and cuddly type. She's also fiercely loyal to O'Neill, which can make for some uncomfortable situations.

"Of course. She's got all the background on the KPC case."

We've reached the corner. To the right, a large, transparent dome peeks out from behind another apartment building. We cross the street and stop in front of the translucent curve. A sign above the door reads Bellevue Station.

"Bellevue?" I look around, but all I can see are nearly identical apartment blocks. The mountains, visible as a gray smudge from my room at the O'Neill compound, are hidden by the buildings. "Where's the view?"

Bill shrugs. "Old name. I think it's actually the guy who built here first. Or used ironically, maybe. This part of Grissom is not beautiful."

O'Neill nods to our security guys, and we enter the station. People move purposely through the building, taking lift tubes down to the pods or buying snacks at the vendor row at the back of the dome. Bill purchases a group pass and flicks the code to each of us. Then we scan through the entry gate and head for the slide ramp.

"Everyone talks about the swamps of Grissom," I say. "But I've only seen desert."

O'Neill ushers me onto the green line slide. "There are swamps in the northern continent. You do not want to go there."

"Hey, stand right!" someone yells from behind us.

Bill glances over his shoulder and frowns past me. "You, security guy! Move over. Let people by."

I turn. Andron stands beside O'Neill, blocking the slide ramp and creating a barrier between me and the anxious commuters behind. "Can we let them by?" I ask. "This thing goes on forever."

O'Neill glances at the android and nods. He moves forward, pressing me against the side rail. If we weren't in the middle of a commuter station, it would be cozy. Andron steps closer, turning his back to me. People mutter as they push past, but I can't pick out any specific complaints.

Once the crowd thins, Andron steps away, standing in the middle of the slide ramp again.

"He really doesn't understand how these things work, does he?" I ask O'Neill.

"He does." O'Neill takes a half-step, so he's not squishing me anymore. It's nice to be able to breathe, but I miss the warmth when he moves away. "Normally, he'd block the slide ramp at the top and not allow anyone on until we exit at the bottom, but we don't have a big enough team to manage that."

"Normally, we wouldn't be riding public transport." I laugh at the idea of my mother taking a transit pod anywhere.

"True enough. We need to adjust our operations." He nods at the hulk as we reach the bottom of the ramp. "The line for pods is over there."

The slide ramp deposits us in a large underground room. Holo-ads pop up as we cross the cold floor toward another gate. We swipe our transport codes to the gate, and it opens to allow us through one at a time. Ferrigi goes first to check for terrorists, I suppose. Although how they're supposed to have known we'd come this way is beyond me.

I step through the gate and follow Ferrigi down a short hall. A series of closed doors lines the left wall. The right is blank. The fourth door is open, and the agent stands in the opening. "This pod is clear, Sera."

"Thanks." I step through the door into an oval pod with six seats in two facing rows. The lower half of the pod is dirty white, while the upper part is transparent. Dingy white pods flank us front and rear—they must be translucent from the outside. A few meters from the side, there's a featureless gray, plascrete wall.

Bill's already sitting in the rear-facing seat on the far side. I cross the small pod and drop into the chair facing him.

"Take the middle seat, please, Sera," Ferrigi says from the door. "There's another access hatch on that side."

With a sigh, I move over, glaring at the hapless door in the far wall. O'Neill steps around me and takes the seat I just vacated. Andron drops into the seat on my right, and Ferrigi finally leaves his post at the door to join us. The door swooshes shut, and a display above the door lights up with the number fifteen.

"This pod departs Bellevue Station in fifteen seconds," a firm, androgynous voice says. The countdown flicks to fourteen. "Please take your seats. Failure to do so will result in delayed departure and late fees being assessed to your ticket." Invisible micrograv restraints compress around my legs and hips.

"They take punctuality seriously here." I watch the display tick over to zero. The pod slides sideways toward the blank wall and clicks into place. It accelerates, pushing us back into the seats. Bill and Ferrigi lurch forward then drop back into their chairs as the pod reaches top speed. Dozens of pods slide past us as we zoom out of the station. The walls close around, forming a dark tube.

"Andron, Ferrigi." O'Neill leans forward to address the two men across from me. "I've forwarded some suggested modifications to your operating procedures. They should be more effective for this urban environment. Let me know what you think."

"Yes, ser." The words snap out of their mouths in perfect unison, and they flick their holo-rings to life.

I shake my head and glance at O'Neill. "I think I'd prefer Vanti. She knows how to do this right."

"Vanti tends to play by her own rules." His eyes twinkle. "Cupcake truck, anyone?"

"That was a very effective cover," I protest.

"No argument. She's good at what she does. Just a bit unpredictable." His lips twitch as he turns to Bill. "Long story."

"I figured." Bill nods. "I messaged Kate. She's meeting us at al-Petrosian's office."

"That's not a great idea," O'Neill says. "We don't want to spook him."

"Routine investigation," Bill says. "Kate wanted to talk to him, anyway. We can do it together and save everyone time."

"Why did Kate want to talk to him?" I ask.

"Same reason you did. He certified my ship."

"Why did you ask me to help you if Kate's already working all of this?" O'Neill asks. "If she's got it under control, I'd prefer to have Triana away from potential danger."

Bill flushes and glances at the security guys. They're both engrossed in the files O'Neill sent. Or at least appear to be. I suspect they're listening to every word we say. Best way to keep your principal safe is to know what they're up to, right?

"I called you because Aretha wanted you to come home."

O'Neill stares at Bill. "What?"

"Wait a minute," I break in. "Akiko got me deported. Then, when Ty came back to SK2, Aretha tried to pull him away again? Is this all about getting him away from me?"

"It might be," Bill mutters. "Aretha didn't think you'd come along. And she did think Ty would help me."

"What is wrong with those women?" O'Neill demands.

I put a hand on his arm. "They're your family. They're trying to do what's best for you. And since you quit working for the board, there wasn't any reason for you to stay on SK2. Except me." I smile, feeling all warm and melty at the thought that he stayed only for me.

"I still have a job." He stares at me. "Did you think I left board sec? I quit working for Dame Morgan."

"But you said you resigned." The warmth drains from my body. "You packed up your compartment and moved out."

"That's when I thought you were dumping me." He shifts in his seat to face me better. "Once we got the whole deportation thing ironed out, I asked Don Said if I could come back."

"But why were you living in Mother's guest compartment?"

"It's not easy finding a place I can afford on SK2." He chuckles. "You should know that."

I do. A maintenance tech makes way less money than board security. The place Kara and I had on Level 6 was better than our studio on Level 2, but it took months on a waiting list to get in. Everything on the station is fully occupied.

"I'm on leave without pay right now," O'Neill says to Bill. "I already used up my vacation time. But when family asks for help, you go."

Bill's face turns red. "We thought you'd quit. That you were just hanging around the station because of her." His eyes dart to me then away.

O'Neill rakes a hand through his hair. "Well, we're here now. You're going to get help, whether you want it or not. And if there's a connection between this al-Petrosian and the one we put away, you're going to get a lot more help than you expected."

"This pod will arrive in Levaward Station in fifteen seconds." The countdown appears above the door again. The invisible restraints, which had loosened while we traveled, tighten across our laps.

"Arriving in five. Four. Three. Two. One. Welcome to Levaward Station. Please collect your belongings before departing the pod."

The clock clicks to zero then goes blank. The pressure across my hips vanishes, and I stand, turning toward the door. The men get to their feet, blocking the doors.

We wait. Nothing happens.

Then an explosion throws us to the floor.

FIFTEEN

O'Neill shoves me under the seats, his chest and shoulders protecting my head from the outside world. Dust sifts down, dropping grit into my eyes. I blink, tears blurring my vision. Blood pumps in my ears, drowning out the ringing left by the blast. "What happened?"

"Stay down," O'Neill says, pushing me against the wall. The struts supporting the seats dig into my back and legs, but I don't say anything. I flick through my audio implant channels, trying to find the frequency the men are using. They must be talking via the implants—there's no way they're silent right now. Unless they're injured.

"Are the hulk and the android okay?" I whisper. My stomach clenches at the thought of the death and destruction an explosion that size could cause.

"They're fine." O'Neill rolls away and springs to a crouch. After a minute, he reaches out to me.

I take his hand and let him extract me from my hiding place. My back burns as my shoulder comes away from the strut—I'll have a bruise there. "How's Bill?"

O'Neill glances around the pod and pulls me to my feet. "He's good. No injuries. We need to get out of here."

"Station door is blocked," Andron says through the implant.

Hah, I found the right signal.

The pod has cracked across the top. A chunk is missing behind our seats, and dust fills the air. I peek through—a ragged hole gapes in the wall between the tracks and the station. The lights inside our pod have failed, but the one behind us glows, giving the whole scene an eerie atmosphere.

The screech of plastek being forced rips at my eardrums. "Off-side door is opening," the hulk says. "I can't get it all the way open, but we can get through."

"Get out there and check for threats." O'Neill's voice is calm, decisive. "Stay off the pod-rail in case they're still sending traffic through."

"Roger." There's more ear-splitting noise as the hulk pulls the doors farther apart. "Clear. There are three other pods in the station. I'm going to check on them." There's silence for a few moments, then his voice comes back. "No one is responding when I pound on them. Returning."

"Triana." Ty's whisper comes through the audio. "Let's go. Set your audio to channel thirty-four."

"Already there." I grin and swipe some dust off his shoulder. Bill coughs. "Sorry, Bill."

He waves me off. "Let's get out of here."

I slide through the gap in the off-side door. Taking the hand Ferrigi holds out, I jump the meter to the ground. The soft glow of the other pods through the dust gives the tunnel an eerie atmosphere. Bill and Andron—still inside our pod—show as faint shadows on the translucent material. The other pods appear to be empty.

"Stay to the left of that red line." Ferrigi releases my hand and points at the floor. A small blaster has appeared in his other hand. "That's the pod track, and if one comes through here, it will smash you like a bug. Stay behind me."

We make our way along the narrow path, past the three other pods, and into the empty parking stalls beyond.

"Don't stop here—when emergency vehicles arrive, they'll pull into the unoccupied spaces." O'Neill points over my shoulder. "There's a mainte-nance catwalk up there. Ferrigi, take Triana there while we get one of these doors to the station open."

The hulk turns to take my right arm in his left hand—the one not holding a blaster. "This way, Sera." My shoulder pulls and aches when he moves my arm.

"Are you sure we want to go in?" Bill asks. "There was an explosion in there. Aren't we safer out here?"

O'Neill exchanges a look with the other two agents and nods. "Good call. Let's see if we can access the surface another way."

Their feet clatter on the metal ladder as they follow us up to the catwalk that runs alongside the pod tunnel.

A glimmer in the distance precedes a waft of oily smelling air. "Pod coming!" Bill calls out.

O'Neill pushes me against the wall, standing between me and the narrow railing at the edge of the catwalk. Burning sears my back—I must have wrenched something pretty good.

"I'm not going to fall off," I mutter.

"The station just blew up." He doesn't look at me—his eyes are trained on the approaching light. "That could be anyone. Andron, watch our six."

"If they were trying to sneak up, wouldn't they leave their light off?" I lean against the wall. My legs are starting to shake—probably a delayed reaction to the explosion. My heart is still pounding in my head, but the ringing in my ears has eased. I take a shaky breath.

Ferrigi stands to my left, legs apart, blaster aimed at the oncoming light. O'Neill takes a half step away, giving me a little breathing room. "Get down, Triana," he whispers over his shoulder.

I slide down into a crouch, the rough wall tearing at my bruised back. At the bottom, my legs decide it's time to rest and slide out from under me, dropping my butt to the coarse metal grating. The floor is cold—it seems to leech all the warmth from my body.

"Triana?" O'Neill's voice sounds sharp.

I try to answer, but it's too much effort. He knows where I am. If I look up, I'll be staring right at his fabulous rear end. I try to lift my chin, but my head doesn't want to obey my commands. A heavy weight settles on my shoulders and chest. My eyes close. I'll just rest while they figure things out. What's the point of having bodyguards if you can't let them do all the work once in a while?

"Triana!"

I blink at O'Neill's face, right in front of mine. "Wha—?"

"Where are you hurt?" He picks up my arm and moves it around. I don't feel anything. It looks funny, just flopping around so bonelessly, but I can't muster the energy to giggle. Plus, I'm so cold.

"Ty, there's blood on the wall." Bill's voice seems to come from far away. "She's bleeding."

O'Neill lowers me to the catwalk. A pod whooshes by, the light stabbing through my closed eyelids. Then it's gone. Two or three more scream past, red and blue lights flickering. Emergency vehicles? I don't care—someone else can worry about that.

"Triana." O'Neill's hands hold my face, blessedly warm against my cold cheeks. "We think you took some shrapnel to the back. We're calling a med team. I'm going to roll you over."

When they ease me onto my stomach, a thin piece of fabric protects my cheek from the rough grating. Someone's shirt? It's still faintly warm. I breathe in. Smells like O'Neill. I rub my cheek against it, feeling safe and protected. Ty will take care of everything.

SIXTEEN

I'M LYING on the deck of a sailboat under the warm sun of Sally Ride. Water sloshes against the hull, and a bird squawks overhead. The salt of the sea breeze tickles my nose but disappears under a stronger one—roasting meat and garlic. O'Neill must have fired up the barbeque.

"Would you like a margarita?" Vanti appears suddenly, her head blocking the sun. "We're supposed to get a blizzard this afternoon." She holds out a puffy snow boot with a tiny umbrella and a straw sticking out of the top.

I look around, but the deck has disappeared under a layer of Christmas ornaments. When I sit up, tinsel slides off my chest and shoulders, leaving strands of metallic icicles clinging to my thick sweater. A vague sense of dread pours through me like honey. I hate this stuff—it wraps around the vacuum bars and destroys my bots.

Vanti, now a meter-tall food-delivery bot with spectacular copper hair, grins. I'm not sure how I know she's smiling—the bot doesn't have a face.

"This is a dream, isn't it?" I ask.

"Of course." The voice sounds just like Vanti when she's playing her college recruiter role—relentlessly cheerful. "Would you like fries with that?"

My eyes peel open. With the hiss of an air seal breaking, the curved translucent surface above me hinges up. A med pod. Light stabs at my eyes, forcing them shut. I blink furiously, trying to see who's waiting for me.

The room is small and bright. White walls gleam and the smell of antiseptic fills the cool air. I glance down at my body, which is covered by a thin blanket. Med pods can treat some injuries while the patient is fully clothed, but mine is apparently not one of them. I clutch the blanket to my chest and sit up slowly.

O'Neill sprawls across a chair in the corner. Stubble covers his chin, and his skin looks waxy. His perpetually perfect hair sticks out at all angles. He's wearing the same clothes he had on when we visited Bill, so not too much time has passed.

"Are you okay?" I croak.

His eyes pop wide. "Triana?"

"I'm fine." I think for a moment. It feels true, and if I just came out of a med pod, it probably is. "I'm fine," I say again with more conviction. "What happened?"

"A piece of the pod must have sliced into your back." He gets up and crosses the small room. His fingers trace a line down my back. "We didn't notice it until we were on the catwalk. Didn't you feel it?"

I shrug, and a tiny pain zings through my shoulder. "I thought I bruised it when you pushed me under the seat. I guess I was operating on adrenaline."

"We got lucky." His arms slide around me, pulling me close. "You lost a lot of blood. Luckily, the emergency responders got there quickly, and they brought us here."

"Where's here?" I don't really care. He's holding me against his chest, warm, strong and comforting, while his hands slide over my bare back. Through the thin blanket, I can feel his solid chest, his heart thumping fast against my cheek. I burrow closer.

Behind him, the door whooshes open. His hands drop as he spins to meet the threat. I scrabble at the blanket as it slides away.

"Oh, it's you." His shoulders relax, and he rises from the half-crouch.

I get the blanket secured and peer over his shoulder.

"Sorry to interrupt," Vanti says. "But there's press gathering outside. Someone must have leaked the Runner's involvement."

The Runner. That's their *so flattering* code name for me. Aretha and Akiko would love it. "Can we please change my code name?"

"Hi, Triana." Vanti doesn't smile—she saves that expression for her under-cover personalities. She holds out a pile of clothing. "I brought you some gear. Griz, let's give her some space to get dressed while we plan our escape."

O'Neill nods. His fingers graze my cheek in a warm caress, and he leans in for a fast kiss. "I'll be right outside."

When the door closes behind them, I use the facilities and get dressed. I try to avoid the mirror, but the horror of my unchecked hair is unavoidable. My frizzy red curls stand out in all directions, like a clown after a hurricane. Fortunately, Vanti's got my back. I find a pair of her industrial-strength hair ties in my pocket. With the mess contained to the back of my head, I can face the world.

I wave the door open and step out. O'Neill and Vanti glance up from their conversation, and he holds out his hand. I cross the narrow waiting room. It's deserted except for us and Andron standing guard by the exit. The door behind Vanti opens, and she spins, hands up. A white-coated med tech stops in surprise.

O'Neill moves Vanti aside. "Is she cleared to go?" He nods at me.

The woman looks at the holo-file in her palm then at me. "I need to do a final check."

"Really?" Vanti crosses her arms over her chest. "You don't trust the med pod."

"Not for high-profile patients." The tech shrugs. "I'm sure she's fine, but everyone knows SK2 folks are litigious by nature."

"If the pod says I'm fine, I'm fine," I mutter.

"The Ice Dame is gonna want proof," Vanti says.

"Send her the med pod file." I glare at Vanti. "I'm not a child, and I can be released under my own recognizance or whatever."

"Let Dr. Tyson do a final check," O'Neill says. "Please? We want to be sure."

I roll my eyes and stomp back into the examination room. The doctor

—they really must be worried about a lawsuit if they sent an actual doctor—runs her scanner over me. She peers into my ears and throat and even pulls out an archaic stethoscope to listen to my lungs and heart.

"Satisfied?" I heave a sigh. "Wouldn't it be more effective to have me sign a waiver?"

"Oh, I have that too." She swipes a file out of her holo-ring and flips it to me. "Standard release paperwork. Oh, and here's a snack. The agents said you'd be hungry."

I grab the chocolate and rip it open. "First sensible thing you've said." I run the waiver through the LegalCheck app and swipe my hand through the accept icon. "Can I go now?"

"You're cleared." She smiles a professional smile. "Thank you for choosing Blenheim Hudson Foretelli-Smythe Summit Medical and Technical Group."

"I didn't really get a choice," I mutter as I wave the door open. "But you're welcome."

"We're going out the back," Vanti says as I emerge again. "Through the kitchen, to avoid the press. Dame Morgan will issue a statement once we're clear."

I try not to roll my eyes again. O'Neill takes my hand, his fingers warm against mine. His hair has magically fallen into place again, as always. "How long have we been here?"

"Couple of hours," O'Neill says, pulling me down a deserted hall behind Vanti. Andron falls in behind. "Bill went home. Luckily, Kate reached the inspector's office early, so she wasn't caught in the explosion."

"Where's the hulk?" We turn and start down another empty corridor. "And where's everyone else? This is a medical center, right?"

"We asked them to clear the halls along our route," O'Neill says. "Ferrigi is by the back door."

We pass through an empty kitchen. Gleaming white cabinets line the walls. Pots full of bland-looking food lay abandoned. I yank my fingers out of O'Neill's grasp and turn off the heat under a soup pot that is close to boiling over. Nobody wants to clean that up.

We work our way through a storage and delivery bay to a large loading dock at the rear of the building. Ferrigi stands in an open doorway, watching. He turns his head and mutters through the audio implant. "Clear to exit." Late afternoon sunlight streams in around him.

The O'Neill family carriage stands half-hidden behind a delivery truck. At least it looks like the one we rode in earlier. It's a boxy, black vehicle with a translucent gray top. We move forward as a block, with me in the middle and the four security people surrounding me. I feel like an actor in a cheesy political drama.

A drone buzzes around the corner of the building. With a wave of O'Neill's hand, the carriage door opens. He checks inside, then Vanti pushes me into the vehicle. The others pile in behind me, and the door slams shut. Before I'm strapped in, the carriage moves forward.

At the end of the blocky building, we reach a quiet street. We turn out and slide up to the next intersection. As we turn away from the medical center, I peer toward the front of the building. A half-dozen people stand out front, and a bank of drones veers toward us, homing in like a swarm of hornets.

"We've got incoming!"

SEVENTEEN

Vanti flicks her holo-ring. "Counter-measures."

"This is a family car; we don't have counter-measures." O'Neill's hands fly through the interface, adjusting our route.

"Sure, we do." I fling a file at the vehicle's dash. "Take that, you little bastards."

"What did you do?" Andron asks.

"I disrupted the carriage's signal—like swapping out a ship's transponder." I keep my eyes on the screen as I answer. "That got rid of the drones locked onto our signal. Looks like a few of them might be using visual."

The cloud of drones has stopped, with only a few of them still following us. I flick the carriage signal at a passing vehicle, and the swarm of flying cameras take off after the other vehicle. The occupants of that carriage are in for a surprise when they stop. I whisper, "Sorry."

"Nice," Vanti says.

The remaining drones mill around us like hungry shoppers in a food court.

"Maybe we can lose them in a parking garage," I suggest.

Vanti flings a grin over her shoulder at me. "Just like old times. Got any of those around here, Griz?"

O'Neill grunts. "This might work." He flips a map onto the translucent front window. A red dot expands into a circle then disappears, like an animated target.

"Sanctuary?" Vanti laughs. "They don't track visitors, do they?"

"Nope. Part of their tax-exempt status—they have to offer complete privacy." He pokes the bullseye with his finger, and a blue line appears on the map, leading from our current location to the church. "We'll go in, switch the signal again, then exit. That should throw them off."

"I'm not sure why they're bothering." Vanti nods, leaning back in her chair. "They know who you are, right? Surely they know where your family lives."

"It's another obscure legal thing," he says. "They can't just show up at my family's home, but if they follow a subject there, it's fair game."

"That is so messed up."

The late sunlight disappears as we slide down a ramp into the parking garage. The lights inside the vehicle brighten.

"Won't they just wait outside for us to come back out?" I ask. "If they're tracking us visually."

"Yeah, we should ditch the carriage." Vanti leans over O'Neill's shoulder to hit the parking icon.

"Wait, what?" O'Neill stares at her.

"We'll set it to head for home later tonight." She opens the door. "They won't wait that long, right? Injured Morgan heir isn't *that* big a story." She winks at me and jumps out.

O'Neill scrambles after Vanti. "How are we going to get her home?"

"Taxi." As she speaks, a fleet of small blue carriages pull up next to us. She flicks an address code at the first one, opens and shuts the door, and waves through the pay screen. It slides away. "You wanna come with me and Triana or send one of the boys?" She nods at Andron and Ferrigi.

O'Neill's teeth grind as he stares from Vanti to the taxis and back. "I'll go with you." He turns to the two surprised guards. "Send these taxis to random locations. Then wait for an hour and take the transit system back to the house. We'll use the vehicle recall later tonight when it's safe to bring the carriage home."

The men nod in unison and start sending instructions to the next two taxis. They roll away.

"Grab some lunch if you want," Vanti says. "I've heard the Grissom Sanctuaries are famous for their delis." She jumps into the little blue carriage and scoots across the bench seat. "Come on."

O'Neill and I follow her into the vehicle. As our carriage trundles away, I turn to the redhead. "There's a deli? Can't we stop there first?"

Both agents laugh. Vanti looks at her holo-ring's clock. "Forty-seven minutes. You win."

"Were you betting on how long it would take for me to ask for food?" I raise my nose and give her my best Ice Dame glare. "How long did you say?"

"I predicted less than twenty," Vanti says. "I guess I didn't take your medical condition into account. The med pod always makes me nauseous."

"I didn't take the bet." O'Neill holds up his hands in innocence.

"That was stupid." I grin. "You could have won big." I turn to Vanti. "He snuck me a candy bar in the exam room."

"Cheater!" Vanti leans forward to peer past me at O'Neill.

He grins, unrepentant, and slides his arm around my shoulders.

The taxi wanders through a residential neighborhood at a leisurely pace. When we stop at an intersection, Vanti flips open a couple of apps. "Looks like we got away. Let's take a couple more detours then head back to the family compound."

We settle back into the uncomfortable seats. "How did you get this taxi so fast?" I ask.

"Lyfter." Vanti smirks. "I have a couple of accounts on all the popular crowd-sourced transports. You never know when you might need an inconspicuous getaway car. And the paparazzi have no reason to connect me to either of you. Yet."

"Alias?" O'Neill asks. When she nods, he turns to me. "She's travelling as a tourist, not board security."

"Surveillance is harder to avoid here than on Kaku, where it's all carefully marked to protect your privacy." She combs her fingers through her perfect copper hair. "I have a couple of pre-packaged aesthetic mods in case we need to make a quick change."

"Pre-packaged?" I stare at her. Aesthetic mods can change hair, skin, even eye color. They're done in licensed salons, using expensive equipment, by highly trained aestheticians like Kara. "Aren't those dangerous?"

"That's what your roomie would like you to believe," Vanti answers. "Cheap pre-packs could put the lower-tier aestheticians out of business. Lucky for them, the aesthetics lobby has a steady grip on the senate economic committees. These are only available through select channels."

"Black market mods?" O'Neill asks. "I'm not going there."

"Afraid you'll end up with green dreadlocks again?" Vanti smirks.

"Green dreadlocks?" I repeat. "Again?"

As we make our way back to the O'Neill home, Vanti tells me the story of their first undercover assignment. She's a surprisingly good storyteller, although O'Neill constantly interrupts her to "set the record straight."

"I did *not* enjoy wearing those ridiculous skin suits," he protests.

"Right." Vanti waves him off and finishes her story. At the end, she shudders. "And that was the last time I willingly worked on SK2."

"Trapped in an airlock is no fun," I say with a shudder of my own.

The taxi pulls into a narrow alley and stops in a parking spot by a vine-covered wall with a vehicle-sized, plain brown door. Beside it, a gate blocks a tunnel much like the front entrance to the O'Neill home. We climb out, and Vanti flicks a few more icons on her screen. "That'll wipe the carriage's local memory. The trip is stored in Lyfter's master data-banks, of course, but those require a court order to access."

"Or a good hacker." I raise my eyebrows.

She nods. "Or a good hacker. We'll just hope none of the paparazzi have bothered hiring one. We should probably come up with some alternate travel arrangements."

"I've heard some crime syndicates use big drones." As O'Neill waves his holo-ring at the access panel, I mime something swooping down from the sky. "They fly you away like a huge package."

"No thanks," Vanti and O'Neill say together. The gate pops open.

"Spoilsports." I follow them into the compound.

TWO HOURS LATER, the paparazzi are camped out in front of the house.

96

"I thought you said they aren't allowed to come here unless they follow us?" I peek through the gap in the shutters. "I don't want to be stuck in here forever."

"The law says something about 'newsworthy subject' and 'no assumptions of location.' I guess they've started interpreting that more liberally." O'Neill pushes the office shutters closed and pulls me away from the window.

"They followed your sister home." Vanti strolls in, a tall, frosty glass in her hand. "Aretha said they picked her up outside her place of business, and she couldn't shake them."

"What makes her 'newsworthy'?" O'Neill mutters.

"I happen to be working on a high-profile contract dispute right now." Aretha also has a tall glass. She raises it to Vanti. "You aren't the only important person in the building."

"Never said I was, Sis." O'Neill nods at me. "She's the one."

"Thanks for throwing me under the shuttle," I say.

"Aren't contract disputes kept under wraps while they're ongoing?" O'Neill's eyes narrow. "How'd the press know you're working on it?"

"That's a question I've been asking myself since I got home." Aretha looks at Vanti. "Maybe someone leaked something."

Vanti raises an eyebrow. "It would have to be someone who actually pays attention to what you say."

O'Neill takes the glass out of Vanti's hand with a laugh. "Nice burn."

She smirks and throws herself down in a chair.

"What *is* this?" O'Neill makes a gagging face at Vanti as he hands the glass back to her.

"It's a TereshTini." Aretha raises her glass and takes a sip from the double straws. Her eyes go wide, and she sticks out her tongue. "Gah! That's awful!"

Vanti winks at me. "I must have gotten the recipe wrong. Triana said they're good."

I take Vanti's glass and sniff. Ugh. "You definitely got something wrong." I let my lips quirk a bit, so Vanti knows I appreciate her support.

"Let's figure out what's going on." O'Neill sits on the couch across from Vanti and pats the seat. Aretha dodges between us and sits next to him. I try not to roll my eyes as I take the chair next to Vanti.

"Bill's ship blew up." Aretha flicks a file onto the table projector and adds a little rectangle that says, "Bill's shuttle. Boom." She smirks and changes the background to a video clip of an explosion. "Obviously, someone was out to get Annabelle."

"But it blew up after I got off," I protest. "If they were after me, they're really bad at it."

"Maybe they're just inept." Aretha shrugs.

"Wait, I think we need to go back a little further," Vanti says. "First, Triana got deported. That doesn't usually happen here."

O'Neill's head shakes. "That was a misunderstanding."

Vanti looks at Aretha's pink face. "Really?"

"Really." O'Neill flicks the display. "Today, the Levaward pod station blew up. Did you get any intel on that?"

Vanti nods, and more files appear on the display. "Small bomb placed near the doors to the pod exit. At Levaward, the pods unload passengers in one location and pick up new ones in a different spot. That helps funnel traffic during high-density hours—when lots of shuttles are land-ing. That's why no one else was hurt—the two pods you saw had dropped passengers a few minutes earlier, but there were no available spots in the pickup lane. So, they had to wait in the drop off queue. The timing was excellent for preventing collateral damage. Which tends to rule out terrorists—they usually want to cause as much mayhem as possible."

"Which means this is more likely an assassination attempt, not an act of terror." O'Neill makes a face at me. "Not that that's any better as far as Triana's concerned."

"Thanks." I give him a sour smile. "But how did they know I was coming? That's not the kind of thing you can do on the spur of the moment, and we didn't even know we'd be going there until Bill suggested it."

EIGHTEEN

WE ALL LOOK at each other in silence. Finally, Aretha speaks. "No. Bill wouldn't be in on this. He took the blame for that shuttle crash."

"Maybe that's why he set this up." Vanti drums her fingers on the arm of her chair. *"Pilot error* can't be good for business. He blames Triana and wants to take her out in revenge?"

"No!" O'Neill and Aretha say together. While Aretha gives Vanti the stink eye, O'Neill continues. "I'm not saying he didn't have the opportunity, but I know he didn't do it. Besides, he was with us—he could have been injured or killed, too. Who else would have known we'd go to the shuttle field?"

"It's not a secret that you're helping him investigate the investigation." I think about that for a second but can't come up with a better way to say it. "If someone is really out to get me and they know I'm hanging out with you, then all they have to do is predict where your investigation will take you. Going to the regulator was an obvious step. The only issue is timing. Maybe they've got surveillance on Bill's apartment."

"Could they have set that bomb to detonate remotely?" Aretha asks.

"No *'could'* about it." Vanti leans forward to highlight some text. "Electronic analysis shows a receiver and wireless connection. That thing could have been triggered from anywhere on the continent. Or in orbit, for that matter."

"But how did they know when?" O'Neill shoves his fingers through his wavy hair, and it falls into place as always. "Was someone watching Bill's apartment?"

"Watching Bill. Watching you. Monitoring the regulator's calendar." Vanti ticks the possibilities off on her fingers.

"The regulator—al-Petrosian—didn't know we were coming," I say.

"Al-Petrosian?" Vanti sits up suddenly.

"Not Wil." I put a hand on her arm. She glances at me, and I yank my fingers away. You never know if you'll still have all of them after touching Vanti.

She grins. "Better not be. That guy caused us a lot of trouble. Relative?"

"I requested a full check on him but haven't heard back yet," O'Neill says. "I don't have my usual contacts here on Grissom."

Vanti gives him a scathing look, which he ignores.

"You could have asked me," Aretha says. "I know everyone."

"You were busy trying to deport my girlfriend." O'Neill's teeth grind together.

"Ugh. I feel like we're just going around in circles." I fling myself back in my chair. "Where'd you make that TereshTini, Vanti? I think we could use a pitcher—of good ones."

A PITCHER of TereshTinis and a full dinner doesn't help. Neither does thrashing through the same information over and over. Finally, we decide to give up for the night. Aretha pulls out some playing cards, and Brad, Serena, and Angie join us for a game.

"You've got the room next to Triana," Serena tells Vanti. "I moved your friends down the hall. Where are they, anyway?"

We look at each other. "They haven't come back yet?" O'Neill jumps up. He stalks away, flicking his holo-ring.

"They were supposed to take a transit pod back here," I say. "It's not like them to disappear." Actually, I don't know them at all, but I can't

100

imagine the SK2 board hiring anyone who wasn't one hundred percent reliable.

"No sign of them." O'Neill returns, running his fingers through his hair again. "Vanti, check with Sanctuary surveillance."

"There isn't any," I say. They look at me. "That's the reason we used their garage, remember? Sanctuaries don't track worshipers."

"That can't be true," Vanti grumbles, swiping at her holo interface. "I mean, I know that was my idea. And they definitely don't track who enters their facility. But surely there are cams outside the building? And what about the deli? If they paid for dinner, there'll be a record."

"Good luck getting that at this time of night," Aretha says.

Vanti grins. "We have a secret weapon."

"I'm not sure hacking into planetary security is a good idea," I say. "I already got deported once, remember?"

"What do you suggest, then?" Vanti crosses her arms and pins me with a stare.

"I'll take a look." I heave a sigh. "But if they come after me, you have to fight them off."

"Deal."

O'Neill, Vanti, and I move back to the office. The big desk has a state-of-the-art holo-ring interface. As I fling files into the holo, I wonder how much this thing cost. That gets me wondering where the O'Neill family gets its money. I mean, I know they're wealthy—look at this house. And they have the meter-long list of last names any "good" family claims. But where did the wealth originate? And how much of it flows to Bill? I remember that *Ancient Tēvē* quote, "Follow the money."

After hacking around a while, I find an unencrypted vid cam outside the Sanctuary. It hangs from the awning of a store across the street—probably part of their cheap security system. But it's badly aimed, and the front entrance of the Sanctuary is in full view. Maybe someone else wants to watch who enters and leaves the protected space.

"Hey, Ty," I call out.

He looks up from his huddled conversation with Vanti. "You got something?"

"No, but if hulk and the android were on duty, wouldn't they use a company account to pay for lunch?"

He rubs his eyes. "They might. Good craft would require them to use cash, but inside a Sanctuary, they might take the chance. Especially since they aren't here covertly. Good thought. I'll see if I can access the records." He swipes open a screen and starts digging.

"Here they are leaving the Sanctuary," I say a few minutes later. "Android has a sammie in his hand, so they obviously bought something." I follow them down the street, jumping into the traffic surveillance system. This is secure, of course, but getting into a transport network is child's play. My old friend Stervo could do it in his sleep.

I yawn. Even though I had a good nap in the med pod, I'm tired. The med techs warn you that's going to happen, but it's always a surprise. Plus, I'm betting the TereshTini was a bad idea. I yawn again. "Come on, guys, where are you?" I mutter.

I jerk awake when O'Neill touches my shoulder. "You should go to bed." His fingers knead my tense muscles, and I sigh.

"I'll just sit here and let you do that for a while," I say, closing my eyes. "Then I'll be ready to start looking again."

"Can't you load one of your facial recognition loops and let it follow them?"

My eyes pop open. Of course I can. "I can't believe I didn't think of that. Lemme get it set up." I toss one of my apps into the mix and set the parameters. Then I tether it to the transport network and set up a relay to send me the results. "Done. I'm going to bed."

We shut off the lights in the office. The rest of the complex is quiet—everyone else seems to have gone to bed. "How late is it?" I ask.

"A little after midnight," O'Neill says.

"Where's Vanti?"

"She went to bed an hour ago. Didn't you notice?" He slides an arm around me and guides me toward the stairs. "Right after you started working on the facial tracking thing."

"That was an hour ago?" I tip my head and rub the back of my neck. Stars peek through the dark fronds of the trees overhead. The rings are visible tonight, and they glitter in a thick streak across the darkness. "Wow, those are beautiful."

We stand at the bottom of the steps, staring up at the sky. I lean against O'Neill, his warm body helping my tense muscles relax. His arms wrap around me, his hands caressing my stomach and the side of my hip. I turn in his arms. As our lips touch, a soft knock echoes through the quiet courtyard.

"Someone at the front gate." O'Neill pulls back reluctantly.

"Maybe hulk and the android are back?"

He shakes his head as he turns away. "They'd better have a darn good reason for not reporting in." I follow him through the tunnel. A heavy wooden door hides the gate. He checks the cam pointed at the front steps. "Not our boys—it's peacekeepers."

"Should I hide?" I joke, but I'm not really laughing.

"They can't drag you out of our house." He swipes an icon and connects to the intercom. "Identification, please."

The officers flick their credentials to the house system, and it verifies. O'Neill opens the wooden door and peers through the gate. "What can I do for you?"

"There's been an incident," the taller one says. "We need you to come down to the station."

NINETEEN

O'Neill's eyes narrow. "Why don't you come inside and tell me what this is all about?" He pulls the gate open.

"Is letting them inside a good idea?" I whisper.

He nods but keeps his eyes on the officers. "Please come into the office, Peacekeeper Timons." He steps back, still watching the men, and points to the first door in the dark hallway.

I pull it open and discover it leads to a small, white room. A utilitarian desk sits in the far corner, with a couple of uncomfortable looking chairs arrayed in front. Ty closes the front gate behind the officers and follows the two men into the office. He sits behind the desk and gestures to the chairs. "Please, tell me what this is all about."

The taller man sits, but the other remains standing. He casually backs toward the outer wall where he can watch all three of us and the door we entered through. Vanti would be impressed by this one.

He stumbles over the edge of the carpet and falls into the wall.

Maybe she wouldn't. But that gives me an idea. I round the desk to stand behind O'Neill. The tall back of his chair hides my hand as I ping Vanti on my holo-ring.

"Ser O'Neill y Mendoza bin Tariq—"

O'Neill cuts him off. "O'Neill is good enough."

The senior guy nods, an efficient single jerk up and down. "Ser O'Neill, we have detained two gentlemen who claim to be in your employ."

"Do these gentlemen have names?" O'Neill asks.

The man consults his holo. "Kairon Andron and Lou Ferrigi."

Lou Ferrigi? My lips twitch, but I manage to keep my expression blank.

"They work for the Station Kelly-Kornienko board of directors, not me." O'Neill leans forward in his chair. "Are they all right?"

"They're fine, Ser O'Neill." He leans back in his chair, staring at O'Neill. Waiting. For what? Does he think O'Neill is going to crack under the pressure and start spilling... something?

O'Neill waits him out. After what feels like a couple of hours, he glances at me. "There's no reason for you to be here, Sera Morgan." His eyes lock onto mine, but I'm not sure what message he's trying to convey.

I cover another yawn. "I'm fine. I couldn't sleep with strangers in the house, anyway."

O'Neill bites his lip as if he's trying not to laugh. He knows I can sleep just about anywhere. He gives me a mock glare. "As you wish, Sera." Obviously, he wants me out of the way.

I yawn again. "Maybe you're right. I've had a long day. I think I'll grab a cupcake and hit the sack."

His lips twitch again, and this time, he lets the smile out for a second. "Enjoy your snack, Sera." He stands and ushers me to the door. When he opens it, Vanti gives a little finger wave from down the hall where the visitors can't see her. O'Neill nods again and shuts the door.

"What do they want?" I hiss as I hurry to the agent.

She holds a finger to her lips and leads me to the other office—the real, attractive one. She shuts the door behind us and crosses to the tall curtains by the fireplace. I had assumed they hid another window, although now that I take the time to look, I realize the external windows don't have drapes. And this isn't an external wall. She twitches the fabric aside to reveal a heavy wooden door.

A call comes in through my audio implant. Vanti. She has this amazing ability to speak through the comm while making no audible sound and without moving her lips. It's kind of freaky.

"Andron and Ferrigi were picked up a few hours ago." Her voice is loud and clear through my implant. "No charges have been filed, but they're considered 'persons of interest' in the Levaward Station attack."

"Of course they are. Why aren't we?" I whisper.

She frowns and puts a finger to her lips. "I'm listening on the other channel." She flicks her ring and swipes something at me.

A male voice cuts in. "—leaving the scene. No one else was there."

"Did you check the cams and passenger manifests?" O'Neill asks. "Because there were at least three other people there."

"Would you care to explain how you know that, Ser?" The peacekeeper's voice sounds threatening.

"Because I was one of them." The chair creaks as he shifts. I can almost see him leaning forward across the desk. "Sera Morgan, my cousin Bill Hillis, and I were there. We filed a report from the medical center."

Silence. Then the man clears his throat. "Ah, yes, I see." He sounds embarrassed. "Your report went to headquarters. Our people must have forgotten to sync the data system. Well, then, there's no reason to detain your, er, friends."

"Coworkers." O'Neill's voice is pleasant but firm. "I trust you'll send them back here. Perhaps arrange for transportation?"

"I—uh—yes, of course," Timons says.

"Thank you, Peacekeeper. Is there anything else I can do for you?"

Timons clears his throat again. "Just don't leave the local area." He chuckles, but it sounds fake.

"We wouldn't dream of it," O'Neill says. "My sister is getting married in a few days. We'll be here."

"If you don't mind me asking, Ser, why is Sera Morgan here? And why wasn't my office informed of her visit?"

"I do mind you asking," O'Neill says. Doors open, and feet shuffle. "Unless the law has changed very recently, Grissom citizens aren't required to register guests at the local Peacekeeper office. She's here on a valid visa. That's all you need to know."

"I beg to differ," Timons says, his voice indignant. "If she's going to be the target of terrorist attacks, I most certainly need to know!"

Silence.

Then O'Neill speaks again. His voice is low and calm. "Has the Levaward Station attack been labeled a terrorist action directed at our guest? If it has, then the shoe is on the other foot. As her security manager, I need to know whatever you've discovered."

Timons blusters. "No, no, I misspoke. There have been no determinations. And of course we're happy to share our information. Just contact my office. Here's a link. We don't want a foreign citizen injured on our planet, now, do we? I'll send your employees home. Maybe they'll do a better job from here on out."

The door shuts, and the audio goes dead. Vanti raises an eyebrow. "Interesting."

The wooden door opens, and O'Neill comes in. "Analysis?"

"That was very strange." Vanti wanders across the room and throws herself down on the stiff couch. "Almost felt like that guy was in on whatever this is."

"Agreed." O'Neill pulls me up from my chair. "I wish we knew what they were up to."

"We'll figure it out." I yawn again. "I need to sleep. Maybe my subconscious will come up with the answer."

"Oh, I forgot to tell you." O'Neill gives me a sheepish grin. "Mom wants some help with the wedding."

"Wedding?" I stare at him. "This is the first I've heard of a wedding."

"No, it's not." Vanti pushes the door open. "Griz told that peacekeeper his sister is getting married."

"But we came to Grissom to clear Bill. You didn't say anything about a wedding." I give O'Neill the stink eye.

"Two aliens, one stone," Vanti mutters.

O'Neill snickers. "Exactly. Bill gave me the excuse to come now. But, honestly, I was going to—well, originally, I had quit my job and planned on staying on Grissom. Then you and I... I went back to SK2. So, this gave me a convenient way to attend the wedding and help Bill."

"If I'd known, I would have packed a hat." My eyes narrow even more.

"A hat? You've been watching too much *Ancient Tēvē*." O'Neill ushers me up the steps. "No one wears hats to weddings anymore. Unless it's for the Grissom royal family."

"Grissom has a royal family? I don't remember that from my history classes."

"No, we don't." O'Neill says as we reach the second floor. "But I'm sure people would wear hats to their weddings if we did."

I roll my eyes and try to hold back another yawn. "I'm sure you're right. I'd come up with a hilarious response if I weren't so tired."

When we reach the third floor, Vanti says good night and leaves us alone in the corridor. "Which of these rooms is your sister's?" I whisper.

O'Neill opens my door, and we step into the cool darkness. "None of them. Hers is on the second floor. But Andron and Ferrigi are two doors that way." His arm brushes against my shoulder as he points.

An electric thrill runs down my back.

His breath is warm against my neck. "And Vanti's next door, of course."

My blood goes cold. "She's probably got a vid of every room in the building," I mutter. I kiss him quickly and turn away. "Too many eyes and ears."

"Yikes. You sure know how to kill the mood." He chuckles, pulling me closer. "But, yeah, this place is crowded. Maybe we can sneak away after the wedding."

"You never finished telling me about this thing." I flick on a light and plop down on the bed. "What's the deal?"

He shrugs. "Mom just needs help with last minute stuff. No big deal. But it will give you something to do while Vanti and I continue the investigation."

"Oh, so it's a great way to keep me out of trouble? Like a toddler or something. Thanks, you can see yourself out."

"That's not what I meant." He sits and puts an arm around me. "But don't forget you were badly injured today. You could have been killed." He gives me a little shake. "I need to know you're safe so I can focus on doing my job."

"I thought your job was to keep me safe." I sound like a cranky little girl, but I don't care. He's treating me like a child; he should expect me to behave like one. *Vicious circle*, the little voice in my head whispers, but I ignore it.

"Andron and Ferrigi's job is to keep you safe." He leans in to kiss my cheek. "My job is to help Bill. Then we can enjoy the wedding and get back to SK2."

"You're for sure coming back?" I turn and lock eyes with him.

His gaze roams over my face, pausing on my lips before returning to my eyes. "You can't keep me away."

———

No, I'm not going to tell you what happens after that. It's not really any of your business.

TWENTY

THE NEXT MORNING, we meet in the lounge for breakfast. Between O'Neill and the twins, the AutoKich'n is getting a workout. I pour myself some coffee, add plenty of cream and sugar, and sit beside Vanti while waiting my turn.

"Are you going to eat?" I glance at her cup of green tea.

She shudders. "I'll have a protein bar later. You?"

"As soon as the boys get out of the way." I grin. "Breakfast is the best meal of the day. Well, besides dessert."

She snorts. "Dessert isn't a meal."

"That's why you're so grumpy all the time, Vanti. You should eat more dessert."

"Just don't eat the pudding," O'Neill puts his plate of eggs and sausages on the table across from me.

Vanti's lips twitch, and she shakes her head.

"That must have been funnier in person." I glower at them as I make my way to the AutoKich'n.

The two grin at each other but don't say anything. Vanti and O'Neill have known each other since the academy. The pudding joke goes back to that first assignment on SK2, but the nickname, Griz, goes back even further. They won't explain that one. Usually, their inside jokes don't bother me, but sometimes…

"When did you two get home?" O'Neill asks as the twins sit down and start shoveling food into their mouths.

"Late?" Yuri says with a shrug.

"Late." Ro nods. "All business."

"Business?" O'Neill raises an eyebrow. The twins do it back at him. I look away, disgusted. Why can everyone but me do that?

"They work for the same media company," Serena says as she marches into the room. Her mother, Angie, follows behind, wearing a bright yellow sweater and pink pants. She heads for the sideboard and loads a pile of pastries onto her plate. Serena takes the plate, removes all but one of them, and puts it on the table for the old lady.

"Don't forget—you're on cam duty for Lili's wedding." Serena pins a steely eye on the boys as she fixes Angie's coffee.

Ro salutes with a strip of bacon and shoves it into his mouth.

"We're on it." Yuri grins and takes a huge bite of pancake.

I program my request into the AutoKich'n and drink the rest of my coffee while it cooks. When the machine dings, I pull out my plate of French toast with poached eggs. A small puddle of syrup covers the top slice with a pat of butter right in the middle. I take a deep breath. Cinnamon. Maple. Delicious.

As I sit down, the hulk and the android slink into the room. They both look sheepish and avoid our eyes.

"Get some breakfast," O'Neill says. "We have a busy day ahead of us."

"Do they get to go with you?" I glare at O'Neill over my French toast.

"Nope." Vanti sips her tea. "They're on babysitting duty." She acknowledges my evil eye with a tip of her cup. "Sorry, I mean they'll be here, holding down the fort. And accompanying you, should you need to go anywhere."

"They were so useful on the last trip," I grumble. "No offense."

The hulk's lips press together. "You're not wrong."

"Sorry." My face burns. It's not their fault we got bombed, and there's no way they could have predicted it. "But if I stay here, you can help O'Neill."

"One of you will remain on duty with Sera Morgan at all times." O'Neill thunks his cup down on the table. The coffee sloshes. "The other will stay nearby for backup."

The two men snap to attention and salute then gather their breakfasts.

"I can help with your investigation." Angie taps her forehead. "I've got a top-notch thinker up here."

O'Neill smiles. "I think Vanti and I have this one covered, Grandma, but thanks."

"Now we have that settled, let's get down to business." Serena sets her toast and tea on the end of the table and flings a file onto the dining room's window. It glows brightly, expanding into a complicated chart showing projects, locations, and names. "Ty, you and Lindsay need to be back here by two."

"Vanti, please, Sera O'Neill." Vanti says. "Only my mother calls me Lindsay. And the administrators at the Techno-Inst."

Serena nods. "Deal, but only if you'll call me Serena." She turns to the twins. "You've got everything you need for the ceremony?"

Ro gives her a thumbs up between bites. "We're good. But we gotta run. Gotta get to the Roosevelt Center before Senator Van Valkenburgh starts her speech."

Yuri jumps up, still pushing bacon into his mouth. "Bye, Ma! See ya, guys." He and Ro hurry out of the room.

"Senator Van Valkenburgh?" Vanti raises her eyebrow again. She catches my eye and her lips twitch. She knows I hate that I can't do that.

"The boys are covering her press release," Serena says. "Some big announcement about nothing. We have important work. Triana, you're going to help Mother with flower arrangements. Thank you for offering to help. Akiko and Aretha are both working, and Ty is useless with artistic things."

"Where's Dad?" O'Neill asks.

"He's working with the caterers." Serena turns to me. "He's an amateur chef. He's hired a team to do the catering, and he insists on 'helping' them. We had to pay extra for that." She smiles.

Ty groans. "He should really leave that stuff to the experts."

"You know your father." She takes a bite of toast and flicks the file. A single line glows red. "The centerpieces, bouquets, and boutonnieres will take the longest, but we can't start them until the flowers are delivered. Grandma, we have a final dress fitting this afternoon, but you'll be ready to take a break by then. How are you with crafty stuff, Triana?"

I stare at Serena. After a second, I find my voice. "Uh, I might be able to program a robot to stick flowers in a vase, but that's as good as it gets."

"We'll teach you." She turns to Vanti. "You sure you don't want to help, too? I've heard you're good with your hands."

"You should see her cupcakes," I say.

Vanti smiles her college recruiter smile. "I would love to, Serena, but Griz needs my help." She's out of her seat and dragging O'Neill from the room before anyone can respond.

"See you this afternoon!" O'Neill calls out.

"Don't be late." Serena turns back to the table. "Cupcakes? Maybe we should have hired Vanti to do the cake. You should see the monstrosity Jie's family has commissioned for the wedding. Lili and I laughed so hard..."

"The cupcake thing was a bit of a joke," I say. "Long story."

Serena looks disappointed for a moment, then she nods. "You can tell us while we work on the flowers. Finish your breakfast and let's get to it."

TWENTY-ONE

I AM the galaxy's worst flower arranger. I've pricked my fingers so many times, I feel like I've been folding cactus origami. After accidentally tipping over two different buckets of flowers and somehow setting the florist's wire on fire, Angie puts me in a corner with a wide bowl of short-stemmed flowers and a roll of sticky green tape. "You'll do best making boutonnieres. Most of the boys won't care if they're a little lumpy." She shows me how to hold the greenery and flower together and wrap the tape around the stems.

I take one of the heavily scented flowers and lay a fern next to it. "Tell me about Bill."

Serena glances up from her four hundredth centerpiece and gives me a shrewd look. "Aretha told us what happened to you."

I stick a cloth magnet against the tape and wrap another layer over it. "Did she?"

"And she told me her role in the whole debacle." She snips the bottoms off a handful of stems and rapidly pokes them into the glass bowl. It looks random, but each centerpiece she finishes is both beautiful and unique.

"Really?" Should I ask if she admitted to her own role? I might be able to use that information as leverage later, if necessary.

"Yes, she told me she set the whole thing up." She places the bowl on the huge table overflowing with flowers and sprinkles some glittery stuff over it. The sparkles adhere to the flowers and leaves, creating a fairytale effect. "I need to check in with Brad. You two keep working." She dusts the glitter off her fingers and hurries out of the room. A gust of fresh air pushes out the heavy floral perfume for a brief second.

"That's not—" I break off. Maybe Aretha's protecting her sister. I guess if she wants to take the fall for Akiko, that's her prerogative.

"Well, Aretha didn't plan the explosion, obviously." Angie grabs a handful of flowers and wraps them into a perfect bouquet. "That seems more like Gwen's work."

"Gwen?" The just finished boutonniere falls from my numb fingers, and the cloth magnet sticks to the leggings halfway down my shin. "You mean Gwen Watson? Bill's wife's partner?"

"Exactly. She was a demolition expert before she became a peacekeeper."

"What? Does Ty know?"

"I'm sure he'll figure it out." Angie smiles and pulls another handful of flowers from the bucket beside her chair. "He's good at his job."

"We need to tell him!" I flick my holo-ring. "How did you know about that?"

"Gwen's aunt is in my social club." Angie pauses to deliberate over two identical flowers. "She was so proud when Gwen graduated from Peace-keeper academy. And so happy she wasn't going to blow things up anymore." She slides one bloom into the bundle, weaving it through the rubbery leaves.

I send a message to O'Neill, suggesting he check Watson's work history.

Got it. Demolitions. How'd you know?

Grandma Angie.

He sends back an emoji with a confused face.

"You're right," I tell Angie. "He found it. Is there anything else he should be finding?"

"Not that I know of. I'll let you know if I hear anything. I told you I'd be a good investigator." Angie grins. "I need a drink. You want one?"

"Uh, I'll wait until after lunch."

"Suit yourself." She pours a glass of whiskey then returns to her flowers. "I don't normally drink this early, but flower arranging is easier if you're just the tiniest bit buzzed."

I look at the half-full glass. "*That's* going to get you a tiny bit buzzed?"

She tilts the glass and gazes at the golden liquid. "I'm not going to drink it all at once." She chugs back half the contents. "Perfect."

We work in silence for a while. I manage to break the stem off the flower I'm trying to wrap. With a shake of my head, I drop it back into the bucket. "You're Serena's grandmother, right?" Angie nods, and I continue. "There's a generation missing."

"My daughter, Evaline, will be here Saturday. She's out on one of the fringe worlds for her job."

"One of the fringe worlds? What does she do?" I grab another flower and a piece of the green stuff. Wrapping tape around the stems shouldn't be this difficult. I can solder a micro board in my sleep! The tape sticks to itself, blobbing together under my fingers. I pull it off and start again.

"She's in the CEC—Colonial Explorer Corps." She sets her bouquet into the bucket holding the finished ones and takes a swig from her glass. "She doesn't do the initial trip—those people are gone for decades. She's in the second wave once they have the jump beacons set up. She analyzes minerals for potential development. She's probably going to retire soon."

The sticky tape has wrapped around my pinky finger, and I can't get it loose. I shake my hand, hard, but I just succeed in hurting my wrist.

Angie reaches over and pulls the stuff free. "Try again, dear."

"Maybe you're right about the booze," I mutter.

"Have a sip." She holds out her glass, but it's mostly empty. "Oops, time for a refill." She goes to the cupboard, her legs steady. After that much whiskey, I'd be staggering like a freshman at Techno-Inst on a Friday night. She brings the bottle back to her chair and pours another generous serving.

The potent smell of the whiskey splashing into the glass hits my nose, pushing out the pungent florals. The scent brings up the memory of Kara's grandfather's wake. I hold up my hand. "I think I'd better wait until after lunch, at least."

"More for me, then." She sips and smiles. "Give me those flowers. I'm done with the bouquets."

I carry the buckets of flowers and foliage to her chair. The tape has wrapped itself in my hair, so I don't have to go back for it. A savage yank leaves me with a short piece of tape and several strands of red hair now stuck to my hand.

Angie grabs the roll still hanging from my frizzy curls and easily detaches it. "You can stick the stems into the little water things." She hands me a box of green vials but takes my two finished products away. "Don't bother with those two, dear. I'll redo them."

I work out how to poke the stems through the membrane at the top of the vials. Angie's already finished three boutonnieres by the time I figure out how to do the first one. The next few go easily, and soon I'm caught up. "All of this," I gesture to the flowers, "is normal for a wedding?"

"You've never been to one?" With quick, precise movements, she trims and wraps. Her fingers are steady, her eyes clear. I glance at her glass, and it's half empty again. Remarkable.

"No, they aren't really done on SK2. People over there don't seem to go for lifelong commitment." I stare at the box. Two more flower bundles wait for vials. This woman is a machine. "And short-term contracts are business arrangements. Some people throw a party—especially for the first one. My roommate, Kara, just signed a ten-year contract with her partner." I shiver. "It was a nice party, but ten years is a long time."

Angie laughs. "Safwan and I were married for sixty-three years. If he hadn't been killed in a freak rainstorm, this year would have been seventy-eight."

I gape at her. Seventy-eight years. Wow. "I've seen weddings on *Ancient Tēvē*. They usually get divorced two or three years later. Makes the whole thing seem kind of pointless."

"Oh, that happens sometimes." She nods and points a flower stem at my box. "You're getting behind."

There are four more boutonnieres in the box. She must have a stack of completed ones hidden under her chair. I look, but there's nothing.

"But I think your *Ancient Tēvē* probably plays up the ones that don't last. After all, conflict is more interesting than peace. At least to an audience." She raises her eyebrows at me. "Are you and Ty going to get married?"

I gulp. "I dunno. I mean, he's supposed to get down on one knee with a ring and skywriting and a jazz choir or something, right?"

Angie laughs. "No one really does that. I guess it was the custom a few centuries ago, but not anymore. Mostly people just have a conversation and decide to do it." She peers closely at me. "He's obviously head-over-heels for you. And you love him, right?"

I nod. "Yeah, but forever?"

"It only happens one day at a time." She wraps the last flower and tosses it onto the pile in front of me. "You just have to choose love every day. That's not so hard."

I stare at her for a moment. Maybe she's right. Choosing love every day can't be that hard.

Angie's voice startles me out of my funk. The box of half-finished flowers is now empty, and the boutonnieres all have vials. She must be part witch. "Now that we have those done, I think we should help with the investigation. Call a carriage and let's go."

TWENTY-TWO

"I'm not supposed to leave the house," I say as Angie jumps up from her chair.

"When has that ever stopped you?"

"How do you know me so well?" I brush little green bits from my clothes and find a lumpy boutonniere still stuck to my leg.

Angie grins. "I think you and I are a lot alike. Plus, Ty loves to talk about you."

"But if someone is targeting me, going out in public is risky." I wave the floppy flower around. The blossom snaps off, falling into the empty flower bucket.

Angie takes the sad greenery from my hand. "You've got the boys for protection. I'm sure they're getting tired of hanging out here, too." She pulls open the door and calls, "Yoo hoo! Lou! Kairon! Where are you?"

How does she know their first names? I follow her out into the courtyard. The heavy scent of flowers fades, replaced by the fruity tang of live plants. I sneeze a couple of times.

"Were you looking for us, Lady?" Ferrigi steps out of the tunnel leading to the front gate.

"Yes." Angie steps into his path. Ferrigi is huge, and he towers over the old woman. She points at him and cranes her neck to peer into this face. "We need to go to the dress fitting."

"I wasn't told Sera Morgan would be leaving the compound." Ferrigi crosses his arms and stares down at Angie.

"She's going to the wedding, so, of course she needs her gown fitted." She shakes her head as if she can't believe his naivete. "Not leaving the house. Silly man."

I have a gown for the wedding, and it fits perfectly. Ty must have clued Hy-Mi in because it was there in my trunk, clearly labeled in the Dress-Success app.

Ferrigi nods, indecision plain on his face.

"Check with my grandson if you want," Angie says. "I'm sure he won't mind you interrupting his work."

Ferrigi clears his throat. "That's not necessary, Lady Angie. Give us a couple of minutes to get our gear together." He strides away, flicking his comm line. "Andron, we got a job."

"You are a master spy," I whisper. "I'll bet Vanti could learn a few tricks from you."

Angie smiles. "A hundred and two years in the 'verse teaches you a few things."

"A hundred and two?!" I stare at her. I'd figured late eighties.

She laughs and smacks my arm. "No, I'm only ninety-three. Got ya!"

I do some quick math. "But that means you got married to Safwan when you were fifteen."

"Oh, I was kidding about that. We were only married seventy-three years ago. Two years after Evaline was born."

"Did he really die in a freak rainstorm?" How does a rainstorm kill someone, anyway?

"Oh, no. He's alive and well. You'll meet him at dinner tonight." She grabs my arms and pushes me toward the stairs. "Go get whatever investigative stuff you need. I'm gonna hit the little girls' room."

I stare at her as she totters off across the courtyard. Is she senile? Most age-related mental deterioration can be eliminated through medical treatments, but obviously these people don't go in for rejuvenation. Maybe they prefer to get a little batty when they age, too. I hurry up to my room, debating the wisdom of leaving the house with a crazy old woman to investigate what could be a terrorist action.

Of course, we will have the hulk and the android with us. Not that they've proven their reliability. Which reminds me. I left the facial recognition loop running in the office last night. I grab my stash of local currency and slide it into a pocket. The paper bills are clumsy, but sometimes you don't want to leave a trail. What other "investigative stuff" do I need? If Vanti were with us, she'd have weapons and grappling hooks and invisible string or something. Maybe I can sneak into her room and borrow something.

I close my door behind me and stroll casually down the balcony to the next one. The handle turns easily, and I step into the dim room. The shutters are ajar, letting in some light. In the middle of the neatly made bed, there's a small box holding down a piece of paper. My name is scrawled across the page.

Triana,

I know you. When you go out, at least take the boys with you. And be prepared... Here are a few things that might come in handy. Don't tell Griz I gave them to you. This note will self-destruct five seconds after you read it.

Vanti

P.S. Just kidding about the self-destruct. How would I do that?

I pick up the box and open in. Inside, there's a tiny first aid kit, mini-stunner, two small darts inside clear tubes, and a sleeve of capsules. Knowing Vanti, the darts are probably dipped in a sedative. I'm not sure how I would deliver them—I don't have a dart gun. I leave them in the box. The stunner and med pack fit into my empty jacket pocket.

The capsules have tiny writing on them. Oh—these are the pre-packaged aesthetic mods she mentioned. I shiver but shove them into the hidden pocket in the waistband of my leggings. I can't imagine using them —I could end up looking like anyone, just a day before Lili's wedding. I'm sure Serena wouldn't appreciate that, especially if I end up in any of the pictures.

I hurry down the steps. Andron and Ferrigi are waiting in the courtyard, but Angie isn't back yet. "I need to check something in the office." The guys nod, resigned to waiting. I guess that's not uncommon for them.

I cross the dim office and sit behind the desk. The loop I set last night has produced a string of vid links. Views from cams stationed all along the street—some of them government owned, some belonging to individual stores or residents. My loop accessed everything. I smile faintly, pride in my data mining skills making me all warm and happy.

I quickly swipe through the vids. Andron left Sanctuary. Ferrigi left a few minutes behind him. They walked down the same street—on opposite sides—and passed the first transit station. A few minutes later, they arrived at the second transit station, which they both entered. While they waited for the next pod, a pair of peacekeepers entered and spoke to them. The four of them turned around and headed back to the surface. A Peacekeeper vehicle pulls up, and they climbed inside.

Not very exciting. I reach out to swipe off the last vid but freeze. Just in view of the cam, there's a tall, blond man. I slide the vid back. He was standing there when Ferrigi descended into the station. I follow the link to that cam and watch the whole sequence. The man watches both agents go into the station. Then he speaks to the peacekeepers, pointing toward the station door. He loiters there and watches as the four men return and get into the carriage. He's wearing casual clothes, and he's got a smirk on his face—a smirk I'd recognize anywhere.

Bobby Putin.

"It can't be," I whisper. In a flash, I'm sending a message to Attica Prison on Sally Ride. I connect to the local SK'Corp office and authorize the exorbitant fee to have them relay a real-time call. I wait impatiently as the signals connect.

"Attica. How may I direct your call?" A thin woman in a stiff, dark uniform answers.

I put on my best top-lev voice. "This is Annabelle Morgan. Please connect me to the warden immediately."

The woman's eyes widen as she swipes through several identity confirmation alerts on her screen. "Yes, Sera." The holo goes black, and an electric blue Attica Prison logo rotates lazily in her place.

The view goes black again then resolves to a distinguished looking man in his late sixties. He's probably younger, but this job requires gravitas, so aesthetic mods lend him an aura of age and authority. "Warden Peters. How may I help you, Sera Morgan?"

"I need to see Bobby Putin." My voice comes out high and thready. I clear my throat and try again. "I've just seen his doppelganger, and I want assurance it's not him."

"Sera, I assure you I spoke with Ser Putin just this morning. He's still safely locked—"

I cut him off. "The court records of his conviction and sentencing are clear. If a representative of the Morgan family demands confirmation, you're to provide it, no questions asked. I am Dame Morgan's official representative. You've seen my credentials." I gesture at his desk. He would have had to review and accept several confirmations while I waited on hold. "Show me the cell."

He holds up his hand in surrender. "One moment, please. Do you wish audio?"

"NO!" I take a deep, shaky breath and try again. "I don't want him to know I checked. I just need to see that he's there."

"Yes, Sera."

The view goes back to the logo then clears to a prison cell. I recognize it from my visit when he was sentenced. The cam sits just above eye-level in the visitor's chamber, facing a transparent wall. On the other side of that wall is Bobby's domain. Fifteen square meters, all but the bathroom in full view. Even the bathroom has a cam, but I don't want to see that.

Bobby has acquired some nice furnishings in the months since his conviction. He has an enormous bed lofted overhead, with a staircase made of shelves leading to it. The shelves overflow with old-fashioned books. A plush couch sits under the bed, with a half-dozen plump pillows and a low table. The other end of the room holds a desk with a comfortable chair and a beautiful lamp. A door at the back leads to the bathroom. He's hung expensive-looking prints on the walls, and a thick carpet covers most of the floor.

Bobby lounges on the couch, paging through a large, colorful book.

Soft music plays in the background. If it weren't for the transparent front wall, this could be any top-lev apartment.

"Triana!" Angie pushes open the door. "Triana, where are you?"

At the sound of her voice, Bobby's head pops up. He grins directly at the cam then gives a little finger wave.

TWENTY-THREE

TERROR GRIPS my stomach in an iron clench. Trembling, I slap the interface and shut down the call. The warden is going to get an earful from me—as soon as I get over the shakes. I double check the connections —to make sure I'm not still being charged for the interstellar call—and close all the files except the vid that spooked me in the first place.

"Triana, dear, you look terrible." Angie totters across the room and takes my hand in her warm ones. "And you're cold. What happened? Who is this nice young man?" She peers at the paused video.

I try to speak, but nothing comes out. Holding up a finger, I hurry to the liquor cabinet. I fumble with the bottle, unable to unscrew the lid. Angie takes it from my hand and pours a shot of something. I'm too freaked out to notice what. I toss it down. My throat sears, and I choke, tears pricking my eyes. Angie pounds my back until the coughing stops. Warmth spreads from my belly up into my chest, and a nice fog filters through my brain.

"That was not a nice young man." I stagger to the closest couch and drop onto the hard surface. I forgot how uncomfortable this couch was. "That was someone who looks very much like Bobby Putin."

"The top-lev serial killer?" Angie asks.

I nod. "When we were on S'Ride, I thought I saw him several times.

Seems there was a fad to get aesthetic mods to look like top-levs." I shudder. "Imitation Bobby Putins everywhere. One of them must have come here."

"But it's not him." Angie perches on the edge of the sofa and pats my hand. "He's in prison."

"Yes. I checked. He's still there." My heart rate has slowed in a sea of alcoholic fumes. "It freaked me out, but I'm okay now."

"Maybe we should stay home." Angie's tone belies her words—she really wants to go.

"Don't be silly," I say. "Bobby's on S'Ride in the Attica Super-Max. That vid is just a weirdo look-a-like who hasn't gotten modded back yet. Or maybe he enjoys looking like a serial killer." I laugh. It comes out kind of hysterical, but that's okay. Thanks to the drink, I'm feeling cozy and a bit floaty. "We're perfectly safe, especially with the avenger boys to protect us."

Angie raises an eyebrow but doesn't ask. "Let's get going, then. I'll leave a message for Serena. We'll meet her at the bridal studio at two." She jumps up and pulls on my arm.

I heave myself off the sofa and follow her out the door.

"We're ready to go!" Angie sings out across the courtyard. "Come on, avenger boys!"

Andron and Ferrigi exchange a look then steer Angie toward the rear of the house. "We're taking one of the family carriages," Andron says. "I'm not doing the public transport thing again."

"Works for me!" Angie skips a little as we walk through the rear passage. We take one of the side doors into a big garage. Four bubbles—or carriages, as they insist on calling them—hang from their charging cables in the ceiling. Angie marches straight toward the largest: a six-person deluxe model. "Let's go!"

"Are you sure we should take that one?" Ferrigi asks. "It's a luxury model."

"My husband and I bought this carriage." Angie draws herself up to her full height, her eyes on level with Ferrigi's solar plexus. "I can ride in it whenever I want."

"Right. Sorry." He waves at the access panel, and the door unfolds into a shallow ramp. "After you, Lady Angie."

I follow Angie into the carriage. "Is that true?"

Angie makes a face. "Don't be ridiculous. I haven't bought a carriage in decades. That's the best part of being the matriarch, though—you can do whatever you want."

We take seats at the back of the vehicle, while Andron and Ferrigi get in front. "Where to, ladies?" Andron asks.

Angie and I exchange a look. We hadn't gotten that far in our planning. "Let's go to the station where you got picked up," I say. "It's a good starting point."

"I thought we were going to a dress fitting," Ferrigi says, his eyes narrow.

"We are," Angie says. "We just want to drive past there on the way. Come on, you can humor an old lady. We won't get out of the carriage."

Andron and Ferrigi mutter to each other for a few seconds, then Andron swipes the interface. "Palizo Station." The system repeats the name then asks us to fasten our restraints. When our straps are all cinched down, the garage door opens, and the vehicle slides out. The transparent upper half of the bubble darkens, dimming the hot sun and protecting us from prying eyes.

We skim down a narrow alley behind two other large homes. The backs of all three houses are covered in flowering vines. "Those things grow on every building on the planet," Angie says. "It takes an army of gardeners to keep the front of the house clear."

"But they're pretty," I protest. "Why get rid of them?"

"The blossoms fall off later in the summer—it's a mess." She clucks her tongue in disgust.

At the end of the alley, the carriage curves out onto the street and loops around to the front of the house. A half-dozen paparazzi drones stationed in front of the house turn our direction then ignore us. I guess they don't have an accurate inventory of the family's vehicles.

We settle into our seats as the carriage picks up speed. It merges into a more heavily trafficked street. "I'm surprised those drones didn't follow us." I peer through the overhead. "I was sure they'd recognize me."

"They can't see inside the carriage." Angie pats my arm. "And you don't really look like yourself, anyway."

"What do you mean?" I put a hand to my hair. My springy red curls feel remarkably docile. "What did you do?"

"Your friend Vanti gave me one of her black-market aesthetic mods. I slipped it to you when you weren't looking."

I stare at the old woman. "Is that why you kept trying to get me to drink something? What do I look like?"

With a grin, Angie hands me a mirror. I catch a glimpse of white and close my eyes. I almost can't bear to look. Finally, I pry my eyes open and face the mirror.

Pale gray eyes peer from between heavy laugh lines. Soft white curls wave back from a wrinkled forehead. Maybe I'm experiencing a drunken hallucination. I reach up, and the woman in the mirror touches her nose. "You made me old," I whisper.

Angie's grin widens. "It's perfect! Who would suspect a pair of old ladies out for lunch?" Her voice is low, and she glances at the two men as she speaks.

"They don't know who I am, do they?" My eyes dart from Angie to Andron and Ferrigi. "That's why they were willing to come with us. They think I'm safely back at home."

"Don't be silly, dear," Angie says. "Their job is to protect you. They weren't going to leave you at home alone. But they both agreed this was the safest way to do it."

I look in the mirror again. Even my own mother wouldn't recognize me. Of course, she'd never in a million years allow herself to look this aged, so the possibility I might would never cross her mind. But even Kara or O'Neill wouldn't—

"How long does this mod last?" My voice is strangled.

"Until you do another one, I guess." She considers me for a few seconds then shrugs. "I didn't ask."

"But I have to attend Lili's wedding tomorrow. I can't go looking like this!"

"Sure you can." Angie laughs. "You'll have to fight off the old geezers, though. You're pretty hot for eighty-five."

"Eighty—did you tell Vanti the mod was for me?"

"I might have suggested it was for an old friend."

I drop my head into my hands. "Whatever." I look up. "I can just find an aesthetician to reverse it. And you're right, it's a genius disguise."

"Here's the station." Andron spins his seat to face us. "Not much to see."

We peer out the window. I half expect to see the man who looks like Bobby Putin, but of course, he's not there. The station is completely unremarkable. "Can we go to the Sanctuary? Or, better yet, let's backtrack our steps to the subway station that blew up."

"That's out of the question," Ferrigi says. "This little detour was bad enough, but I'm not taking you to a crime scene."

"You're definitely the party pooper of this couple." Angie waves at the two men.

"We aren't a couple!" Ferrigi's eyes bulge a little.

I giggle. "Would you rather be paired up with one of us?" I give him an outrageous wink.

Angie flutters her eyelashes. Ferrigi turns purple, while Andron chokes back a laugh.

"Where's the dress place?" The hulk glares.

"I can almost imagine him green, can't you?" I ask Angie. She snorts a laugh.

"I have the address." Andron pats the hulk's arm. "I won't let the old ladies be mean to you anymore."

I can't hold in the giggles. Ferrigi glares, and the giggles turn to laughter. The more I try to get it under control, the funnier it all seems. I laugh so hard my stomach hurts. Then it goes queasy. "Maybe we can get some food? I had a huge shot of something on an empty stomach, and I lost count of how much Angie drank."

"I so deserve a raise. No one told me I'd be babysitting two drunk old ladies." Ferrigi turns his seat around, putting his back to us.

"There's a nice restaurant right up the street," Angie says. "One of my favorites. Turn right up there."

The car drops us in front of a little diner and trundles away to park. Andron opens the door, and Ferrigi follows us inside. As the hostess seats us, I overhear a woman telling her companion, "When we're that old, I want two hot hunks to take us to lunch."

We sit in a booth, with the guys on the ends of the benches and Angie and me against the wall. Andron turns out to be an entertaining conversationalist, but Ferrigi remains stoic. They watch both entrances to the restaurant, even when they're talking or eating. The food is tasty but unremarkable.

"We should get moving," Ferrigi says when the bill is presented.

Angie swipes her holo-ring at the payment icon, and it turns green. "I need to visit the little girls' room." She makes shooing motions at Andron. "You coming, Lois?"

"Lois? Oh, yeah, I need to go, too."

Ferrigi takes my arm as if to help me out of the wide bench. "No funny business, Sera. Vanti warned me about you."

"Did she?" I try to raise one eyebrow, but aesthetic mods don't seem to change muscle action. "We'll be right back. Don't get your knickers in a wad."

He gives me a confused look and steps out of the way. I follow Angie to the restroom located near the back door. We take care of business then pause over the sinks.

"I think we should sneak out the back," Angie says as she washes her hands. "Give those boys a good run for their money."

Thanks to the alcohol, comfort food, and time, my encounter with Bobby has faded to a fuzzy memory. "If we had a place we wanted to investigate, I'd totally agree with you. But I have no idea how to get to that bombed subway station, and I'm sure it's been blocked by peacekeepers. I do my best sleuthing via the net, anyway."

She screws up her face. "We have a golden opportunity, though. We shouldn't waste it. I have an idea." She opens the door and peeks into the hallway. With a cheeky grin over her shoulder, she turns left and stops. "Oh."

Andron leans against the wall beside the back door. "You ladies weren't planning on ditching us, were you?"

"We paid for your meal," Angie says. "We don't owe you anything."

A grin flashes across his lips. "You're right, but I owe her mother." He points at me. "If I lose her, I lose my job."

Angie winks. "I'd hire you."

"For what? A bridge partner?" I shake my head at Angie. "You're more trouble than I am." I turn to Andron. "I want you to remember that later."

"That doesn't sound good. You planning on causing me trouble later?" He sweeps a hand back toward the restaurant's main room.

I sigh and shake my head. "No. I rarely plan the trouble I get into."

TWENTY-FOUR

THE CARRIAGE SLOWS as we approach the city center. The bridal studio is located in a wide pedestrian square near the courthouse.

"Here on Grissom, even the contracting ceremonies are done with a bit of pomp," Angie says. As we exit the vehicle, a woman dressed in an enormous white gown with a three-meter long veil emerges from a boutique. Three women in hideous purple floral dresses buzz around her, arranging bits of the gauze and silk. The woman in white pauses for a vid, twisting and turning for a flock of drones to catch every angle, then she saunters across the square toward the blocky government building. A group of men in bright red suits wait on the steps.

"Is that where we're going?" I nod at the store she just left. A huge sign over the door proclaims it Beyond the Veil Bridal.

Angie sniffs. "No, they're a bit tacky. Lili chose The Knot. It's over behind that crowd. Much nicer."

"Beyond the Veil sounds a little morbid. Isn't that what they call the afterlife?" I hurry after Angie—the woman can move!

She laughs. "Yup. Hey, look, there's Yuri!"

Andron hurries to catch up to Angie and holds out his arm. "Hang on. There are too many people here. Something's up."

"Yeah, that's Yuri," Angie repeats. "He and Ro were covering a senator's press conference, remember?"

"How can you tell it's Yuri and not Ro?" I squint at the man. He's standing inside a bubble of holograms, directing drone coverage like a symphony conductor.

She shrugs. "I just know. Family instinct. Yuri!" She ducks under Andron's outstretched arm and trots across the square. Andron makes a comic lunge, missing her entirely. He stumbles and backpedals furiously. With a little hop, he regains his footing and takes off across the plaza.

"Stay together," Ferrigi barks, herding me toward them. "We need to find an alternate route."

We catch up to Angie and Andron, standing outside Yuri's virtual bubble. Twenty or more vids surround him, each showing a different view of an empty stage and a huge crowd. As we watch, he flicks one and swipes it behind his back. The others reform to fill the space.

"Can't talk, Grandma!" he says. "Yuri's up by the stage."

"I thought you said this was Yuri," I mutter.

She shrugs. "I was wrong. Let's get closer."

"Let's not." Ferrigi grabs Angie's wrist. "We need to find an alternate route to the venue."

"We can't." I point at one of the screens in Ro's bubble. A sign reading The Knot is clearly visible behind the stage.

"They must have a delivery door." Ferrigi pulls Angie away.

"Let go of me, young man!" Angie hollers. People in the back of the crowd turn and stare. Angie swings her arm and twists her hand against the hulk's thumb.

Ferrigi cries out and drops her arm. "Hey, I'm trying to protect you!"

Angie steps back into a martial arts crouch, her knees creaking loudly enough to hear over the restless crowd. "I don't need your protection." She brings her hands up, ready to fight. The bag swings wildly from her wrist.

"Angie!" I touch her shoulder. "We don't need an audience." I nod toward the crowd as more people turn to gawk.

"I don't like being manhandled!" Angie winks at me and whispers. "I'm making a distraction. You sneak around to the front and see what's going on. I got this."

"Angie, we don't need a distraction. We can just walk up there."

Andron has circled around behind me and is ready to jump in and grab Angie. I wave him off. "Don't." I turn back to the old woman. "Come on, let's just go."

Angie grabs my arm and pulls herself up. "I coulda taken him."

"He's on our side." As I turn, I glance at Ro. He grins and points at his screens. He's got three cams trained on Angie, catching her impromptu mixed martial arts demo live. "That's not going out on the net, is it?" I whisper harshly.

"Course it is." Ro grins and swipes in another drone to catch the crowd's reaction. "Don't want dead air while we wait for the senator."

I close my eyes and shake my head. At least I'm not recognizable. But anyone tracking the avenger boys could figure it out. Maybe.

"Come on." I drag Angie toward the edge of the square. A few in the crowd clap, and Angie stops to take a bow. Laughter and more applause follow. I wait on the sidelines, rubbing my temple, as Angie darts out and takes another bow.

She comes back while the crowd continues to cheer. "Always leave them wanting more. Let's go." She waves one more time then steps under the awning of the nearest shop and trots down the sidewalk.

Andron hurries after her. "We were waiting for you."

"Let's go, Sera," Ferrigi mutters. "Stay together."

I glare at him. How'd I get left with the bossy one?

The narrow aisle under the awnings is cordoned off. We walk along the shaded strip, slowing to look in shop windows. Angie and I stop at one to gaze at the amazing assortment of pastries. A young woman in a dark green suit with Van Valkenburgh emblazoned on the chest hurries up to us. "Please, keep moving. If you want to stop and watch the senator, we'll find you a place in the square."

I exchange a perplexed look with Angie. "We stopped to look at the cakes, not the senator," she says. "These are much more interesting."

The young woman's face goes red. "We're required to keep these aisles clear. Please, keep moving." She flicks her holo-ring, and a bright red icon with the word Security across it pops up.

"No thanks." Angie waves at Andron and Ferrigi. "We brought our own." She links her arm through mine and strolls away.

I bite back a laugh. "You old troublemaker."

"Hey, watch who you call old, ya crone," she retorts.

We wander to the front of the square where the crowd pushes against a meter-high stage. As we approach, a line of massive, green-suited men and women step forward to block the walkway. They stand shoulder to shoulder, their eyes hidden behind dark visors.

A short woman appears. Her hair is dyed the same green, and she's wearing a matching suit. She hurries behind the line of guards and climbs the steps to the stage, a small entourage following behind. At the same time, a voice announces, "Ladies and gentlemen, Senator Van Valkenburgh." The green line falls back to block access to the steps, and the crowd cheers.

"Look, there's Yuri!" Angie darts around the green suits toward the rear of the platform. "Yuri!"

"Angie!" I lunge after her, certain the guards will see her as a threat and take her down. The green suits let us by, but behind me, I hear a scuffle.

Several voices bark, "Halt!"

"Sera!" Ferrigi calls.

I look over my shoulder. Four of the green suits have blocked Andron and Ferrigi. They look as immovable as the cliffs at the Ebony Coast. "Angie, they've—"

A wave of heat flings me across the walkway, slamming me into the stone building. Fire erupts everywhere. Screams are cut off by a resounding boom.

TWENTY-FIVE

SMOKE BILLOWS, stinging my eyes. Heat presses against my face and arms. My skin feels singed. A muffled roar presses against my ears. I blink, tears spilling out of my eyes. Green suited legs stumble past, a mass of people hurrying away.

I check in with my body parts, but everything seems to be there and working. I peel myself away from the wall and roll to my hands and knees. A stray breeze whips some smoke away, and a clear space forms just above the ground. I crawl across the walkway, the rough surface ripping at my hands and knees. Angie's white hair, mussed and dirty, waves in the hot breeze, but she doesn't seem to be moving.

"Angie!" I call. I can't hear anything except my voice echoing inside my head. I crawl closer. "Angie!"

As I reach her side, she groans and rolls over. Her face is dirty, her eyebrows have been singed off, and blood drips from a cut above her left eye. She grins. "That was exciting."

At least I think that's what she's saying. I can't hear anything but a roaring in my ears. I try activating my audio implant and swipe my hand through Angie's call icon.

"Hello?" Her voice sounds tinny, but I can hear it.

"Angie, are you hurt?"

"I'm fine, but Yuri might be feeling a bit bruised. I landed right on top of him." She points as Yuri levers himself up.

I swipe Yuri into the call. "Are you hurt?" I ask again.

Yuri looks at me, his confusion obvious. "I hear Triana. Who's that?" He points at me.

Angie laughs. "That's Triana. She's in disguise."

Yuri turns back to Angie. "You saved my life, Grandma." He points at a huge hunk of rock. "I was standing right there."

"Huh, and here I was thinking you cushioned my fall." Angie starts to get up but wavers, putting a hand to her head.

"Stay down," I say. "Let me stop the bleeding." I scoot closer and pull Vanti's first aid kit from my pocket. Snapping the flat package open, I take a look at the printed inventory. Wound Clean. Good. Pressure Patch. Perfect. I wipe the blood away and peel off the patch's protective coating. Another swipe with the cleaning pad, and the patch goes on. It tightens across her skin, pulling her eyebrow up and closing the gash.

Angie touches her temple. "Feels like a mini-face-lift! Bonus."

The smoke has thinned, and Yuri stands. "Are you all right?" He reaches a hand down to me.

"A little bruised from hitting the wall." I take his hand and let him pull me up. "I don't know if we should try to move Angie."

"I'm fine. Stop talking about me like I'm not here." She grabs Yuri's hand and pulls herself up. She totters, so I grab her other arm.

"Let's see if we can get her inside. The bridal shop is just over there—if it survived." I point over the stage. Around us, the smoke has cleared. The wall of green suits has vanished, and presumably the senator with them. A twisted hulk of metal is all that's left of the steps. The bunting on the front of the platform burns, giving off acrid fumes. Through the muffling roar in my ears, I hear faint cries and moans.

"Good. Were you two here alone?" He guides the old woman around the back of the stage.

"Oh, crap, no!" I turn, looking for our security detail. "Get her inside. I need to find them."

Leaving Angie with Yuri, I dash back to the mangled steps. A man lies on his side, his legs pinned under the metal, but it's not Andron or Ferrigi.

I crouch beside him, checking for a pulse. "This guy is alive!" I holler, but I don't know if anyone can hear me.

"I'll see if I can send emergency services to you," Yuri says via the audio link.

"Thanks. Did you find a safe place for Angie?" I ask absently as I try to remember my first aid training. I don't think Vanti's kit is going to help this guy.

A hand grabs my shoulder. I jerk away, spinning around on my haunches.

Ferrigi is there, saying something I can't hear. I tap my ear and turn back to the man. Ferrigi grabs my arm again. I glare over my shoulder then notice a man in white behind him. The blue star on his uniform identifies him as medical personnel. I scoot out of the way then slowly get to my feet.

Ferrigi says something else, but I ignore him. I swipe my communications icon and bring him into the call. "Where's Andron?"

"He's okay. Checking in with the peacekeepers." Ferrigi takes my elbow and urges me away from the emergency personnel. "We need to get you to safety."

"I'm fine—" I start to say, but he doesn't stop pushing. "Angie and Yuri are in the shop. Let's go there." I yank my arm out of his grip and head around the back of the stage. Ferrigi follows.

The Knot's windows must be made of blast-plas; they're scratched but not shattered. I wave the door open and stumble inside. Cool air with a faint citrus tang greets us. Angie huddles on an overstuffed white couch, her blackened clothing leaving dark streaks on the pristine material. I hope it's easy to clean. Yuri stands beside her, swiping through his holo-screens. My audio connection goes dead.

A blonde woman in an elegant blue suit approaches, her eyes wide and frightened. Her voice reaches me like an echo in a long tunnel. "This shop is by invitation only."

I stare at her. "A bomb just went off outside your store, and you want to check your guest list?"

She wrings her hands, her eyes darting from me to Ferrigi. His black clothing is torn and burnt, and I'm sure I don't look very reputable, either.

"It's not that. But our current client had some security concerns, so, as you can imagine, an explosion just outside…"

"If your current client has security concerns, you shouldn't mention them to random strangers," Ferrigi growls.

I put a hand on his arm. "We're with your two o'clock client." I flick my identification to her. "And I know they would want you to extend relief to anyone who needs it."

"Yes, of course." She glances at my ID. The blue verified symbol pops up, and her eyes fly back to my face. "Sera Morgan?"

"Since I'm possibly the target of that security concern, you can understand why I'd feel the need to travel incognito." I touch my white waves, which, if Angie is anything to go by, probably look like they belong to a corpse.

"Quite so. Would you and your party like to move into the fitting area?" She steps aside and gestures to a blue door at the rear of the small shop.

"I need to find Ro." Yuri jerks as if he's just woken up. "I'm sure he's fine. He was at the back of the crowd. But I can't get through on the comm."

"Where's Andron?" I ask as Yuri hurries past. "Be careful, Yuri!"

He waves and dashes away.

"He's coming," Ferrigi says. "Had to give a statement to the peacekeepers. They aren't going to like us being involved in a second explosion in two days."

I start to giggle but choke back the hysteria. "They will not be pleased. Where's everyone else?" I swipe my comm system up but can't get a connection. The four-way call with Yuri, Angie, and Ferrigi has crapped out. Luckily, my hearing is returning.

"Comms were probably affected by the blast. Or overridden by emergency services. I'm shocked your local call worked." Ferrigi offers Angie a hand and ushers us both toward the blue door. "And we're a little early. I'm sure the others will be here soon."

The blue door shuts behind us with a whomp. "It's sound-proof," the blue-suited woman says. "We get high end clients who don't wish to be overheard." She nods to another blue door at the rear of the building.

"Most of our prestigious clients come in through the back—that's why I was so surprised to see you out there."

"We didn't know." I shrug and look around. Huge mirrors cover the walls and an alcove in the back of the room. A small stage raises the alcove a half-meter above the floor. To the left, a white door probably hides the dressing rooms.

This room has several of the white couches—on closer inspection, I can see they're Lether. That stuff wipes clean with a damp cloth. My lips twitch—I guess I'll always be part space janitor. Knowing I won't damage the material, I plop down on the closest one.

"My name is Carolina. My partner, Vera, will assist you with the fitting." She opens a hidden cupboard and pulls out a tray with several bottles of sparkling wine and a dozen beautiful crystal glasses. She sets it on the table and expertly pops the cork on the first bottle. "Please, enjoy this while you wait for your party." She pours three glasses, sets the open bottle in the old-fashioned bucket, and retreats through the blue door.

A white panel pops out of the wall, hinging like a door. Ferrigi spins toward it, his hands up and ready. It swings wider, revealing another woman in a blue suit. This one has dark hair in a fancy updo and dark eyes. "I'm Vera," she says, giving Ferrigi a cool look. "Can I offer you something besides the bubbly?"

Ferrigi shakes his head and retreats to stand beside the blue door.

"Do you have anything non-alcoholic?" I ask.

"Of course." Vera disappears through the virtual curtain cast across the doorway. She returns a moment later with two bottles of sparkling water.

"I don't suppose you have something stronger?" Angie asks. When Vera gives her a small head shake, she grabs a glass of the wine. "This will have to do." She chugs it down and holds it out for a refill.

I stand and take a glass to Ferrigi. "It's just water. You gotta stay hydrated."

He eyes it suspiciously then takes a sip. With a nod, he follows Angie's example. I grab the bottle and refill his glass.

I tip my glass back and take a gulp. Dust drifts into my eyes and empty glass. I glance at Vera. "Could you show us to the ladies' room? We'd like to clean up a bit."

"Of course, right this way, Sera." She opens the white door, which leads to a short hallway. Ferrigi pushes past me to inspect the various empty dressing rooms. The last door on the right reveals a large bathroom. We wait for Ferrigi to check for enemy bridesmaids, then Angie follows me in, the half-full bottle of bubbly in one hand. She shuts the door in Ferrigi's face.

I stare at the mirror in horror. My left eyebrow is missing. Soot covers my wrinkled forehead, and my white hair is filthy. The Knot thoughtfully provides a full range of facial care products, so I wash my face. A quick session in the InstaFab booth gives me a tidy if not fabulous hairstyle.

Angie sits on the white bench along the wall, the bottle dangling from her fingers, her eyes closed.

"Angie, are you all right?"

Her eyes pop open, and a watery smile crosses her face. "I...don't know. I've never been blown up before. It's got me a little frazzled."

I take the bottle from her and hold it up to the light. "But you aren't drinking."

"I think this is too serious for alcohol." She sets her crystal glass on the side table and runs a hand through her thick white curls.

"You should get cleaned up." I drop back onto the couch, and a cloud of fine ash poofs up around me. "You'll feel better."

She coughs dramatically and gives me another weak grin. "I think I look pretty bad-ass covered in soot. But the dress fitting might not go as planned."

"Why don't you use that shower? I'll get you something to change into." I nudge her with my shoulder toward the small, elegantly appointed stall. There's a changing space with another of the Lether benches and an inner booth with a sonic shower, a full range of beauty products, and buffing towels warming on a rack. "I'll bring your dress in here." I look at my dirty clothing. "Or maybe I'll have Vera bring it in."

She rises with a grunt and heads into the little room. I grab the champagne and push open the door.

Ferrigi escorts me the five steps down the hall and opens the outer door. He makes me wait while he scopes out the room then allows me to enter.

Ty's mom and sisters have arrived, and they're oohing and aahing over the champagne and a tray of appetizers on the low table. They look up in surprise when I enter.

"May I help you?" Serena sets her glass down and rises from the white couch. She gives me a second look, her eyes catching on my torn and dirty clothing. "Who are you and what happened?"

TWENTY-SIX

"There was a bit of an explosion outside," I say. "Angie needs some new clothes."

"Angie? Is she okay?" Serena pushes past me to the bathroom.

"Who are you?" Aretha stalks toward me. "I know that voice."

I start to give her my best "what's wrong with you" look then remember I don't exactly look like myself. "It's me, Triana. I, uh, had a makeover."

"Triana? What are you doing here?" Aretha touches my hair in wonder. "And why would you...?"

Still sitting on the couch, Akiko crosses her arms, her lips pursed. "She used some kind of mod to sneak out when she should have stayed safely at home. You know you're at risk! I can't believe you would put Grandma Angie in danger!"

I hold up both hands, trying to ward off her anger. "It was Angie's idea!"

"She's a million years old," Akiko scoffs. "Maybe senile. Unfit to make that kind of decision. *You* should know better!"

I glare at her. I want to argue it's Angie's fault, but Akiko's right. I know better. I should have stayed at home. "I'm sorry."

"I'm not." Angie stands in the doorway, wrapped in a white robe with the boutique's logo embroidered in pink on the chest. "If we hadn't been here, Yuri would be dead. That bomb had nothing to do with Triana. It was aimed at Senator Van Valkenburgh." She pushes Ferrigi out of the way, stomps across the room to Akiko, and drops into a martial arts crouch. "And if you call me senile again, little girl, we'll see who's unfit. I can take you."

I bite back a grin. I'll bet she could. Akiko is soft and plump. Angie is a terror.

"Grandma." Serena takes Angie's arm. "Let's not start any physical altercations."

"What did you mean about Yuri?" Aretha takes the bottle from me and fills her glass.

While Angie explains about the explosion, I retreat to the bathroom again. I find another robe and make use of the shower. After transferring my cash and Vanti's tech to a robe pocket, my filthy clothing goes into a refresher—if it survives the cleaning, I'll put it back on before we leave.

I think about what Akiko said. Angie is as mentally acute as anyone, and the explosion would have happened whether we were there or not. But Akiko was right about me. I shouldn't have let Angie convince me. Ty and Vanti don't need my help in their investigation, and by being here, I put them all at risk. Maybe I should get Andron and Ferrigi to take me home. Not just to the O'Neill's compound but back to SK2.

Akiko would be thrilled by that. The thought makes me grimace. I've learned my lesson there. I won't just disappear—I'll talk to O'Neill first.

Mind made up, I tighten the belt on the robe and stride out of the room.

As I return, the blue door at the back of the room opens. Ferrigi pushes me against the wall, shielding me with his body.

"We've delivered the bride!" a voice calls out.

The hulk relaxes, and I peek over his shoulder. The O'Neill women surge up from the couch, swarming around Jie and Lili. O'Neill and Vanti stand a few steps behind them. I shove Ferrigi out of the way and stumble across the room. "Ty!"

His head snaps in my direction, but his eyes pass over me, searching the room. "Triana? Where are you?"

Vanti's face crinkles into one of her rare smiles, reminding me I look nothing like myself. I stop short of throwing myself into O'Neill's arms. "I'm right here." I spare a glare for Vanti. "Someone slipped me a mickey."

"What are you doing here?" He grabs my arms and peers into my face. "Wow, that is—I've seen you in all kinds of disguises, but this one is truly disturbing."

"Thanks. Hopefully, someone has the antidote." I give Vanti the evil eye. "I told you before I don't trust these black-market mods."

The sly grin disappears from her face as O'Neill turns toward the redhead. "What did you do?"

"I didn't do anything." She studies her fingernails. "Well, I might have loaned one of the mods to your grandma. They're one hundred percent reversible, though. Just turn it off."

"What do you mean, turn it off?" I demand. "She slipped something into my drink. You can't turn those off; you have to wait them out. Or get them reversed."

"No, she didn't spike your drink." Vanti holds out a hand. "Do you have them?"

I reach into my pocket and pull out the sleeve of capsules and a loose one. "You mean these? This red one fell out of the packet."

O'Neill gasps.

"Yeah." She takes them and tucks the packet away but holds up the red capsule. Her own hair whitens, and wrinkles form on her perfect skin. "They aren't aesthetic mods. Good thing you didn't swallow one! They form a visual cortex over your body. Kind of a hologram but anchored to your skin." She does something to the capsule, and her face returns to normal. "Fast, easy, and non-invasive."

I touch my hair, and a red curl flops into my face. Blinking in amazement, I turn to the mirrored wall. I'm back to normal. Well, except for the soot still engrained in my hairline. And the drawn on eyebrow. So much for the InstaFab. "Angie just slid one of these into my pocket?"

Vanti nods. "Yup."

"If I'd taken off my jacket, then I would have changed back." I look at the mirror again. "That would have been disconcerting in public."

"You're supposed to wear them as close to your skin as possible." Vanti hands me the device. "I usually tuck mine into my bra."

"I wasn't given a choice. How do I activate it?"

"Squeeze."

I squash my fingers together and watch as my face wrinkles and my hair whitens. "That's incredible." I squeeze again. Back to normal. "Why did Angie say she spiked my drink?"

Vanti shrugs.

O'Neill laughs. "Who knows why Grandma Angie does anything? I should have known better than to leave you alone with her. The two of you are trouble."

"To be fair, you thought your mom would be there." I glance at the others and lower my voice. "Did you hear about the explosion?"

"Yes." O'Neill lowers his voice, too. "Ro and Yuri were there. They're both fine."

I let out a breath. "I knew Yuri was okay—Grandma Angie saved him. But we hadn't heard from Ro."

"A couple of the senator's security detail were injured, but the bomb was in a weird location." Vanti's dispassionate tone is kind of comforting —as if she's recounting something that happened long ago or far away. "Yuri was in exactly the wrong place. Of course, terrorists love collateral damage. But I'm sure they would have preferred to hit their mark."

"Let the peacekeepers take care of it," O'Neill says. "We need to focus on who's targeting Triana."

"If anyone really is," Vanti says. I can tell they've had this discussion several times already. "That subway bombing could have been random. How would they have known she would be there at that time?"

The sharp smack of clapping hands interrupts our conversation. The chatter around the hors d'oeuvres dies, and Vera moves to the center of the room. "Will the gentlemen be staying for the fitting?"

Jie and O'Neill exchange a panicked look.

"No. Definitely not." Serena makes shooing motions at Jie. "Go away. You can't see the bride until tomorrow."

Jie grabs another item from the canape tray and hurries toward us. "You heard the woman. Let's get out of here."

THE RINGS OF GRISSOM

Vera looks pointedly at Ferrigi. "And you?"

He points at me. "If she stays, I stay."

"I'm going!" I smile at the ladies on the couch. "This is a family thing. You don't need me here. And now that Angie is safely in your hands—"

"No thanks to you," Akiko mutters.

O'Neill takes a step forward. "Akiko."

Her face pales, and she looks away. "Sorry."

Vanti touches my arm. "Do you want to put some clothes on before we go?"

I look down at my robe and sigh. "But it's so comfy." I glare at her. "Don't leave without me."

"Wouldn't think of it."

"We'll wait outside." Jie kisses Lili and hurries O'Neill toward the door.

I narrow my eyes. "Better yet, why don't you come help me." I grab Vanti's hand.

"Ferrigi, you can wait with O'Neill. Vanti can protect me from Vera." Without waiting for an answer, I drag her into the bathroom.

My clothes hang inside the refresher, clean and pressed. They still look horrible, with stains, tears, and burns, but I put them on.

"I wouldn't have left without you." Vanti hands me a blue capsule. "Just to be safe."

I squeeze the blue device and watch in the mirror as my red hair lengthens and turns brown with green streaks. My face elongates a bit, and my eyes turn green. "Why is my eyebrow still missing? Shouldn't the cortex thingy hide that?"

"The cortex uses your own features to create the illusion. If you're missing something it's looking for—they can build customs, but I didn't know you'd burn off something important." She opens a drawer and roots around inside it. "Here, fix that one. What did you do, stick your head in an InstaFab?"

I look at the logo on the wall of the booth.

Vanti laughs. "Oops. They aren't exactly the best in the business. Here, let me fix it."

She rips the packaging off a single-use eyebrow pencil and with a few quick strokes, draws in a new one. Then she takes a couple swipes at the other side.

"Is there anything you can't do?" I peer in the mirror. "These look better than my real ones."

She shrugs and heads for the door. "We learn this stuff in undercover school."

"Undercover school? Is that a real thing?" I follow her out.

"No." She leads the way into the larger room. The men have disappeared, and Lili stands on the little stage. She's wearing a silvery sheath that clings to her figure. The skirt has a slit on one side and a train that flares behind her. "Ooh, that's lovely."

I've never heard that tone of admiration and longing from Vanti before. She's always so cool and professional. Her Techno-Inst recruiter persona was bubbly and high-energy, but it was all surface. This is different.

Vanti steps closer, reaching out to finger the fabric of the train. Suddenly, she snatches her hand back, as if the material might burn. Her face goes blank, and she straightens.

"Hey, would it be okay if Vanti and I stay?" I ask Lili. "We can send the guys home." Without waiting for an answer, I hurry to the back door.

I poke my head outside quickly, at waist height, like I've seen Vanti and O'Neill do a thousand times. Jie and O'Neill sit at a small outdoor table. Thick vines cover an open framework over their heads, providing shade for the small courtyard. Ferrigi stands by an arched wooden doorway, watching for external threats, I guess.

I can't believe I got all that in a single glance. Figuring the coast is clear, I stride out. "Vanti and I are going to stay here. You guys can head back." I glance at Ferrigi. "All of you. Vanti can protect me. She's done it before."

O'Neill does a double take. "Not sure I like these techno-mods. I didn't recognize you. Again."

"That's a good thing. I'm perfectly safe. You boys go home." I kiss him on the cheek. "We'll come back with your mom."

"The hulk and the android are staying." His eyes sparkle when he uses my nicknames. "Vanti's good, but she can't watch inside and out on her own. And there were terrorists in the area. Check in before you leave. I want to know where you are at all times."

I give him a disbelieving look. "Like you aren't tracking me?"

He grins. "You got me. But call anyway." He kisses me more soundly on the lips then lets me go. "Come on, Jie, let's get out of here."

I duck back inside and come face to face with Vanti. "What was that all about?" she asks.

"I decided I'd like to stay." I gesture at the women behind her, all still marveling over Lili's dress. "I've seen lots of wedding prep on *Ancient Tēvē*, but I've never done this in person. Looks like fun."

Vanti's eyes narrow. "Really? Are Ferrigi and Andron staying here?"

"They've got the external. Your only job is to keep me safe from Vera." I grin. "And Akiko."

Vanti returns my grin. "That might be harder."

TWENTY-SEVEN

WE SETTLE BACK on the couch and watch the rest of O'Neill's family try on their dresses for the big day. Lili's traditional silver dress sparkles amid their midnight blue gowns. All of them look fantastic. The longing in Vanti's eyes compresses my heart like a vice.

"You should try one, Vanti." I turn to Vera. "What do you have that would fit her? She doesn't have to match, but she needs something that will complement."

"No, I'm working." Vanti jumps up to stand near the door. "I shouldn't be goofing off."

I glare at her. "You work for me—or at least for my mother. And I want Vera to find you a dress." I nod at the salesclerk. "I'm sure you have something that will look spectacular on her."

Vera smiles her professional smile. She knows my credit limit would allow me to buy the whole store. "I have just the thing."

She hurries through the white door and returns a few minutes later. "I've put it in the dressing room. This way, please."

"That's a nice thing to do," Angie whispers to me. "I wonder if she's—" She breaks off. "Is she seeing anyone?"

I shake my head. "She doesn't talk about her personal life. Why do you ask?"

Angie shrugs. "I wasn't sure if it was the dress itself she wanted or what it represents."

When the door opens again, all conversation stops. Vanti is attractive even when she's wearing her usual black tactical gear. But I've never seen her like this. Her copper hair is swept into a fancy updo, leaving a few wisps waving around her face. The emerald green dress sets off her pale skin and bright hair to perfection. It clings to her slender figure, then flares at the waist into a full skirt. The deep plunging neckline reveals a long, gold necklace.

"Wow, Vanti, you look amazing." I push her up onto the low stage. "Look in the mirror. You look—wow."

The other women murmur agreement. "I'm not sure she should be allowed to look that good," Aretha says. "She'll outshine Lili!"

"Oh, this is just for fun," Vanti says. "I'm not getting this—I have to work."

"Nonsense," Lili says. "You look amazing. You should definitely get that dress."

"Lots of room for weapons in that skirt," Angie adds.

While they argue, I flick a message to Vera. She nods. Done.

WHEN WE GET HOME, the men are waiting. O'Neill, Jie, Ro, Yuri, and Brad sit in the lounge, drinking beer. As Andron and Ferrigi trudge up the steps toward their room, Brad calls out, "Grab a beverage, boys. You're off duty."

They exchange a look with Vanti then clatter back down.

"Not completely off duty," O'Neill says as he hands out drinks. "We'd like to do a hot wash."

"Hot wash?" Aretha asks.

"Military term." Vanti mixes wine and sparkling water then slouches into a chair. "Means we're going to go over everything that happened and figure out what went wrong."

"And how we can do better next time." Ferrigi perches on the edge of a chair with a glass of plain water.

"If you're going to talk work, I have somewhere else to be." Serena grins at the group. "I'll let you know when dinner is ready."

"I'd better go help." Brad downs the remains of his drink and puts the glass into the AutoKich'n. "I could use some help—got something special planned for tonight." He rubs his hands together, looking from face to face.

Lili jumps up. "I don't want to think about the explosion. Someone could have been killed." Brad puts an arm around her, and they wander away.

"I'd better make sure she's all right." Jie grabs another beer and follows his fiancée out of the room.

"Anyone else?" O'Neill holds up a bottle.

Andron gives Ferrigi's water a quick glance then takes the beer. "Got the Buzzkill if I need it," he mutters, patting his pocket.

"What happened is someone tried to blow up the senator, and we didn't get killed." Ro clinks his beer bottle against Yuri's. The two nod and drink.

"Right." Ferrigi frowns. "But our response could have been better. If the ladies would just follow orders—"

"That's not the tone of voice you should use when referring to a lady." Angie's face is straight, but her eyes sparkle. "Especially not one old enough to be your great-grandmother." She looks at O'Neill. "Or who *is* your great-grandmother."

O'Neill holds up both hands. "I would never." His hands drop. "However, Lou is correct. Running toward a crowd at a political rally is not the best move."

"We didn't run." Angie's eyes narrow. "And the rally wasn't our problem. Maybe someone should have done better recon." She folds her arms.

"Yes," Ferrigi says. "We would have, if we'd been given any advance notice."

"You could have checked the location while we were in the carriage." Angie's tone heats up. "Or at lunch. Or while Triana was working on the surveillance thing."

Ferrigi opens his mouth, but O'Neill cuts him off. "What surveillance thing?"

My face heats. "It was nothing. I'd left the facial recognition loop running last night, and I thought I recognized—there was another Putin look-a-like in one of the clips."

Vanti looks up from her spritzer. "Bobby Putin?"

"It wasn't him. I checked." I squirm. Just thinking about him grinning at the camera makes me queasy.

"Doesn't it seem like a bit of a coincidence that there's an inspector named al-Petrosian involved in Bill's crash, and she sees a guy who looks like Bobby Putin hanging around our guys?" Vanti points at Ferrigi and Andron.

O'Neill's jaw tightens. "When you put it that way, it does sound suspicious. And we never got to visit the local al-Petrosian."

"I thought that's where you all disappeared to this morning." I give O'Neill the stink eye. "Where'd you go, if not to see the inspector?"

"We went to his office," Vanti says. "He wasn't available. We also checked out the scene at the transit station. Nothing new there. And we chatted with the peacekeepers investigating the explosion. They've got no new leads. They're trying to track the electronic components recovered from the blast, but no luck yet."

"How about I see if I can get al-Petrosian's home address? We can pay him a little visit tomorrow morning before the wedding." I glance at Angie. "There isn't anything we have to do in the morning, is there?"

"Serena and Lili will be busy, but you'll probably have some free time." The old lady holds out her empty glass, and Ro grabs the whiskey bottle on the table to refill it. She grimaces. "I'm sure they'll try to keep me out of the fun. You should break me loose to help—I'm a great spy."

"Tha's crazy! You're a terrible spy!" Ferrigi complains. "You don' follow directions. You jus' run off, getting into trouble!"

"Are you sure that's water he's drinking?" I whisper to Aretha.

"Ro! Yuri! Who poured that man's drink?" Aretha glares at her brothers.

Ro and Yuri dissolve into laughter, clicking their bottles together again. "That's always funny," one of them says between the giggles.

O'Neill rolls his eyes and jumps up to rummage in a cupboard in the corner. He returns and hands the Buzzkill bottle to Ferrigi. "I should buy stock."

"We already did," Ro says.

"It just keeps climbing." Yuri nods at his twin. "Best investment ever."

Vanti's lips twitch, but she keeps her face straight. "Let's get back to business for a few minutes, okay?" The twins nod solemnly, so she continues. "Triana will find al-Petrosian's home address. I'd like to pay him a little visit."

"Already on it." I've connected my holo-ring to the hackbox I set up on the household net. It allows me to connect to the external net without tracebacks. It also allows me to work from anywhere inside the O'Neill compound. I tune out the others as I focus on my hacking. As a precaution, I jump through some external nodes to muddy any attempt to trace me. Then I set a loop to worm into the local net provider. I could try to hack into the planetary databases, but government authorities tend to take a dim view of hackers. I've already got a record on Grissom; I don't need to make it worse.

Ironically, net providers are usually a little sloppier with their security. And since everyone is connected to the net, it's way easy to find people's personal data by trolling the providers. Here in Virgilton, there are only two net providers, and one of them offers inferior service. So, I start with the other.

A few clicks and a password cracker, and I'm inside their customer database. The billing data isn't available here—that would take more time—and cracking financial systems carries a much higher criminal penalty. "Here it is. He lives on Rosequartz Way."

O'Neill shakes his head. "I really shouldn't let you do this kind of stuff."

"Let me?" I raise my eyebrows at him. "Oh, please, ser, may I hack this database?"

A grin flickers over O'Neill's lips, and the twins cackle loudly.

"Someone cut them off." O'Neill glares at the boys.

Yuri holds up his bottle so we can see the label. "It's alcohol free."

"We don't need a buzz to have a good time." Ro shoots a pointed look at Ferrigi. Andron looks away, as if he's hiding a grin.

"I'm not here to have a good time. I'm here to do a job. Protect her."

Ferrigi points at me. "And that is being complicated by terrorists and juveniles."

"We aren't technically juveniles," Ro says.

"We're well over the legal age," Yuri agrees.

"Boys." Aretha has been uncharacteristically quiet. "Stop baiting him. If you aren't going to help, go away." She waits, but they don't move. "Fine. Let's—"

She's interrupted by the door alert. Everyone looks at everyone else.

"Were we expecting guests?" O'Neill asks.

"They're here!" Serena calls out as she crosses the courtyard. "Come meet Jie's family!"

TWENTY-EIGHT

"I GUESS we should have expected that." Hours later, Vanti and I sit on the top step, staring down into the courtyard.

"Expected them?" I ask, nodding at the knot of people gathered by the tunnel leading to the front door.

"Haven't your *Ancient Tēvē* vids taught you anything?" she asks. "The groom's family always shows up right before the wedding."

"I guess." I rub my temple. "I can't believe they stayed so late, though. Don't they have a wedding to prepare for?"

O'Neill steps out of the gloom of the second floor and starts up the steps toward us. "Yes, but the groom's family gets the easy part. They basically just have to show up."

I cross my arms. "According to my much-maligned vids, there should have been a rehearsal dinner tonight. Attended by all the participants of the wedding. That would have left the rest of us free to work."

"Rehearsal? Why do they need a rehearsal? The ceremony's pretty straightforward." He drops onto the step next to me and slides an arm around my shoulders. "You just do what the guy tells you to do."

"The guy?" I lean against him, his warm body making me forget the discomfort of the hard steps.

"Sure, the wedding guy. The officiant. Whatever." His voice rumbles in my ear. "You two managed to sneak away—I'm surprised you aren't over casing out al-Petrosian's house."

Vanti and I exchange a guilty look.

"What?" O'Neill pushes me away so he can see my face. "What did you do?"

I shrug. "We took a little walk. He lives just a few blocks away. But there was something going on over there, too."

"Too many people," Vanti confirms. "So, we came back here and did a little network sleuthing. He's clean. No unexplained deposits in his credit accounts. No off-world travel in years. No suspicious behavior."

"You don't think he's too clean, do you?" I glance from one to the other. "Maybe he's hidden his 'evil twin' deeper than we were able to look."

"Possible. Anything's possible." Vanti wrinkles her nose. "But my gut tells me it's not him."

"Where does that leave us?" O'Neill pulls me close again.

I snuggle in and start ticking people off on my fingers. "Bill could have done it. We haven't investigated his assistant yet—what was her name?"

"The backup pilot?" O'Neill's arms tighten around me as he flicks his holo-ring to pull up a note page. "Luin. We ran a full check on her—it came up clean. Same with Watson. No connections to anything shady."

"Have you talked to the Peacekeepers about the bomb in the square?" he asks Vanti. "I doubt that one targeted Triana, but you have to admit it's odd that there were only three explosions on Grissom in the last five *years*, and she was nearby for all three of them."

"I got their report," Vanti says. "I have a friend. The same equipment was used—same type of remote triggering. She—my friend—wasn't able to get anything from the flight investigators, but I'd be willing to bet that explosion also used remote triggering."

"I've seen the report." O'Neill shifts behind me, and I can hear the grin in his voice. "I have friends, too."

"I thought you told Aretha you didn't have any contacts on Grissom." I twist around to look at him.

"That *is* what I told Aretha." He settles me against him again. "I have a few connections. How could I not? I grew up here."

"What did they tell you?" Vanti asks.

O'Neill's arms close around me again so he can flick his holo-ring. "Here's the report—I haven't had time to look at it yet."

Vanti's ring lights up, and she flicks the file open. I relax against O'Neill while she reads, my eyes drifting shut.

"There it is!" Vanti's jubilant tone shakes me out of my stupor. "Exactly the same as the other two. In fact, the serial numbers on one of the recovered components are only one off from the one recovered at the transit station. Definitely the same perps."

I sit up. "So, we've got three explosions, all tied to the same equipment. Where did that come from? Who bought it?"

"Stolen." Vanti scowls. "All of it. Nearly a year ago."

"A year?" I look at O'Neill. "But we only met a little over a year ago. I can't be the target. I didn't have any connection to Grissom that far back."

O'Neill runs his hand through his hair. "I don't know. Let's get some sleep. Maybe something will shake loose overnight."

Vanti stands. "I'll be up early—I'm going to try to get to al-Petrosian first thing."

"And by 'get to him,' you mean talk to him, right?" O'Neill stands and pulls me to my feet. "Just talk to him. He's a government employee, and we're security for a company based in foreign territory. Hacking into their computers is bad enough. We don't need to mess with their public servants. We'll all end up in jail, and I doubt our friends will be able to get us out."

"Yours might not, but I know the right people." Vanti grins then shakes her head. "I'm just going to ask him about inspecting Bill's ship. Like I said, I don't think he's in this. But no stone left unturned, right? Especially when we've got no other leads."

"WHAT ABOUT WATSON?" I ask. Vanti, O'Neill, and I sit at the breakfast table. The house is quiet—no one else is up yet. "She's a demolition expert, and she works with Bill's wife."

"We're still looking at her." O'Neill butters a piece of toast. "On the surface, she's clean, but she would be, right?"

"If this doesn't have anything to do with Triana, maybe we should turn over what we know about Bill's accident to whoever is investigating the incident with the senator." Vanti peels the wrapper off one of her protein bars and breaks off a tiny piece.

"I told Aretha—and Bill—that I'd help clear him." O'Neill rumples his hair. "I can't just leave him with pilot error."

"Why would anyone believe that?" I ask. "If there were electronics found at the crash site that indicate a remote detonation, then pilot error is a stupid conclusion."

O'Neill points his knife at me. "Exactly. Someone is covering up for the terrorist by pinning that crash on Bill. And they're doing a crap job."

"Yes. If we point the investigators toward that information, we can let them clear Bill." Vanti breaks off another tiny bit, chews, then swallows. "That way, you can enjoy the wedding."

O'Neill's eyes narrow. "It's not like you to hand an investigation over to someone else. What's going on?"

"Yeah, what?" I ask. "Did you learn something from al-Petrosian this morning?"

"Oh, I haven't been over there." Vanti waves that away. "He was a long-shot. I'll swing by after breakfast."

"That's not breakfast." I point at the barely nibbled protein bar then gesture to my plate of pancakes with butter and jam, bacon, and coffee. "This is breakfast."

She shrugs. "I prefer these. Look. I'll run over and chat with al-Petrosian, then I'll send the reports we have to the peacekeepers looking into the other explosions. You two enjoy the festivities." She picks up her protein bar and disappears before we can say anything.

"That was weird," O'Neill says.

"I thought so, too. What's she up to?"

"I don't know, but I aim to find out."

I make a sticky pancake toast and bacon sandwich out of my breakfast while O'Neill pours our coffee into travel mugs. Then we head out through the back gate.

Vanti is nowhere in sight, of course. We purposely gave her a head start. I bring up my mapping app, but O'Neill waves it away. "I grew up in this neighborhood. I know a shortcut. We're headed to the old part of town."

We stride through shadowed alleys and cross brilliantly lit streets. The sun is still low in the sky, but birds are singing like mad, and a cool breeze plays in the trees. "It's going to be stinking hot this afternoon," he tells me.

"It's always stinking hot on Grissom," I reply.

"Not really—just in the summer." He grins. "Farther north—up by the CEC academy—it's not as bad. But that's all government-owned land."

"Why did the original settlers come here then?" I peer down the dusty alley. We're on the outskirts of Virgilton, and the dry plains stretch out to distant mountain ranges.

"Food. There are three good growing seasons on this part of the planet. And most of the north is too swampy for agriculture." O'Neill indicates a turn, and we head down a bright street. Tall white walls with wide arched doors line both sides of the stone-paved road. Everything looks old. "You just have to stay inside in the sum—"

"Is that Vanti?" I point at a redheaded figure. She's standing in the middle of the street, arms crossed, staring directly at us.

O'Neill laughs. "Of course it is. She's probably tracking us." He quickens his pace, and I stretch my legs to keep up.

"I should have invited you along, I suppose," Vanti says as we approach.

O'Neill raises an eyebrow. "You think?"

"Come on, they're expecting us—well, me."

TWENTY-NINE

VANTI TURNS and pushes open a tall wooden door. We follow her into a walled courtyard. A wide gravel path winds through local plantings. A fountain tinkles in a corner. I do a double-take—I'm pretty sure it's a hologram. I don't feel any spray as we swing past it.

There's another tall wall—this one several stories high. Much like the O'Neill house, this blocky building has an iron gate latched across a dark tunnel. Vanti waves at the access panel then looks up at the very obvious camera. A few moments later, the gate unlocks.

"Who's they?" I follow Vanti into the dark corridor, O'Neill bringing up the rear. "And why are they expecting you?"

"Al-Petrosian and his partner." Vanti strides through the dim tunnel and out into a slightly brighter courtyard.

The sun is still low, so heavy shadows fill this space. Like the O'Neill home, balconies look down on the central courtyard. This building is taller and narrower. The courtyard holds a small seating area and one thin tree with thick fronds at the top. The fronds stretch almost fully across the courtyard, protecting the occupants from the sun at mid-day. A small pond takes up about half of the open space, and bright flashes of movement draw my eyes to the water.

"The gang's all here, I see," a male voice says. A small man emerges from behind the stairway leading to the second floor. "You are Agent O'Neill and Sera Morgan. I am Vern al-Petrosian. I'm surprised you allowed her to come." He nods at me.

"I don't have any control over where she goes," O'Neill says. "I just try to keep her safe."

"Seems like a risky business for a security professional." Al-Petrosian gestures to the chairs and takes a seat. "I, for one, don't care for risks."

"It works for us," O'Neill says.

"You might want to hire a new security manager," he says to me. "I wouldn't employ someone who gives me that much freedom. It's dangerous."

"Thanks for your advice." I give him my best condescending Ice Dame look.

He spreads his hands. "I'm a government inspector. Being risk-averse is in my nature."

"While we'd love to hang out and discuss risk mitigation all afternoon, we're on a bit of a timeline today." Vanti taps her wrist in the ancient time's a-wasting gesture. "Where's your new partner?"

"I'm here."

I spin around as a woman emerges from the gloomy cloister behind me.

"Watson!" I jump out of my seat. "What's she doing here? What do you mean by partner?"

O'Neill steps between me and the peacekeeper. "Sera Morgan isn't going anywhere. And if you try to deport her again, I will report you for accepting bribes."

She glares at O'Neill. "I've never taken a bribe!"

"Maybe not credits, but you deported Sera Morgan because my sister told you to. You must have received some kind of compensation."

"Please, Ser O'Neill, have a seat." Al-Petrosian touches O'Neill's arm then taps the chair. "All will be explained."

"Vanti, what the hell's going on?" O'Neill's voice is barely audible. He's probably talking to her via audio link. I can't hear her answer, but

O'Neill's shoulders relax a fraction as Watson stalks past us and sits between Vanti and al-Petrosian. O'Neill waits until she's seated then pulls my chair a little closer to his. We sit.

"Agent Fioravanti visited me yesterday with an interesting story." Al-Petrosian waves dramatically at Vanti.

"You visited him yesterday?" O'Neill asks. "When?"

"After everyone else went to bed." She shrugs. "I was busy earlier. Talking to her." She nods at Watson.

"Could someone please explain what is going on?" My voice crackles with frustration.

Al-Petrosian holds up a hand. "It's Officer Watson's story."

Watson shifts uncomfortably. She stares at a spot behind me as she launches into her tale. "I was an explosives expert for many years. Made my living taking down old buildings. It's exciting but a bit dangerous. My family kept after me, trying to get me to change careers. I went to the Peacekeeper academy, but after I graduated, I wasn't sure I wanted to do the job. It seemed so boring."

"Peacekeeper is a boring, safe job?" I glance at Vanti then O'Neill. "Is Grissom that safe? There've been three explosions since I got here."

"That's not normal," Vanti says, nodding at Watson to continue.

"So, about nine months ago, I took a sabbatical." Her hands twist in her lap as she speaks. "I took a cruise and ended up on Sally Ride. While I was there, I met a guy." Her eyes flick to me, then away. "He was charming, handsome, smart. So attentive, but a little mysterious. We went places and did things I'd never have attempted on my own. It was so exciting." She sighs.

My heart rate speeds up, thumping loudly in my ears. Somehow, I know where this story is going, and but I can't get a word out to interrupt.

"After a month or so, he convinced me I should come home and take the peacekeeper job. He said he'd come to visit. Maybe to stay. I was stupidly in love with him. I would have done anything to be with him, so taking a job I'd trained for was easy. He continued to send me messages— always promising he'd be coming soon." She swallows, hard. "Then I saw a news story about Bobby Putin."

I gasp. Even though I'd half expected it, the statement shocks me.

She nods. "My mystery man was a top-lev serial killer. The next time he contacted me, I called him on it. He didn't even try to deny it. But by then, he'd managed to gather enough incriminating evidence to keep me under his thumb." She holds up both hands in denial. "Not that I'd done anything illegal—well, not on my own. Turns out some of those exciting things we did on Sally Ride were *not* exactly legal. And he had vids to prove I'd done them. Vids that he carefully stayed out of." Her jaw clenches.

She takes a deep breath. "He wanted me to do a couple of simple jobs for him." Her eyes flick to each of us again then settle on me. "He wanted to scare you. He had me put the bomb on Bill's ship." Tears form in her eyes.

"You were willing to bomb your partner's husband's ship because Putin had dirt on you?" My hands clench around the armrests of my chair. "You could have killed him!"

"No!" She jerks like she's been punched in the gut. "No. I'm an expert. Those shuttles are built to withstand a blast. I set it so there was no risk to him. Same with the transit station. No one was there—I used my connections to get the station closed for maintenance before your pod arrived."

"And you knew we were coming sometime that day because Kate told you." O'Neill's face is grim. "Is she in on this?"

"No, of course not. Kate is completely innocent! But we knew you'd want to talk to Ser al-Petrosian, so it was just a matter of getting her to let me know when you'd arrive. It was too easy."

"And that's what tipped me off." Vanti leans forward. "I knew someone had set up the station maintenance—it wasn't hard to trace that back to Watson. That's what I was doing yesterday morning." She glances at O'Neill. "I convinced her to come here and talk to you."

"Why here?" My brow wrinkles. "Is Vern involved with Wil?"

"Me? Who's Wil?" al-Petrosian asks.

"The terrorist I told you about," Vanti says. She turns back to us. "They are very distant cousins. But this was a safe place for Watson to meet us. We have to assume anywhere she goes on a regular basis is being monitored by Putin."

"How do you know she doesn't have a tracker on her?" I ask.

"I checked. This isn't my first assignment. I know how to keep locations safe." Vanti sits back in her chair and gives me a superior look.

"Why did you call them partners?" O'Neill asks.

"Because they are. Now." She grins at al-Petrosian. "Vern says he's risk averse, but there's a little wild man inside him trying to get out. Watson has reported to Putin that she's been contacted by Wil's distant cousin and he wants to help."

"What's your plan, Vanti?" O'Neill asks.

"I'm trying to draw out the other players. That bombing in the square wasn't Watson. Someone else is involved."

"Wil's organization was very good at compartmentalizing," I say. "We may never find out who the other players are. Unless you're going to try to get them to bomb me again."

"No!" O'Neill cries.

"I wasn't volunteering," I mutter.

"Let's face it, the wedding is probably the most likely time for them to strike." Vanti folds her hands in her lap. "Large gathering. Public location. High profile guest. They've proven—with the senator's bombing—that they don't care about collateral damage."

"He doesn't want to hurt anyone," Watson argues.

We all turn and stare at her as if she's crazy.

"Really—that's the only reason I went along with it." She nods repeatedly, as if she can convince us—and herself—by sheer force of will. "He said he just wanted to scare her. He told me to make the explosions nonfatal. He specifically told me to make sure no one was in the transit station."

"He's a convicted serial killer," I say. "He tried to kill me more than once."

Tears fill her eyes. "He's not like that."

I gape at her. "You know he's a killer. He's been blackmailing you to blow things up. How can you say he's not like that? That's exactly what he's like!"

"I'm sorry." The tears spill down her face. "I—he—I'm so confused. I know he's bad, but some part of me keeps trying to convince the rest of me that he's really the charming, amazing man I fell in love with."

"Trust me, he's not." I wrap my arms around myself. O'Neill reaches out and rubs my back.

The other woman sniffs. "I have to keep reminding myself. Sometimes I think he did something to my brain."

"Could he have used some form of hypnosis or brain wave manipulation?" O'Neill asks Vanti.

"We'd have to get her to a certified facility to check." Vanti flicks her holo-ring.

"What?" Watson's face goes red. "What are you talking about?"

"The technology that's used to help trauma victims can also be used to create false—not memories exactly, but emotional attachments." Vanti grimaces. "It's—obviously, no one wants criminals—or politicians—doing that, so it's kept quiet. But Putin has nearly unlimited resources. He could—"

"Wait a minute," I break in. "How's he doing all this? He's locked up in Attica. I checked yesterday. He's definitely there. And he doesn't have access to the outside."

"He's not supposed to have access to the outside." Vanti glowers. "But who knows what he set up in advance? He put Gwen into position long before we finally got him. I'm sure he has contingency plans for his contingency plans."

"I'm sending a team to Attica to do a full sweep." O'Neill starts swiping through interfaces on his holo-ring.

"No. We don't want to tip him off," Vanti says.

"I'll tie it to Triana's call yesterday." O'Neill smiles. "Obviously, someone wasn't following protocol because she specifically asked for no audio connection. And yet, they turned that on, allowing Putin to know she was checking. That's grounds for a full sweep right there." He raises an eyebrow at me.

I nod. "Yup, they blew it. Send a copy of the call with the team, so they have evidence."

O'Neill nods. "Done and done." He flicks a few more things, then shuts down his comm interface. "Now we just need to get Lili and Jie to reschedule their wedding."

"They aren't going to like that." I shake my head. "They've been planning it for as long as I've known you. Remember? Your mom called to tell you about the engagement the first night I…"

He smiles, his eyes warm. "I remember."

THIRTY

As we walk to the O'Neill house, we come up with a plan. Vanti will set up surveillance of the wedding venue while O'Neill convinces his relatives to move the whole thing to the family compound. I'm so glad I'm not the one who has to tell his sisters.

"We'll have someone meet the guests as they arrive and redirect them to the house. Luckily, the venue has an underground parking complex, so anyone watching from outside won't know what's going on. And, of course, by the time guests arrive, whoever's setting this up should be long gone," he says.

"Surely they'll set up cams." I love poking holes in others' theories. "And they'll see the carriages leaving instead of waiting."

"It's the best we can do." He runs his hands through his hair. "I need a positive game face for this discussion. The ladies will not be happy."

"But where will they do the wedding?" I ask.

"Our courtyard is big enough for the reception."

"Why didn't they have it there in the first place? Seems like a beautiful place for a wedding."

"Jie's family wanted it at their club," O'Neill says. We turn down the alley behind the family compound.

"In all the old vids, it's the bride's family who makes all the wedding plans."

"Yeah, but there can be a lot of negotiation in the process." O'Neill grins. "Real life one, *Ancient Tēvē* zero."

I slap his arm as we walk into the house. "Funny man. Good luck."

"There you are! Good," Serena calls out as we walk in. "Ride over to the club with the last of the flower arrangements. You need to make sure the catering team is setting them up properly. I was going to do it, but there's a problem with the music!"

"Mom, we need to talk." O'Neill puts his hands on Serena's shoulders. He turns her toward the lounge, speaking softly as they walk.

"WHAT? We can't change everything at the last minute! This is crazy. It's all being delivered to the club! They'll charge a fortune to move it here. How—"

"Serena." I hurry after them. "I'll take care of it. It's my fault they're targeting the wedding. I'll handle the costs. Come on, Ty, let's get those flowers moved back here." I grab his arm and pull him toward the garage.

"You aren't going anywhere near that venue." He pulls me to a stop.

"It's completely safe." I yank my hand away. "Whatever they're planning is set for hours from now. Your mom needs help. Plus, Vanti is already there, scoping things out."

"Fine, then I'm coming with you." He points at me. "You wait there. I'm getting more firepower."

"You don't have to pay for it." Serena watches O'Neill run up the steps, two at a time. "It's not really your fault."

"If I wasn't here, this wouldn't be happening." I cringe inwardly, thinking of Lili's ruined day. "I know this won't be the wedding Lili was dreaming of, but the Morgan accounts can more than afford the cost. Mother won't even notice the withdrawal." Because it'll come out of my exorbitant allowance, not her funds. But Serena doesn't need to know that.

Serena smiles. "Actually, it will be exactly the wedding Lili dreamed of. She wanted it here. But Jie's family..." She gives me a distracted nod. "Right. So much to do. Thanks for taking care of the flowers, dear." She hurries away.

I stand at the back of the courtyard, watching the flurry of activity. Yelling and wailing come from the lounge, and I slink behind the nearest potted tree. I don't need Lili—or worse, Akiko—noticing me now. Even if it's true Lili would prefer the wedding here, Akiko won't hesitate to point a finger at me for all the mayhem.

The steady stream of people who had been carrying things out reverses direction. The twins pass by, carrying massive boxes back to the lounge. One of them spots me behind the plant and winks. "Good thing Triana isn't here. They'd be all over her." The other twin laughs.

When O'Neill finally returns, carrying an ancient blaster and two stunners, I sneak out to meet him. "Have they been blaming you?" he asks.

"No one's seen me yet, except the twins. And they seem to love anything that causes upheaval. But to be fair, it is my fault."

"No, it's Putin's fault. Don't you ever forget that." He hands me one of the stunners and slides the blaster strap over his shoulder.

I stare at the ugly weapon. "Where did you get that thing?"

"Dad insisted I bring it. It's his old service blaster. To be honest, I'm not sure it even works anymore."

"We can leave it in the carriage." I follow him to the garage, and we get into the vehicle.

He stashes the giant weapon under the seat and swipes in the location. The garage door opens, and the carriage slides out to the alley.

"Cloud the windows!" I say as we roll along. "Why were they transparent?"

"It's a wedding." O'Neill flicks the commands, and the sides darken. "Everyone is supposed to see you transporting the flowers and stuff to the venue. Gotta remind the neighbors that you're spending a boatload of money on a party. Especially the ones who weren't invited."

I laugh.

"When we get there, you stay in the carriage." He flicks an icon on his holo-ring without looking my way.

I stare at him in disbelief. "Do you even know me?" I check the charge on the stunner—it's fully loaded. "You don't have any of Vanti's fancy sedation darts or holo-ring fryers, do you?"

"No. And you won't be getting close enough to anyone to use those, anyway." He shakes his head, a goofy little smile sneaking onto his lips. "Maybe you'd better come in with me. I'd be afraid of what you might get up to if I leave you alone."

I roll my eyes. "You'll probably need my help, anyway. I've saved your bacon a couple of times."

"That you have." His smile widens, and he leans in to kiss me.

Just as our lips touch, the carriage pings. "You have reached the Winter Palace. Do you wish to exit?"

He gives me a fast, hard kiss then checks his stunner again. "Ready?"

"Opening the door." The carriage says, and the doors ease open.

"Not you—never mind. Come on." He climbs out into the empty underground garage. The carriage has stopped near the float tube. As soon as we exit, it backs into the closest parking spot.

Our footsteps echo on the plascrete as we walk. O'Neill flicks his holo-ring. "Vanti. Where are you?" He pauses, nudging me toward the wall. "She's not answering. Check the stairwell."

"Door's locked." I flick my own ring. "Let me see if I can persuade it to open." A few seconds later, the lock clicks. I pull the door open a few centimeters and duck away. No one blasts my head off, so I open the door wider and peek in. "Clear."

"Let's take the stairs." O'Neill checks again then heads up the steps. "Watch our six."

I'm not very good at climbing up the steps while watching down them, but I do my best. Once we get around the first turn, it's easier. We pass three more levels of garage—designated by the huge G painted on the doors, then arrive at the top of the steps. This door opens easily from inside the stairwell.

"I don't see anyone." O'Neill steps out in a crouch. "Stay down."

A flutter of movement to the left catches my eye. I swing my stunner that way as O'Neill calls out, "Halt!"

"What?" A tall, round man carrying a huge layer cake jumps but manages to hold on to the platter. "You scared the frosting out of me! What are you doing yelling at bakers like that?"

"Sorry." O'Neill lowers his weapon, but the baker doesn't notice. I'm not sure he even looked our direction. He powers on, setting the tray on a silver-draped table.

The table holds four other huge, white cakes. They're all covered in swirls and flowers, with sparkling accents and fluffy poufs. "It looks like a marshmallow exploded in a glitter factory," I whisper. "Is this normal for weddings?"

O'Neill wiggles his free hand back and forth. "This is a bit over the top. Jie's family hired Pierre Gâteau Fantaisie to make the cake. He's the baker to the stars."

"And don't you forget it," the baker says. "If you do, he'll remind you. I'm his assistant, Enzo." He waves.

"Nice to meet you, Enzo," I say. "Have you seen a redhead around here? About so tall, thin, pretty?" I hold up my hand to indicate Vanti's height.

"You're the only redhead I've seen in ages. Is that your real hair?" He shakes his head in disbelief. "I know girls who would kill for those ringlets."

My face goes hot. "They're a curse. Sometimes."

"Have you seen anyone else?" O'Neill's eyes constantly rove around the huge room, checking and double-checking for trouble. "Anyone who doesn't belong here?"

"No, just me and the caterers." Enzo hoists the enormous cake again and sets it above an even larger one. The cake bounces a little then settles into place about ten centimeters above the first one. "They're in the kitchen. The wedding planner from hell is in there, too."

"I'll check with them," O'Neill says. "That way?"

Enzo nods. "There are three kitchens. All crazy busy, so watch out for flying knives."

O'Neill salutes Enzo with his free hand. "You coming?"

"I'll stay here," I reply. "I'm going to check the network."

I flick my holo-ring and start swiping through the interface, absently watching Enzo as I break through their pitiful attempts at security. "Are you going to stack all of those?" I point at the other cakes. "In a huge tower?"

"Don't be ridiculous. That would be way too easy." Enzo flicks his holo-ring and makes an adjustment. The cake drops a few millimeters. He closes the interface and points at three of the cakes. "Those are going to orbit around the spherical one. Then there will be trails of cupcakes spiraling upward." His hands gracefully describe arcs and curves. "It's Baker Pierre's most recent masterpiece."

"Looks like a grav-engineer's masterpiece," I mutter.

Enzo gives me an ironic bow. "To be fair, the cake tastes pretty good."

I laugh. The net appears to be untouched. I scan through the last thirty days of activity and can't find anything suspicious. "Oh, you might want to stop. The wedding's being moved. Can you move the cake?"

Enzo stares at me in horror. "Move? I have a grav generator under this table that weighs seventy-five hundred kilos. It took an industrial sized grav lift and three experts two hours to put into place."

"Ironic that a grav generator requires outside lifters to move, isn't it?" I'm trying to distract him, but it doesn't work.

"Pierre is going to kill me! There's no way I can get this thing to another venue before the wedding!" He stares at the floating cake, his face pale and sweating.

"Maybe you can come up with a new design?" I suggest.

"As if it were that easy!" Enzo drops his head into his hands. "I spent weeks designing the equipment."

"You know, that hysterical artiste thing isn't really working for you," a female voice behind us says. I turn as a blonde woman dressed in white strides to the table.

Enzo's hands drop. His face is calm. "You're so right, Seline. Is this move for sure?" At my nod, he turns back to the woman. "Let's come up with a plan."

THIRTY-ONE

I LEAVE THE BAKERS—OR grav engineers—to their business and make my way around the enormous room. Large windows on two sides look out onto a beautiful park. Sprinklers run at full spray, keeping the foliage alive in the Grissom heat. Vanti can't be down there—she'd be soaking wet.

I commandeer a float and work my way around all the small circular tables, collecting the centerpieces that have already been placed. As I reach the last one, the kitchen doors slam open. A stream of black-clad caterers pours out. "Everything goes!" A tall woman in a fuchsia suit follows the caterers. "Pack it all up and move it to the residence. What are you doing?" She stomps up to me, glaring.

"I'm taking the flowers back to the house."

"No, you're not. That's our job." She snaps her fingers, and two of her minions hurry over to take the cart away from me.

"Be my guest. Sera O'Neill sent us over to coordinate the move." I step back, hands up. I've never seen so much rage suppressed so carefully, and I've lived with the Ice Dame most of my life. "But if you've got it handled, I'll just get out of your way."

"You do that," she snaps.

"Have you seen my friend?" I ask another caterer after the pink mobster leaves.

The woman smiles. "Tall, dark, and dreamy? He went upstairs to check the suites."

"Thanks." I wander back to the float tube. Enzo and his assistant have disappeared and the cakes with them. I lift the tablecloth to peek underneath. There's no grav generator hidden there. From what Enzo said, it was too big to move—could it be under the floor?

O'Neill returns. "I can't find her anywhere. And she's still not answering her comm."

"She goes rogue all the time." I take his arm and urge him into the float tube. "You know she'll show up when we least expect it. Probably with Putin's cohort in zip ties."

He frowns. "I feel like we've made a huge mistake. There's no evidence they've been up to anything! Maybe we should have left everything alone."

We step out of the float tube and cross to the garage. Once inside, O'Neill accesses the controls and waves his hand through the "return to base" icon. The vehicle slides up the ramp and onto the street.

"It's fine." I pat his arm. "Lili will be happier having the wedding at home. Jie probably doesn't care, and if his family is mad, well, they can blame me. The caterers and bakers have more work to do, but they'll get paid extra." I rub my temples—I missed something. Something important. What was it?

"Hey, I clicked the 'go home' button." O'Neill flicks the carriage interface, but the word override has appeared on the screen. "What's going on?"

I connect my ring to the vehicle. "Someone has tampered—they've reprogrammed the base location. They shouldn't be able to do that. You're supposed to need a DNA sample from the owner and a password to change that. That's why selling one of these is such an ordeal."

"Can you stop it?"

"I don't know. Usually there's a manual override—a physical switch that allows you to stop the vehicle." I unbuckle my restraint and crouch beside the seat. "The access hatch is jammed. Look, someone soldered it shut." I point at the bead of metal running around the edge of the panel under the dash.

"I knew I should have left you at home!" O'Neill twists around to reach under the back seat. "*Frak!* The blaster is gone!"

Cold pools in my stomach. "Who's doing this? Where are they taking us?"

"Just stay calm. Keep working on that manual override." O'Neill flicks his holo-ring. "I'm sending a message to Vanti—and one to Kate. She can track us and send the Peacekeepers to us."

I pull out the first aid kit Vanti left for me—it's still in my jacket pocket. There's a small pair of tweezers inside. I grab them and drop the rest of the packet back into my pocket. "I might be able to pull some of this off." I pick at the solder clogging the panel's hinges.

"We're back in the old part of town." O'Neill peers through the front of the carriage. "Not far from al-Petrosian's place. There are a lot of warehouses out here—some of the older businesses still operate from this area. How's it coming?"

"I've got one hinge clear, but the—is there a tool kit in here? I might be able to pry the panel free if you can find a screwdriver." The tweezers slide into the gap but bend under the force of my prying.

O'Neill hands me a small multi-tool. "See if one of those blades will work."

I fold out a few of the implements. A saw blade—too flexible. A toothpick—too thick. A fork? I need to remember he has this. Could be handy for cake-related emergencies.

"I think it's too late." His voice is low. Worried. He wrenches at the door handle. "The door is locked."

We've stopped in front of a large blocky building. Of course, what building on Grissom isn't large and blocky? But I'm betting this one doesn't have a courtyard inside. A big door ratchets open, the clunking and rattling audible inside the carriage. It sounds like an old-fashioned chain and pulley system. When the door is clear but not completely open, the carriage slides inside. The clanking resumes as the door slowly rolls down behind us.

Sunlight illuminates stacks of boxes near the door, but most of the interior is hidden in shadow. The carriage pulls into the center of the space and stops. The system powers down.

The light dwindles as the external door lowers. With a louder clank and a soft crash, the last of the light goes. In the darkness, the unmistakable sound of a bolt being shot reaches us. "I guess we're locked in." A shiver runs down my spine.

O'Neill's warm hand squeezes my shoulder. "Move up here—between the front seats. I want you behind me at all times. And if you fire that stunner, make sure it's not pointed at me, okay?"

A slightly hysterical giggle burbles out. "That sounds like something I might do." My hands and feet are cold, and acid churns in my stomach. I pull the stunner out of my pocket. "Bobby isn't here." I whisper.

"What's that?"

"I just need to remember Bobby isn't here. He's in Attica. No matter how scary this is, it's not Putin scary."

O'Neill gives me a fast hug then pushes me behind him. "That's my girl."

The carriage doors all pop open at once. Slick programming, designed to freak us out. I take a couple of deep breaths and will myself not to shake.

A blinding light goes on, shining on the right-side door. "Please, won't you join us?"

Ice water pours through my body. "That sounded like him." I'm not sure the words made any sound.

O'Neill's hand reaches back and touches mine. "Stay behind me." He steps toward the lighted door. I follow as closely as possible, almost stepping on his heels. He walks down the steps and stops at the bottom.

For a second, nothing happens. Then hands reach out of the darkness and grab O'Neill. He twists and gets a shot off but collapses to the ground. The hands drag him away. I scream and lunge forward, but more hands restrain me.

"Thanks for coming, Annabelle," Bobby says, stepping forward into the light.

THIRTY-TWO

MY HEART STOPS.

Then stutters on. "How—how can you be here?"

He holds out a hand to assist me down from the carriage. Like a freaking fairytale character. Anger flares, hot and fast, in the pit of my icy stomach. I straighten, staring down at him. Taking a deep breath, I try to channel my inner Ice Dame. "What do you want?"

His lips curl in an appreciative smile. "I want you."

"How did you get out of Attica?" I demand, hoping he can't hear the shake in my voice.

"Please, join me. I'll explain everything."

I ignore his hand and stomp down the steps. Every movement takes a supreme effort of will as I get closer to him. Sweat breaks out on my temples and upper lip. My breathing speeds up, and I start feeling light-headed. I try to take deep breaths, but my chest contracts. This man terrifies me.

He turns and gestures for me to precede him. A red carpet stretches across the warehouse. A series of spotlights turn on, illuminating the crimson path to a pair of armchairs and a couch, like the set of a vid-net talk show. O'Neill lies slumped in one corner of the couch. His head lolls against the high back, but his eyes are open and angry. Vanti sits on the other end of the couch, her hands secured to her ankles by a long zip tie. A wide piece of tape covers her mouth, and her jaw works as she glares at our captor.

"Isn't this nice, the old gang back together again?" Bobby gestures to one of the armchairs and sits in the other. A small table stands between the chairs, holding two crystal glasses and a bottle of wine from Apollone Vintners—the same wine we drank my first night at the O'Neill home. Could he be any more cliché?

I cross my arms, standing in the center of the space between Bobby and my friends. "What. Do. You. Want?"

"Please sit, Annabelle." When I don't move, his eyes flick behind me, and his chin drops a fraction. Hands grab my arms, and his goons wrestle me into the chair. Vanti grunts when I step on her toes.

"Now that we're comfortable, I'll tell you what I want." Bobby pours two glasses of wine and offers me one. I glare. He holds his glass up in toast then sips. He makes a face. "Not my favorite wine. You were wise to refrain." He sets the glass down.

"I'm sure you didn't invite us here just to insult the wine, Bobby." My pounding heart has slowed to steady thudding, and my breathing has eased. It's hard to take him seriously as a villain when he's behaving so foppishly.

He's undoubtedly trying to put me off balance, so I resolve to stay alert. Vanti makes faces at me, but with the tape across her mouth, I can't tell what she's trying to say. Oh! The internal comm. I drop my hands into my lap, trying to figure out how I can initiate a call without him noticing.

I glance at Vanti again. Her hands are bare—he's taken her holo-ring. O'Neill's is gone, too. But mine is still on my finger. I need a diversion.

"You're right, I'm not here to insult the wine—that's an added bonus. Austere, grippy, tight." He smiles, his slick, creepy, upper-lev smirk. "About what I'd expect from a winery owned by the Mendozas." His eyes flick to O'Neill then back to me.

"I liked it," I say, just to be contrary. And because I did.

"Of course you did." His smile turns condescending. "Your education was severely limited during your years on Kaku. Your mother should never have allowed that."

"We aren't here to talk about my mother or my education." I drop my left hand between my leg and the arm of the plush chair, where he can't see it. Without looking, I flick the duress signal Vanti insisted on teaching me. That should bring help from local law enforcement. "Why are you here, Bobby?"

"I'm here because I want my life back." His eyes blaze as he leans over the table, his face only centimeters from mine. The words spit out of his mouth like acid. "And, thanks to you, I can't get that life back, can I? So, I'll just have to destroy yours in return."

Unreasoning fear flings me back in my seat. He grins. Then he sits back, and the feral expression fades. This time, it's the meaningless smile top-levs learn to dispense to anyone below them on the social ladder. He wears it like a mask to hide his anger, but the fury leaks through. "I've gone to the trouble of vacating the lovely single-room apartment you secured for me, in an effort to make your misery my life's work."

"You were there—just yesterday." I vividly remember him waving at me from his opulent prison cell. "You can't be here—there's no way to get from S'Ride to Grissom in less than a day."

"I haven't been there in ages, dear," he says. "I hired someone to fill in for me."

"You—he was a decoy? How did you fool the DNA checks?"

He waves a finger at me. "I'm not giving up all my secrets. I might need to use that trick again someday. Enough chitchat. Here's what's going to happen. I'm going to make your life a living hell. I'm going to kill everyone you hold dear." His waving finger turns to point at O'Neill and then Vanti. The melodramatic flourish chills me. "And everyone they hold dear. But not all at once, and not all today. I'm going to take my time, so you have plenty of opportunity to suffer. Then I'll pin it on you, so you can enjoy my Attica residence yourself."

"You won't. You can't. We've stopped your plot. And the building is being surrounded right now. You need to let us go, or they'll—" My imagination runs dry as I try to threaten him. He's holding all the cards. I need to keep him preoccupied until my duress signal brings the cavalry.

"You haven't stopped anything. I've been setting up a lovely surprise for your hosts for days. All I had to do was convince you to move the wedding to the family compound, so I can spring my trap. You really should have left everything alone."

"Wait. Are you saying we would have been safe if we'd left the wedding at the venue?" I ask. O'Neill's eyes widen.

"Of course not. I had plans for that, too. But the home is my preferred location. Much more personal." Bobby nods at O'Neill as if he's just offered him a compliment. "You three will stay here while I ensure the event is one to remember. Don't worry, I'll make sure you get a copy of the recording. Vid drones are cheap." He stands. "Oh, and Annabelle, your duress signal didn't get out. You don't think I'd leave something like that to chance, do you? Your friend took care of that weeks ago."

"What friend?" I leap up, too.

"Tacky, dear. One should always remember one's acquaintances." The malicious smile is back. "Your old friend Stervo—you met recently on Kaku? Your old hacking friend."

I stare at him. Stervo had been at Kara's contracting ceremony. "He's contracted to Erco's cousin!"

"Is he? Didn't it seem odd that your roommate's partner would be related to one of your old hacking cronies?"

It had seemed odd, but most of the people on Kaku knew someone at the Techno-Inst. "Are you saying Erco is in on this?"

"Sadly, no." He shakes his head, as if this really bothers him. "You never want to fish too close to the target. But his cousin was easy to bribe."

"They weren't really contracted." I knew she was way too interested in O'Neill to be with a guy like Stervo. I look at my holo-ring. "What did he do?"

"He slid a few hooks into your holo-ring programming. I don't understand all the technical details, but I guess there are ways to gain access if you're in physical contact with the target. You don't remember giving him access to your holo-ring?" He grins maliciously. "That Captio is still so effective."

I drop into my chair. "Stervo did something to my ring then fed me enough Captio to make me forget it?" When Bobby was killing people on SK2, he used CaptioPraevus to make the witnesses forget they'd seen anything. In small doses, it eliminated recent memories. In large, it caused seizures, strokes, and brain damage.

Bobby runs a finger down my cheek then tips my chin up and leans close. "You always were so quick on the uptake." He straightens. "I must go. Vern will take care of you. But don't worry. I'll be watching over you. Forever."

He strides away, barking out orders as he goes. A side door opens, and he disappears through it, followed by a herd of guards and flunkies.

As soon as they're gone, I jump up and hurry to the couch. "Are you two okay?" I pull the tape from Vanti's face, wincing as it rips away. She barely blinks.

"What did they give him?" she asks, nodding at O'Neill.

"I don't know." I reach into his jacket pocket and pull out his multi-tool. "Use this."

"I'm afraid I can't allow that." Vern al-Petrosian appears from the darkness and jerks the tool from my hand.

"You!" Vanti spits. "I knew you were in this up to your eyeballs."

Al-Petrosian's hand flies out, catching Vanti across the mouth with a loud crack. She jerks back without a sound. Red welts swell on her cheek. She grins, blood bright against her white teeth. She spits at him. "Where's Watson? Is she here, too?"

"Of course not," al-Petrosian says. "She's on her way to the wedding with Ser Putin."

"Why are you helping him?" she demands.

I ignore them, focusing on O'Neill. "Ty, can you move?"

His eyes flicker. I lean closer and whisper, "One for yes, two for no." Then I pull back. "I said, can you move?"

His eyes blink once.

Behind me, al-Petrosian laughs, a harsh bark. "You put my cousin in prison. Of course I'm helping him!"

I glance at O'Neill's hands and legs—they're untied. Whoever dosed him thought it would be enough to keep him down for a long time, I guess. Big mistake.

"Your cousin?" Vanti asks. "Wil? If Putin's so keen to help you, why didn't he break Wil out when he escaped Attica?"

I twist around to see his reaction. Vern is staring at Vanti, his hands clenching and unclenching. "There was no one to act as a decoy for Wil."

"Right." Vanti nods. "Putin has enough credits to bribe anyone. He could have paid someone to get the body mods and take Wil's place. But he didn't. Was that the reward for helping him—he'd get your cousin out?"

"He will. He promised!" Vern cries.

"Doesn't look likely." Vanti smirks.

"And he always follows through on his promises," I add.

"You don't know him."

I get right in Vern's face. "No, *you* don't know him. I've known him since we were in diapers. He's a psychopathic narcissist who will say whatever he thinks people want to hear to get them to do his dirty work. He lies as easily as breathing. And he's killed people—lots of people. Not just by setting bombs or ordering minions but with his own hands. He likes it." I'm nose-to-nose with him, spitting the words out like glass.

Vern steps back and stumbles over Vanti's feet. In a flash, Vanti's knees land on Vern's stomach. She rips the multi-tool he's still holding out of his fingers. Two flicks, and the zip ties fall away from her wrists. The knife presses against Vern's throat.

O'Neill pushes me down on the couch and crouches beside Vanti. He pats down Vern, pulling a weapon from his pocket. "He's yours," he mutters to Vanti. Then he jumps to his feet, standing beside me, eyes scanning the darkness.

"How many others are still here?" Vanti growls, pushing the knife against Vern's throat. A red line appears on his dark skin, and a bead of blood swells.

"They're coming!" Vern gasps out.

Footsteps sound, and laser fire blasts through the warehouse. O'Neill drags me from the couch, throwing himself on top of me. I hit the floor with a thump, slamming my head and shoulders into the cold plascrete.

Lying half on top of me, O'Neill fires around the end of the couch. Vern's blaster spits out gouts of light. The stench of burning fabric hits my nose. The corner of the couch smolders.

"Take out the lights," Vanti hisses.

I crane my neck to peer the length of my body. Over O'Neill's butt, I can see Vanti's back. She's flipped Vern onto his stomach, her knee in leaning into his back. She pats him down then pulls something from his pocket. "Griz, holo-ring." She tosses it toward him. He catches it without looking, using his left hand. They are two parts of a single, well-programmed bot.

"Cover your eyes," O'Neill whispers as he twists and rolls away. He fires upward, taking out each spotlight with a single shot. I turn my head away and screw my eyes shut but don't feel anything hit me.

When he moves, I open my eyes again. The bulk of the couch looms dark against the remaining spotlights, still focused on the red carpet. I'm jammed against the solid base of the sofa, O'Neill crouching over my upper body. He pops up over the couch and the blaster whines.

A voice cries out.

"How many?" Vanti asks again.

Someone whimpers.

"I won't ask again." Vanti's low voice sends shivers up my spine.

"Two," Vern gasps out.

"I winged one, but they're still firing," O'Neill says. "I count three."

Vern cries out.

"You lied to me. How many?" Vanti growls.

"Three. There are three. I swear."

Blaster fire distracts me. O'Neill is firing again, and someone screams.

"We need to move," he says. "Triana, get up, but stay low." He fires a couple more shots and takes out another light. "Get to the carriage."

"I'm not getting into that thing," I say. "He's got it rigged, remember? Who knows what will happen to it?"

"Good call." Vanti heaves Vern to his feet. "Don't try anything. I can kill you with this tiny knife in about three seconds. Or with my bare hands. You will walk toward that door." She yanks his hands up behind his back. They're held together with a daisy chain of hair ties.

I've always wondered why she carries them—I've never seen her use one for her hair.

Vern stumbles forward.

O'Neill pushes me behind Vanti, urging all three of us toward the back wall. "See if you can get behind those crates." He gets off a few more shots.

Laser bolts zing toward us from both front corners of the building. We run.

"They obviously don't care if they hit Vern, so he's not much use," Vanti says as we reach the back wall.

"He's still a shield. Stay down, Triana." He pushes on my back to keep me bent low. He grabs Vern's arm to keep him between me and the laser fire.

"There's a narrow space here," Vanti whispers. "I'm not sure you'll fit, Griz."

"I'll take Vern." He pulls the older man in front of him and pushes. "See if there's a back exit. Triana, can you get into the building's net? We need to send the Peacekeepers to the house."

"On it." I sit down behind the crate and flick my holo-ring. It flares, bright in the dark warehouse. I dial down the glare and start working my way into the interface. If Stervo set this up, I can take it down. I was always a better hacker than him.

"Move this crate." O'Neill's whispered command barely registers. "Or I'll walk you down the middle of this warehouse as a human shield." Something heavy grinds. The crate behind me vibrates. Blaster fire resumes.

O'Neill touches my arm. "Move farther in. These crates are getting hot."

I look up from my holos. "Where's Vern?" I swallow a grunt as I lever myself up off the cold floor. How long was I sitting there?

In the glow of my holo-ring, O'Neill's grin looks ghostly. And vengeful. "He's guarding our six. Move."

We hurry deeper into the tight space between the crates and the back wall. "I'm in the system. I just need a few more seconds to crush the blocker."

"Keep moving."

It's very dark back here. The crates tower above us, and the space gets narrower. My shoulders brush against the cold wall. "Where's Vanti?" I can't tell if she's found a way out, but she's out of sight.

"She went up."

I look up. In the dim light from my holo-ring, the wall of crates looks smooth and unscalable. "Up?"

"They know we're back here—they're likely to go over. She'll stop them."

"How? She doesn't have a weapon. Except your tiny knife."

He snorts. "You've met Vanti, right?"

"Yeah." She probably shoots lasers from her eyes. "Uh, it's getting a bit tight. I'm not sure we're going to get much farther."

Lasers whine, and bolts stab at us down the narrow gap.

"Down!" His shove sends me to my knees. I cower behind him as he sends blaster fire back at the enemy. He grunts and drops lower.

My holo-ring vibrates. "Done! I broke the wall. Emergency call going to the Peacekeepers."

"Please state the nature of your emergency," the robo-voice says.

"Tell them terrorism and code word frolic," O'Neill whispers over his shoulder at me.

I repeat the words to the robo-voice.

There's a thud and the laser fire stops.

"Come on, Vanti got him." O'Neill waits while I get to my feet then moves forward.

"Location?" the voice asks.

I send them our coordinates. "Can I talk to a real person?"

"Transferring you now."

Another voice comes on the line, and this one sounds real. Of course, they can make the AI voices sound real if they want. "Anti-terrorism, this is Watson."

Zark.

THIRTY-THREE

I MUTE THE CALL. "Watson just answered the anti-terrorism call!"

"Hell." O'Neill pauses at the last crate to check the body lying there. It's one of Bobby's minions. He's out cold, and his weapon is missing. Beside him, Vern stares up at the ceiling, eyes unblinking, chest rising and falling. Vanti must have had a stun dart hidden on her person. Or she took whatever they used on O'Neill.

"Vanti, sit rep." O'Neill's body blocks the gap, so I'm stuck behind the crates.

"Hello? This is the anti-terrorist office. We have dispatched agents to your location." Watson's voice is calm.

"This is Kara Ortega-Okila," I say, using my best Kakuvian accent. Surely, she won't recognize that name. "We're under attack."

"Please stay calm," the voice says. No trace of recognition. Is that because she doesn't recognize my voice or because this is an automated system?

"They're shooting at us!" I cry.

"Please stay calm and find a place to hide." Definitely an AI. I cut the call.

"—on planet? Peacekeepers are compromised." As he talks to Vanti,

O'Neill reaches back with his left hand and grabs my wrist. "Stay behind me, but we think we're clear."

A call connects, and Vanti's voice comes through my audio implant. "I've already called Andron and Ferrigi. We have a couple other assets at the wedding venue. I've directed them to redeploy to the family compound. We need to get over there to direct."

We hurry across the warehouse, staying away from the lighted carpet. Vanti pauses at the carriage. "Do we dare?" She holds a blaster at the ready and has another one slung over her shoulder. The bruise on her cheek stands out dark against her pale skin.

"I don't trust that thing, and it's almost faster to run from here," O'Neill says. "We're back in the old town."

Run? I hate running. But their priority is my safety, so if I don't run, they'll be forced to stay with me. Which could put O'Neill's family in danger. Or at least keep them in danger longer. I nod. "Let's go."

O'Neill tries to grin, but it comes out more like a grimace.

Vanti does her commando thing at the door, checking for "hostiles." When no one shoots, we follow her into the street. The sun is blazing down—it's nearing midday and even the alleys are in full sunlight.

"This way," Vanti says, heading to the right, a map in her palm.

"No, I know a shortcut." O'Neill takes off the other direction, and I follow, Vanti a few steps behind me.

We run along the alleys, the sun pounding down. I try to stay in the narrow slice of shade, but it barely protects one shoulder. My lungs go into overdrive, and my heart pounds.

Ahead, O'Neill bangs on a door then swings it open. He glances back at me. "You okay?"

I nod, unable to speak. My lungs heave, and pain gnaws in my side. I stumble over the threshold into a dark tunnel. A man holds the door open. He stares at me in bewilderment then bows as I hurry past.

We run into a courtyard much like the O'Neills'. People look up from their pursuits, staring at us in surprise. O'Neill waves and calls out as we go. "Nice to see you! Can't stop. I'll drop by tomorrow!" I stagger along the path in his wake. The occupants call out greetings and wave.

"You really should hit the gym more." Vanti grins as she comes up beside me, her breathing even and calm.

I ignore her and plod onward.

We exit the building and turn left. Traffic fills a wide road at the end of this alley. "What's going on?" Vanti asks.

O'Neill shrugs. "Saturday. People going about their weekend business. Are you okay, Triana?"

I sag against the corner of the closest building, chest heaving, sweat pouring down my face. "I'm fine," I gasp. "Can we get a taxi?"

"We're almost there." O'Neill returns to my side, his expression concerned. "You aren't okay. We can rest for a minute."

"No, you go on." I get the words out between breaths. "Vanti can stay with me—we'll meet you at the house."

He studies me. "I can't leave you here."

"I'll be fine." I gesture at the heavily armed Vanti. "No one's going to mess with her."

He raises his eyebrows at the redhead.

"Go." Vanti's face doesn't move, but her voice is loud and clear through the still connected audio call. She hands her extra blaster to him. "I've got this."

O'Neill takes off, dodging through the traffic. Horns blare, but he doesn't slow. At the far side, he takes off down the next alley.

"Let me know when you're ready." Vanti stares at a map in her palm. "I'm tracking him, so we can use the same shortcut."

"I'm not sure we should run through other people's homes. They don't know us." My heart rate has slowed to only double its normal rate, so I push away from the building and join Vanti at the curb.

"I'm sure Griz will tell them we're coming." The traffic pauses, and we hurry across the street.

Halfway down the next alley, Vanti stops. "Through there." She knocks on the heavy wooden door. It swings wide, the hinges shrieking. "I guess they left it open for us."

I step inside, and Vanti shuts the gate behind us. The tunnel is dark, but Vanti's map lights the way. "You want to toss that to me? So you can keep both hands on your gun?"

Vanti laughs and my holo-ring vibrates as the map arrives. I pop it open and move forward.

A cobweb catches on my face and I frantically swipe it away. The light at the end of the tunnel is dim, but we move forward into a courtyard.

This garden looks nothing like the comfortable space at the O'Neill house. Wild vines climb up the inside of the building, choking the balconies. Dead leaves lay strewn across the paths, and broken fronds hang from the tall trees. The stench of decay fills the garden.

Vanti pushes past me into the damp, rank air.

Birds squawk and explode out of a bush as we pass, their tiny wings creating a wave of sound. We jump over the fallen branches. Vanti swings her blaster in a wide arc, her eyes and head constantly moving. I stagger along the path in her wake, lungs heaving. The stinking air makes me want to vomit. Something rustles in the overgrowth next to the path. Vanti spins toward it, and a dark creature streaks out.

"Cat!" I put a hand on her shoulder. "Don't shoot the cat."

Her lips press together, and she turns away, picking up the pace. We hurry into another tunnel, which opens to a familiar looking alley. The house across the alley has vines growing up the back, with huge purple and green flowers. "There's the house." She puts an arm across the opening, stopping me. "Griz, what's the status?"

"Andron, Ferrigi, and I have done a full circuit of the house. There's no external threat that we can find. I'm going inside. Keep Triana out there."

She raises an eyebrow at me.

"Yeah, not going to happen." I push her arm out of the way, and she grins.

"Before we go in, can you scan for any signals?"

"Like what?" I pop open my hacker tools. "We're looking for something that could trigger an explosion?"

"We're inside." O'Neill says. "Hey, there's Putin!"

Vanti and I make eye contact then race across the alley. She beats me to the back gate and flings it open. "Where are you, Griz?"

I follow her into the courtyard where she stops me. "Wait."

"I'm heading into the lounge. Saw him on the surveillance."

The house is full of people. The caterers have set up tables and chairs in the cloister around the courtyard. A huge tapestry hangs against the wall near the office. Men and women in black move through the space, positioning trays of food and bottles of wine.

The bakers have rebuilt their floating cake in the pavilion. The five huge white layers hover over the wide couch, spinning like a tiny solar system. The cupcakes spiral away in graceful arcs. It's an absurd, extravagant spectacle.

"I want one of those if I ever get married," I whisper to myself.

Vanti snorts a laugh.

"What? It's amazing."

Her eyes soften and she looks at it again. "It really is." Then her jaw tightens. "Let's find Putin."

"There!" My voice squawks higher on the word, and I point. A man stands in the center of the courtyard, the sun glinting off his blond hair. "There he is."

Vanti pushes me into a chair. "Stay there." She races across the courtyard, dodging effortlessly through the crowd. She circles around behind the blond man. I stand so I can see over the crowd, but side-step into the shadow of the closest bush.

The man stiffens then slowly turns.

"That's not him," I whisper.

"I've got a decoy," O'Neill's voice comes through the audio call.

"This one is too," Vanti says. "There's another Putin. And another one! Did he hire all these guys and send them here to die?"

"That sounds exactly like something he'd do." I turn, scanning the courtyard.

"We need to clear the house. He could have hidden an explosive anywhere."

"My mother is going to kill me," O'Neill says. "Then my sisters are going to resurrect me and kill me again." His voice rumbles through the whole house. "Ladies and gentlemen. We have an emergency situation. Everyone, please exit the building."

I stay in my corner, sheltered by the large bush, as confused people filter by. If I were going to blow up a house full of people, where would I hide the explosives? He planned this weeks or even months ago. People come and go through all the time. He could have hidden charges all around the house—a few here, a few there.

"Did your nieces and nephews find anything odd?" I interrupt O'Neill's continued announcements, speaking on the private channel. "If he planted his explosives before the other night, surely they would have found something when they were playing?"

"Kids are pretty good at finding stuff they aren't supposed to find," Vanti agrees. I can see her now that the crowd is thinning. She's directing people toward the rear exit. "Do you think he planted them a long time ago?"

"I don't know. But with the wedding, there have been plenty of people coming and going over the last few days," O'Neill says. He's at the other side of the courtyard, ushering people out the front.

"The flowers!" I say. I turn and dart through the fleeing crowd, heading for the kitchen. Angie had someone move the empty flower buckets there. I dodge the white-clothed tables and scurry through the open door near the dining room. I haven't been in here before—it's only used for storage now. Or the occasional huge banquet. The family uses the AutoKich'ns for most meals.

The big white tiled room is empty. Deep metal trays lay on a long white counter, their glass tops steamed or frosted over. I peek into one—slices of juicy meat. The smell makes my stomach growl.

Focus, Triana. We have bombs to find and a killer to catch. I hurry into the utility room at the back. There are the buckets. Thankfully, someone has drained them. I pick up the first and turn it over. As far as I can tell, it's just a bucket. "What would explosives look like?" I ask.

Vanti sends a series of pictures to my holo-ring. "The clay-style could be shaped like anything, but they require electronics on the outside to detonate. If you see anything that shouldn't have wires but does, let me know. I've called in a friend—we should have a scanner here within the hour."

"An hour?" O'Neill's voice sounds harried. In the background, I can hear female voices arguing.

Vanti ignores him. "I'm checking IDs of everyone we've got out here. The decoys seem to have disappeared."

I continue checking through the buckets and the rest of the kitchen. Nothing. I snag a chocolate covered *petit four* and make my way back to the courtyard. O'Neill and Vanti meet me by the water feature.

"I see you found time to get a snack." Vanti nods at my fingers.

Oops, chocolate. I grin. "It was just sitting there. I needed to make sure it wasn't dangerous."

"You shouldn't be here at all." O'Neill glares at Vanti. "Why didn't you keep her outside?"

"Have you met her?" Vanti heads for the front door. "My friend has arrived. They'll scan the building."

While we watch from the courtyard, a small team follows Vanti into the house. They send drones flying through the halls. Team members hurry to open doors.

"There are some locked doors on the third floor," a short man reports to Vanti.

"Those are probably ours." She hurries away, the little guy following behind.

While they finish the scan, Serena grabs O'Neill's arm. "Can we let people back in? Lili was ready to put her dress on. The guests will be arriving in twenty minutes!"

He calms his mother, walking her back to the lounge. My ring vibrates—a vid message. I pull it up. Unrecognized caller. I send the number to my search app and run a check on the message content. Nothing dangerous. I make a copy and store it in my quarantined backups, then flick play.

Bobby Putin's face appears in my palm.

THIRTY-FOUR

"Ty!" I yell.

In the recording, Bobby laughs. "Are you having fun, yet? I hope you didn't have too much trouble getting away from Vern. He's pretty useless when it comes to physical restraint. But I couldn't make it too easy."

"Got one!" someone yells from the third floor.

"—emptied the building by now. Let me know when you find my little present." Bobby shakes his head. "Oh, wait, you can't. You have no way to find me. I'll just have to watch. It's not over, though. I told you I'd make your life a living hell. I'll slowly threaten and kill everyone you love. Starting with..." He pauses. "You'll just have to figure that part out for yourself."

O'Neill arrives just in time to see Bobby wave and disappear. "What—"

I try to replay the message, but it's gone. As I pull the copy from my quarantined memory block, I ask, "What did they find?"

"Explosives in your room—under your bed. And in Vanti's and the avenger boys'." He grins a little as he uses the nickname. "But the one in your room wasn't wired properly. And the other two were small—they might have maimed anyone inside the room, but they wouldn't have killed."

"He said he's going to target people I love," I say, slowly. "Those explosives were decoys. He's going after someone else. My family. Kara. You." I replay the quarantined copy of the message.

Vanti appears at O'Neill's elbow. "I've already sent a message back to the office. They've doubled up security on Dame Morgan and Ser Chaturvedi. I'll check in with the office on Kaku and have someone detailed to Kara." She turns away as she flicks her holo-ring.

"Can we please get those caterers back inside?" Serena hurries into the courtyard, Angie hot on her heels. "Guests will be arriving any minute!"

"Maybe we should shift back to the venue." O'Neill runs his hands through his hair. "Or cancel the wedding all together. Hold it later."

"He said he was targeting those I love," I say. "Not that I don't love your family, but they hardly seem close enough to be his victims. He also said he's going to make this last for a long time—he wants us to be constantly looking over our shoulders."

"She's right." Serena grabs O'Neill's arm. "You've checked the house—I saw all those drones. Surely, this is the safest possible place. This maniac is trying to rattle you, and he's succeeding. I refuse to live in fear."

Vanti finishes her call and turns back. "They're sending someone to watch Kara."

The tight ball of terror in my stomach relaxes a bit. My head gets kind of light, and I sit down on a chair nearby.

She turns to O'Neill. "Your mom's right. This place is more secure than the venue, and it's just been scanned for explosives and hidden threats."

Before O'Neill can answer, Serena hurries away, calling out to the caterers, who can't possibly hear her yet. "Come back inside!"

As the caterers file back in, O'Neill and Vanti stop each of them for identity checks. Enzo, the baker, and his blonde assistant Seline, straggle in at the end. I wander over as they make some last-minute adjustments to their cake.

"I thought you couldn't move the cake?" I nod at the floating cupcakes. "Where's the seventy-five hundred kilo grav generator hidden?"

Enzo's face goes red, and the woman cackles. "She got you, Enzo! I told you not to exaggerate that much."

Enzo inhales a deep breath and blows it out, hard enough to make the closest cupcakes wiggle. I make a mental note not to eat those. "I've been studying Chef Pierre." He ignores the woman's continued laughter. "When he takes a commission, he claims it's impossible to complete. That there's no way anyone could possibly pull it off—whatever it is. There isn't enough time." He flings his arm up. "The materials necessary aren't available." He flings out the other arm, then drops both and shrugs. "Then he miraculously delivers exactly what the client requested. People go gaga. They think he's a magician. I've been trying it myself, but it always backfires."

The blonde stops laughing. "Chef Pierre is a master at the technique. You could ask for a cookie, and he'd have you believing it was impossible. Then, viola! The cookie appears, as if by magic. Enzo hasn't really perfected the technique." She chuckles again.

"I guess the key is to make your stumbling blocks less heavy." I smile. "I'm glad you made it work. I gotta get dressed."

I leave the bakers and hurry up the steps to my room. When I arrive, the door is open, and my belongings are strewn everywhere. The rugs have been flung back, furniture is dragged away from walls, and my clothing has been pulled from the closet and flung on the bed. I guess I should have expected that—they said they searched. I detour to Vanti's room and knock on the door.

"Come in." The voice is muffled.

I push the door open. A large box lays on the bed. The top has fallen to the floor, and piles of tissue spill across the bed and carpets. Vanti stands at the foot of the bed, staring into the box. "You bought me the dress," she whispers. "Why did you do that?"

"You looked amazing in it." I squirm a little under her intense stare. "That dress needed you."

She chuckles, but tears roll down her cheeks. "I can't accept—I've never had anything so—"

"You should hang this up." I take the dress from the box and shake it out. Vera, the bridal salon lady, must have sprinkled it with magic. It hangs from my fingers, perfect and unwrinkled. "Or not. Just put it on. You'll look amazing."

"Why?" She wipes her cheeks on her shirt sleeve and turns to me. "Why did you buy it?"

"Because we're friends. Because I could, and I wanted you to have it." I hold it toward her. "Put it on."

She takes the dress and lays it back on the bed. Standing with her back to me, she stares down at it. "I really shouldn't."

"It's already done," I say. "They won't take it back. You may as well wear it. Otherwise, it will just go to waste."

Her fingers hover over the dress, as if a force field is keeping them away. Finally, she touches the skirt. In a flurry, she twists around, flings her arms around me and squeezes hard. Her arms drop away, and she spins back to the bed before I can hug her back. "Thank you," she whispers.

"You're welcome. Put it on. I want to see you in it." While she slips into the dress, I pick up the tissue paper, blinking to keep from crying, too. "Hey, why is my room such a mess, but yours isn't?" Aside from the box and tissue paper, everything is in its place. "They even pulled back the carpets in my room."

She clears her throat. "You're the principal. Your safety is our priority. Do you want help putting it back?"

"No, that's fine."

"How do I look?"

I turn. "You look fabulous. I need to get dressed, too." I move toward the door, but something Bobby said flickers on the edge of my memory. "Did they search your room at all?"

"Of course. But they know better than to mess with my stuff." She smirks.

"What about Ty—did they search his room?"

"They searched all the rooms." If she says anything else, I don't hear it. I'm racing down the stairs.

I stare at the closed doors along the balcony. I don't know which one is his. "Ty!" I yell as I pound on the first door.

It opens. "Why aren't you dressed?" Akiko asks. She's wearing the midnight blue gown she tried on yesterday. The style looks fabulous on her curvy form. Aretha, dressed in a more severe style in the same color, peeks over her shoulder.

"Where's Ty?"

"His room is down there." Aretha points. "You should get dressed," she calls after me.

I race along the balcony and pound on the third door. Aretha didn't specify which one. "Ty!"

Ro pops out. Or maybe it's Yuri. "Sorry, wrong room. He's next door."

I run to the next one, but it opens before I can knock. O'Neill stands there, wearing dark blue dress pants and an unbuttoned white shirt. My breath catches in my throat as I stare at his bare chest.

"Triana?" He grips my shoulders. "Are you all right?"

The room has gotten too hot. Air isn't reaching my lungs, and my head swims. I open my mouth, but nothing comes out.

"Triana?" He shakes my shoulders, but his face swims in and out of focus. "Ro! Get a MedChek!"

My legs tremble and disappear from beneath my body. I slide sideways, the walls swinging around me.

THIRTY-FIVE

I BLINK AT THE CEILING. This isn't my room—the light is all wrong. And this ceiling is blue not white. I turn my head. Vanti sits in a chair near the window, her beautiful green skirt filling the chair. The room is quiet, but the clink of glasses and chattering of people provides a soft layer of white noise.

"You should be at the wedding," I whisper.

Vanti's head snaps toward me, but I can't see her face with the evening light streaming in behind her. "How do you feel?"

I sit up. "I'm okay. What happened?"

"Food poisoning." She stands and moves closer. "Some of the desserts were literally poisoned. You happened to get one of them when you filched a snack. The MedChek recommended an antidote that put you right, though. Otherwise, you'd be at the clinic in a pod."

"Where's Ty?"

"I made him go down for the wedding." She shrugs. "It's his sister getting married."

"Did they throw out all the food?"

"Yeah. The girls were not happy. But we ordered a bunch of stuff from local restaurants. Hot wings and barbeque ribs. The twins were thrilled. Jie seemed pretty happy, too."

"What about the wedding cake?" In my mind, I can see the cupcakes orbiting their larger brothers.

"It seems to be okay. The bakers were able to provide vid of the bakery—no one came in or went out except them. And that Chef Pierre guy, but he didn't go anywhere near the cakes."

"So, it's safe to eat?"

"Probably not. We'll have someone test each piece as they cut it." She grins. "We're billing it all to Don Putin."

"He won't pay it."

"He will if we can catch his scumbag son." Her jaw tightens. "And we need to catch him. Having this hanging over your head every day is going to get old really fast."

"You're telling me." I flip back the covers and get out of bed. "Any chance I can get you to retrieve my gown?"

"It's in the bathroom." She points. "You feeling ready to party?"

"I don't know about partying, but I'm ready to go downstairs. Whose room is this?" I look at the dark walls, the Lether chair, and the heavy, old-fashioned books.

"It's Griz's. You collapsed, so he put you on the bed." She smirks. "Don't worry, I was here the whole time. Nothing untoward happened."

I roll my eyes. "I'm not worried about that." I move slowly because my head feels like it might crack open at any second.

"Are you in pain?" Vanti follows me to the bathroom.

"No, just not feeling particularly solid. I'll be right out." I slide the door shut and do my business. Then I shuck my clothing and step into the gold gown Hy-Mi sent for this event. It slides on, smooth and cool against my skin. The asymmetrical neckline frames my face, and the fabric fits snugly against my upper body. The full skirt flares out from my waist in a swirl of liquid gold. I slide on the matching sandals.

My hair is another matter. I stare in the mirror at my frizzy red corkscrews. "What am I supposed to do with this?" I wail.

Vanti knocks on the door. "You need some help?"

I fling the door open. "Why does your hair always look so fabulous, and mine is such a rat's nest?"

"Mine's naturally straight." She shrugs. "I would have killed for curls like these when I was a kid. Let me help." She sits me down in the Lether chair and starts to work.

"Something's been bothering me." I look back at her, but she grabs the top of my head and twists it forward. "I wasn't quite sure what, but it's just there—on the edge of my brain."

"Maybe if you don't think about it, it'll come clear." She wields her comb in silence for a few minutes.

"Ouch!"

"When's the last time you combed this mess?"

"This morning, believe it or not." I flick away a tear. "Ow! Watch it!"

"I'm watching. I'm always watching. It's what I do."

"Yeah, but you're not an aesthetician." Her words jiggle something in my brain. "Always watching—Bobby said he'll be watching! He's watching the wedding."

"He said something about your holo-ring, too, didn't he?" She yanks another strand of hair.

"Yeah." I flick my ring and start a diagnostic running. "But I don't think he can watch me through it. I mean, he could track me. But there's no way to—unless there's a routine that trips nearby cams and sends their signal to him? He made it sound more immediate than that."

"Done." Vanti steps back. "Not too shabby. Go take a look."

I hurry to the bathroom. She's combed out a few of my curls to make ringlets around my face. The rest have been pinned into an elaborate updo. She's tamed the frizz and threaded something through the hair—a narrow strand of fabric that matches my dress. Hy-Mi must have included it. I twist around, trying to see the back.

"Here, hold still." She flicks her holo-ring and takes a pic. "Here's the back."

I stare at the pic, not seeing her amazing creation. "Could he be using my ring to activate other people's cams?"

"Wouldn't he have to hack into everyone's ring to do that? Who else was at that ceremony? Wait, Griz was there, wasn't he?" She flicks the pic away and clicks on the communication icon.

I grab her hand. "Let's just talk to him. My hair looks fantastic. Thank you."

She smiles her tiny smile and heads for the door.

We pause at the top of the last flight of steps. The courtyard has been transformed. Tiny lights glint in nets strung across the open space, creating a flickering ceiling above the guests. The cakes float in the pavilion, lights glinting off the tiny sparkles. Smartly dressed people watch silently, all focused on a single spot.

Lili and Jie stand beside the small pond before a woman in a flowing white robe. Behind her, the tapestry I spotted in the cloister earlier forms a backdrop that looks like a fairy tale landscape. Lili's beautiful silver gown sparkles against the dark blue of her family's clothes. Ty, Brad, Ro, and Yuri tower over Serena, Angie, and the girls. Jie's family, dressed in black, provides a backdrop for his bright red suit.

The white-clad woman stretches her arms wide, and her voice rings out. "Is there anyone present who believes this joining to be unlawful or misjudged?" She stares around the room, eyes narrow in her dark face. "So be it! Jie, do you pledge to honor, love, and cherish Lili as your wife today and every day, for as long as you both shall live?"

"I do," Jie says, his voice strong and steady.

"And Lilian, do you pledge to honor, love, and cherish Jie as your husband today and every day for as long as you both shall live?"

"I do." Lili's voice squeaks a bit, and someone giggles. She grins. "Really, I do."

Everyone laughs.

As the minister launches into a lengthy dissertation on what "forever" means, my mind wanders. I let my gaze travel over the people assembled here, thinking about Bobby's threat. He could hurt me through so many of these people. Ty, obviously. Bobby wouldn't hesitate to take him down, given the chance. But the others mean something to me, too. Serena and Brad. Ro and Yuri. They're like family to me now. Aretha and Akiko are like those sisters you don't quite get along with. And Angie—she's the grandma I would pick for myself, if I could.

I frown. I don't know any of my grandparents. I've never met any of R'ger's family, and the Ice Dame sprang fully formed from the top of SK2, I think. But these people are what family is supposed to be. People who annoy the heck out of you, but you still want to spend time with them. I could happily watch their children grow up and grow old.

Which reminds me. Could Bobby be watching us right now? I pull up my hacker tools and scan the building. Vanti's friends didn't find anything, and I didn't notice any strange transmissions from outside. But maybe Bobby hadn't activated them yet. I turn slowly on my step, running my scanner across the rooms behind me. Around the balconies. Across the courtyard.

There.

"Vanti." I nudge her with my elbow and point my eyes at my holo, carefully held below the balustrade so the wedding guests won't notice. "What is that signal?"

Her eyebrows draw together. "I don't know. It's coming from over there." She juts her chin toward the wedding party.

"Who is that next to Serena? The blonde?" I hadn't noticed her a moment ago. "She's part of the family—she's wearing a blue—no way." I send a message to Angie.

The blonde woman glances over and gives a finger wave.

"That blonde is Angie," I tell Vanti.

The redhead laughs softly. "I knew she looked familiar. She's wearing one of my mods."

"This signal must be what the visual cortex emits." I nod at my holo.

Vanti frowns. "What are you using to read that? I didn't think my mods were detectable, but if you can see it... I need to rethink my undercover tactics."

"It's a program I wrote myself. I'm not sure anyone would think to scan for that frequency. There's nothing useful there. Usually." I swipe my hand across the courtyard, scanning the crowd. "See, nothing. Nothing. Nothing."

"There's something." Vanti points at another blip on the holo. A tall, round man dressed in white stands near the cakes. "That signal looks exactly like the one on Angie. Why would the baker wear a mod?"

"Because it isn't really the baker?" I suggest. "But who would it be?"

Our eyes meet. At the same time, we both whisper, "Bobby."

THIRTY-SIX

"Like the rings of Grissom," the minister intones, "so are these rings symbols of eternity!"

"Where did you get those mods?" I whisper as we slink down the stairs, trying not to attract any attention. Most of the crowd is focused on Lili and Jie, but Angie is peering our direction, her eyes bright.

"I have a supplier." Vanti slides a look in my direction.

"Is there a way to disrupt them? Other than finding the capsule and pressing it?" I reach the bottom of the stairs and try to melt away into the deserted cloister. Unfortunately, a table blocks my way. I stumble into a chair, and its metal feet grate loudly against the stone floor. "Zark."

Vanti pauses in the shadow behind the staircase and glares. She puts a finger to her lips. I raise my hands in a "not my fault" gesture.

We skirt the tables, staying to the edge of the cloister. As we cross by the lounge, a trio of drunk teens shushes each other. They stare at us, frozen in place, as if we'll only notice them if they move. "Take some Buzzkill," I hiss at them. Their eyes dart from me to each other and back to me, but none of them even breathe. I roll my eyes and ignore them.

We stop behind the pavilion that holds the cake. "If you touch the wearer, you can disrupt the field enough to see the person behind the mod. But you have to touch skin-to-skin. Good solid contact." She grabs my wrist to demonstrate. "It's better if your hand is damp."

My hands are sweating. "Not a problem. What if it isn't him?"

She shrugs. "Ask him out? Can you see him from here?"

I shake my head. Holding up my holo-ring, I scan again, but the signal doesn't come through the pavilion. "The grav-lifters on the cake might be interfering."

"Okay, you stay here. I'm going to confront him. Quietly." Vanti reaches into her low-cut neckline for a second. She pulls out a small packet and hands me a capsule. Then her face transforms into an unrecognizable woman. Brown hair, darker skin, brown eyes. Dark hair decorates her upper lip and a large mole pokes out of her chin.

I bite back a smile, wondering what my own mod looks like. "Very pretty. Will you be able to see through his mod if you're wearing one of your own?"

Her face goes blank. "I'm not sure. I guess if it doesn't work, I'll turn mine off long enough to check."

"Do you want me to help?" I don't want to go anywhere near Bobby Putin, and I'm nowhere near Vanti's level of skill, but he's escaped us before. I want him locked up and out of my life.

Vanti considers for a moment. It's so weird to see her expressions cross this unrecognizable face. Finally, she nods. "One on either side. We'll each grab his wrist. If it's him, I'll take him down. I've got my tranq ring." She waves her right hand, the heavy metal ring on her middle finger glinting in the light from the decorations. I know from past experience that it contains a fast-acting sedative and a sharp needle to deliver it. "Ready?" She raises a heavy eyebrow.

I nod. "Go."

We round opposite sides of the pavilion and sidle into the crowd. People glare as I worm my way around them. At the front of the gathering, the minister declares, "I now pronounce you wife and husband. Seal this vow with a kiss."

The crowd cheers. I duck under an arm and around a portly man in a tan suit. I look for Vanti's copper hair then remember she's in disguise. Hopefully, she's closing in from the other side. I find the baker, flick my scanner at him to be sure, then slink up behind him. A brunette squirms in on his other side. Vanti.

Music blares, and people start dancing, cheering, hugging, and singing. I don't recognize the song, but everyone else in this room does. Except the baker. He stands still. Alone.

I take a deep breath to steady my nerves and reach out. My hand slides around his wrist, clammy against his warm skin. The man turns, and I get a weird vision of Bobby Putin overlaid by Enzo the baker. I gasp.

His eyes widen "Annabelle, how nice to see you again." His usual top-lev accent holds a tinge of surprise.

"It's him!" I call out, but my voice is drowned by the music.

"Gwen!" Bobby barks. Seline appears beside him. "Take care of her."

Watson pauses for a second, as if she's not sure what to do. The second seems to stretch out for hours. Until it's broken by a missile in green.

Vanti slams into Watson, taking her to her knees before the peace-keeper realizes what's going on. "Triana, get away!" Vanti cries out. She yanks her hand away from Gwen's arm. A tiny bead of blood appears on the woman's bicep—Vanti used her tranq ring.

Bobby twists his arm out of my grasp and catches my own wrist in his iron grip. He spins me around in front of him in a gruesome mimic of the dancing all around us. Then he pulls me close with a choke hold around my neck. "Drop the tranq, Agent Fioravanti."

Vanti snarls. "Or what? You'll do something to Sera Morgan in a room full of witnesses? Not even your father could buy you out of that."

Bobby's arm tightens on my throat. Darkness tinges the edges of my vision. I've already been poisoned and shot at today. I really don't need to add oxygen deprivation to the list. The black closes in.

"Argh!" The arm around my neck tightens then loosens as Bobby swings around to confront another threat. A blonde woman in a midnight-blue dress swings a chair at him, but he jumps back.

"Angie! Get the avenger boys!" I cry.

Vanti leaps forward, but Bobby swats her out of the way like a fly. She sails into the crowd of dancers, taking two of them down as she falls. She's up again before they realize what happened, heading toward us. Wedding guests start noticing the turmoil, turning to watch.

Bobby's eyes swing from Vanti to Angie to the back exit. Fire sparks in my stomach—he didn't look at me. He doesn't consider me a threat! He's more worried about ninety-three-year-old Angie than me! How dare he?

I launch myself at Bobby, slamming my shoulder into his stomach. He folds with a loud "oof" and catapults backwards into the pavilion. I jerk away as his head connects with the largest cake in the center of the floating display. Thrown off its orbit, it slams into three others in a massive collision. Frosting explodes in every direction. The cupcakes, freed from their tethers, fly outward like water drops from a rock dropped into a puddle.

Guests scream as cake bombs slam into the crowd. Children cheer. Bobby lands flat on his back on the pavilion cushion. The last cake crashes onto his face.

"Nice work," Vanti says. She licks a bit of frosting off her finger. "Mmm. Lemon."

THIRTY-SEVEN

"ARE you sure you should be eating that?" I ask. "Could be poison."

"Not likely," she says, regretfully wiping her finger on Bobby's pant leg. "But you're right—better safe than sorry." She grabs Bobby's arm, slapping a wide metal cuff around his wrist. Where did she have that hidden? "Get up, Putin. You're under arrest."

The pile of cake shifts then falls away. Bobby sits up, his head and upper body plastered in frosting. Splotches of white cover the pavilion and most of the guests standing nearby.

I wipe a glob of white off my bare arm and look at my dress. A splatter of frosting covers most of my front. I stare at Vanti. Her emerald green dress is completely clean. Not a hint of cake.

"How did you do that?" I demand, gesturing at her clothing.

Her lips twitch. "Years of training?"

"Triana!" O'Neill pushes through the cake-splattered crowd. "What happened?" He does a double take. His mouth hangs open.

I smile. "We caught Bobby. And killed the cake." I peek guiltily over my shoulder toward Lili. She's hidden by the crowd.

He scoops a glob of frosting off my skirt. "It looks very dead. But tasty."

"Don't! That needs to be tested before anyone eats it."

"I don't think it's a problem." He sticks his finger in his mouth and nods toward the pavilion.

Bobby sits on the edge of the padded platform, his hands secured behind his back. Andron and Ferrigi stand on either side, weapons pointed his direction. Bobby ignores them, licking the frosting off his lips.

"He wouldn't be eating it if it were poisoned," O'Neill says.

"Are you sure? Maybe he's taken an antidote. Maybe he's decided suicide by poison cake is preferable to life in prison!" My voice gets higher with each word.

Vanti reappears with a boxy device in her hand. Using a serving spoon, she scoops some cake off the pavilion platform and dumps it into a little drawer in the front of the box. The screen lights up then turns green. "It's safe."

"Good thing—we would have had a hard time stopping the kids from eating it." Around us, a dozen children are dancing in the cake splatters, swiping globs of frosting off the tables and chairs. Most of it gets thrown, but a lot is getting eaten, too.

Splat! A cupcake slams into my chest. "Sorry!" a little voice calls. The horde of children swirls away. I peel the cake off my dress and sniff it. "Smells good."

"Children!" Akiko pushes through the crowd, stopping to stare in horror when she reaches us. "What happened?"

I duck my head. Akiko already hates me. Ruining her sister's wedding cake will just make it worse.

"An uninvited guest destroyed the cake." O'Neill points at Bobby. "Triana caught him. Don't worry, we're pressing charges."

Akiko stares at Bobby then looks at me. "Thank you, Triana." I'm not sure if she's being sincere or snide. She doesn't give me a chance to find out but sweeps all the children away. "I'll keep the guests away from here."

"How will she do that?" I ask.

O'Neill shrugs. "I've stopped asking how Akiko gets things done. She has a way."

"Hey, speaking of cake." I nibble on the cupcake. "What happened to Enzo and Seline?"

"Who?"

"The baker—the real guy." My eyes widen. "Or was it Bobby the whole time? Was he at the venue—" My throat tightens.

"Breathe," O'Neill whispers, rubbing my back. "He's right there with multiple weapons pointed at his head. He can't hurt you anymore."

"Are you sure? Did you check, Vanti? Turn off his mod. I want to see his face. His real face." I stare at the man sitting amid the cake.

Vanti holds up a hand. "I'll check." She pats Bobby down and removes something from his pocket. "Here's the mod." As she steps away from him, the Enzo face morphs into Bobby's perfectly sculpted features.

He smiles gently at me. "I'll always be here for you, Annabelle."

I grind my teeth. "No, you won't. You'll be in Attica. Locked away in a tiny box, and I will personally make sure you have no access to the outside, no fancy furnishings, no body-doubles."

O'Neill snaps into action. "Vanti, take him to the Peacekeeper lockup. Andron and Ferrigi, go with her. I want one of you with eyes on him around the clock until he can be moved back to Attica. No chance for his accomplices to help him escape. And make sure they pick up Gwen—and that they still have al-Petrosian."

Vanti flips a little salute at O'Neill and nods to the two men. "Let's get him downtown. Griz, can we borrow a carriage?"

"Sure. It's still in Putin's warehouse, as far as I know." He flicks his holo-ring. "Let me recall it."

Andron and Ferrigi grab Bobby's arms and haul him to his feet. They get plastered in frosting in the process, leaving all three men covered in sticky goo. Vanti looks down at her pristine green dress. "Can I take separate transport? Those two can handle him."

O'Neill laughs. "Sure. Just keep their carriage in sight." He flicks a code to her.

The two men drag Bobby away, managing to get frosting on everything they pass. Vanti follows behind, a weapon in each hand. They disappear into the tunnel leading to the garage. Two cleaning bots trundle out of a hatch nearby.

"Let's let the bots take care of the mess, shall we?" He takes my elbow and turns me away from the pavilion. "Do you want to change?"

"I'm not sure I have another appropriate outfit."

"Anything not covered in frosting will work." O'Neill laughs.

"I have something," Akiko says, appearing again. "Come with me." She takes my other arm and pulls me away from O'Neill. "We'll be back down in a few minutes."

Akiko leads me to a room on the second floor at the back of the house. "Where are you taking me?"

"This is my old room," Akiko says as she shuts the door. "Look, I want to apologize for my behavior. Again. I've been horrible to you, and you've done nothing to deserve that. Let me make it up to you. I know I'm a lot shorter than you, but I have a beautiful outfit that will fit you perfectly."

She opens a cupboard and pulls out a length of flowing cloth. "Blas gave me this years ago. His sister helped him pick it out. It's way too long for me and not a good color. He bought me another one, but he told me to keep this one, too." She leans in and lowers her voice. "He said it was custom, but I think his sister had it made to her measurements. She's a lot taller than me."

She opens the window shutters as I shimmy out of my cake-covered gown. I love that gold dress when it's not plastered in vanilla frosting. I hope it survives the cleaning to be worn again. A soft, warm breeze flows through the room, bringing the scent of the flowering vines hanging around her window.

Akiko throws the fabric over my head and has me turn so she can wrap it around me. The silky stuff slides, cool and smooth, against my skin. The subtle flower pattern shimmers in the light. Akiko pushes me in front of the full-length mirror. The pale flowers complement my skin tone, and the flowing wrap of the dress enhances my figure. My hair has miraculously remained frosting-free.

"You look—"

Ka-boom!

A brilliant flash of light blinds us, and heat rushes through the window. I shove Akiko down, and we crouch on the floor in terror.

The light subsides, and the heat drains away. I straighten and hurry to the window. The vines outside have been singed to a crisp. A billow of acrid smoke wafts upward. Below, a glowing pile of molten slag softens the plascrete.

"Vanti!" I cry. We race out of the room.

"This way," Akiko cries. She leads me down some back stairs I didn't know existed. The door at the bottom jams. I throw myself against it, and it flies open. Akiko and I end up in a pile on the garage floor. I scramble to my feet and race for the open vehicle-sized door.

"Stop!" Vanti flings out her arm, stopping me in my tracks.

"You're alive!" I throw my arms around her. She hugs me back for a brief instant then breaks away.

"Andron and Ferrigi put Putin in there." The words come out in a whisper.

"Were they inside?" My voice cracks.

"No." She nods to the shadows beside the building. It's hard to see in the dim light of the melting carriage, but it looks like medics are working on two men lying on the plascrete. "He pulled the door shut before they could get in—I think he was trying to get away. The thing started to move, and then it went up. He must have rigged it to blow."

"But it got here without exploding," I protest.

"Maybe it was set to go up when passengers were inside." Her voice is strained.

"Are you saying he saved their lives?" I ask.

"It seems hard to believe, doesn't it?"

"Could he have snuck out the other side?" Saving anyone at his own expense is completely out of character for Bobby. He had no sense of self-sacrifice.

"We'll do a DNA check to be sure, but I saw him get in." Her head droops.

I put an arm around her and turn to lead her back inside. From the corner of my eye, I catch movement. The wind whips the melted slag, causing a flare-up. The red light of the fire snags on blonde hair, lifted by the same breeze. "Look! Seline." I point. "I mean Gwen Watson. I think. How did—"

Vanti takes off. She seems to fly through the air, crashing into Watson like a battering ram. The two women smash into the thick vine stems at the base of the building. They disappear behind a screen of leaves that somehow survived the explosion. The vines rattle and shake, huge blackened lengths falling from higher up the wall. Piles of ash and scorched plant rain down onto the plascrete.

The shaking stops. Vanti reappears, dragging Watson with her. Her face and hair have returned to normal, but her white chef's coat is covered in ash and charcoal. It's hard to tell in the moonlight, but Vanti's dress appears unscathed.

"You did it, didn't you?" Vanti asks Watson, but her voice is gentle.

"He deserved it." Watson spits the words.

"He did." Vanti clasps a cuff around Watson's arm. "It's still murder."

"I don't care." Watson glares at me as they pass. "It needed to be done. You should thank me. He would never have left you alone."

A shiver runs down my spine. She's right. He would have haunted me till his dying day. I guess he did.

"It's over." O'Neill appears beside me. "For real this time."

"What about Ferrigi and Andron?" The medics are loading them into portable med pods.

"They'll be okay. The lead medic says they were burned, but nothing the med pod can't handle. They were lucky we had medics on call. Vanti will take Watson to the Peacekeepers."

"What's going to happen to her?" I ask as we walk back into the house.

"That's up to them to decide. I suspect they'll be lenient."

We enter the courtyard. It's a disaster of exploded cake, rioting children, and outraged guests. "Your sister is probably a little upset."

O'Neill laughs. "She barely noticed the furor. She wasn't thrilled about the cake, but we can get a new one. Mom has already decided to hold another party when they get back from their honeymoon."

"Where are they going?"

"A Pleiades cruise to Sally Ride, of course." He laughs at my expression. "They depart on the CSS Caledonia in the morning."

"Is Joan still on that ship?" I pick up a cupcake that miraculously survived the dessert debacle. The delicate design is still perfect. I leave it on a table for someone else. I can't stomach wedding cake right now.

"She is. If the newlyweds ever emerge from their cabin, you can be sure they'll be dancing in the stars." He grins.

THIRTY-EIGHT

Two weeks later, Lili and Jie return from their cruise. Serena pulls out all the stops to plan another, better party. She convinces Chef Pierre to design a new cake, and the real Enzo arrives to set it up. He looks just like the Bobby Putin mod but says he was never in this house before.

"But what about the Winter Palace? I met you there when you were setting up."

"Wasn't me. My assistant, Seline, set up the cake."

"Seline? Was she a new assistant?" Is there really a Seline or just Gwen pretending to be her?

"Fairly new." He arranges the cake. This one is multi-colored and not floating. Plus, there's a whole layer of chocolate, so it gets my vote for best post-wedding cake ever. "She disappeared that night. Never saw her again." He gives me a "go away and let me get my work done" grimace, so I leave him in peace.

Seline disappeared because she didn't really exist. She was a role played by Gwen, whose only purpose was to get access to the O'Neill family during the wedding. Gwen was tried for manslaughter and sentenced to a mental health clinic to work out her problems. She'll never work as a peacekeeper again, but she won't have a record after she completes her therapy. Kate argued on her behalf, and the fact that the only person she killed was Bobby helped.

Andron and Ferrigi are back on duty, but with Bobby out of the picture, it's not much work. Vanti and O'Neill provide plenty of security here in the house. The avenger boys go along when we go out, but we've spent most of the time at home. Yesterday, Angie dragged them out dancing with her ancient girlfriends.

"Who would have thought they'd enjoy line dancing in the afternoon with a bunch of old ladies?" I laugh as we rest in the courtyard before the party.

This morning, we moved the lounge furniture to other rooms. Now, a team is setting up a dance floor, with chairs and tiny tables around the outside edge. A small band will arrive in an hour to take the stage in the corner.

The nets of tiny lights are up again, with more twining around the tall palm trees. Tables and chairs fill the cloister under the balconies. The small space where the wedding took place has been filled with new plants and small benches.

O'Neill tips back his drink. "I'm going to grab a shower and get dressed. I'll see you in a bit." He kisses my forehead and disappears up the stairs.

Vanti's eyes narrow as she watches him climb. "He's up to something."

"Why do you think that?" I stand to take our glasses back to the AutoKich'n.

She follows me. "I don't know. He just feels different today."

"I hadn't noticed," I say. But now that she mentions it, maybe he is up to something. He's been a bit distracted.

"Speaking of distracted, I've been meaning to ask you." I stop at the top of the steps.

"What?"

"Why did Ty recover from that drug so fast? In the warehouse?"

Vanti raises her eyebrows. "Good question. Same reason Gwen recovered so fast when I tranqed her at the wedding, I suspect. She should have been out for hours. But apparently, some people here on Grissom are less susceptible to those drugs. It's a weird mutation seen only in families that have lived here many generations. It's not well-known, but once the docs at Gwen's hospital told me about it, I started doing some research. Now I need to come up with another foolproof weapon."

I shake my head. "New weapons, new disguises. You're going to be busy. But I'm sure you'll figure one out."

———

LILI AND JIE come downstairs just before the party starts, and the family has a quiet toast to their new marriage. Serena has the twins pour sparkling wine for each of us.

"I think I'll get my own." I hold up a hand when Ro offers me a glass.

He laughs. "It's safe, I promise. We only do that the first time."

I take a glass, and he hands the last one to Vanti. She's stunning again in her green dress. She stands beside me, looking more relaxed than I've ever seen her. Ro puts his tray aside and slides an arm around her waist.

"When did that happen?" I ask O'Neill.

He looks at his brother and his former partner and shrugs. "They've been flirting since she got here."

"Really? Vanti flirts?" I glance at the two of them making eyes at each other. I guess she does. How did I miss that?

Brad raises his glass. "To my beautiful daughter and our new son. May you live a long and happy life together."

We all drink and applaud.

Then Serena steps forward. "Okay, O'Neill crew, I'm laying down the law this time." She pins a look on Ro then Yuri. "No spiking the drinks." Her gaze turns to Akiko and Blas. "No cake fights for the children."

"Hey, that wasn't my fault!" Akiko says, but Blas quiets her.

Serena looks at me and Ty and starts ticking things off on her fingers. "No exploding cakes, no serial killers dressed as bakers, no melting carriages."

Ty holds up his hands, the wine glass sloshing with the movement. "No promises."

The family laughs. Serena grins. The door chime interrupts her speech. "Fine. Just make sure everyone has fun."

"This was lovely," I say, resting my cheek against Ty's shoulder. We sway in time to the music, putting all those dance lessons on the *Morningstar* to good use.

Sliding seamlessly into double time, he swings me around the edge of the floor and out into the courtyard. We dance through the flower-scented air, the moonlight making soft shadows through the trees. The stars glitter overhead, with the slash of the rings cutting across the corner of the sky. Other couples hide in the various alcoves—how did I not notice before that this courtyard is built for make-out sessions?

He stops behind the pavilion, tucked between the wall and a tree. "Maybe we can do that someday?"

"What, go on a cruise and have a party?"

"Well, I meant the part before that." He smiles.

I stare up at him. "Did you just ask me to marry you?" I try for humor, but my voice cracks a little. "Aren't you supposed to get down on one knee and hire a flash mob?"

"It's too dark for skywriters, and I thought about fireworks, but we've had enough explosions lately. But I can do this." He gets down on one knee and holds something out. Moonlight sparkles on the tiny diamonds surrounding a sapphire. "Triana Annabelle Morgan Moore, will you marry me?"

Even though I'm not too surprised, my breath catches in my throat. Like all the ridiculous women in vids on *Ancient Tēvē*, tears come to my eyes, and my hand goes to my mouth. "Yes, of course I will!"

He slides the ring on my finger. Or at least, he tries. It gets stuck on the middle knuckle.

"Wait, let me do it." I move his hand out of the way and try to jam the thing on my finger.

"That should fit perfectly," he says as he gets to his feet. "I had Kara measure a ring in your jewelry box."

I stop with the ring half-way on. "A gold ring with a green stone?" It has to be that one—it's the only ring in there.

"I guess." He waits, raising an eyebrow.

"That's a ring my friend Jared and I found on the beach when we were seven or eight years old. When no one claimed it, Hy-Mi had it sized so I could wear it."

We stare at my hand.

"How about this?" I pull it off my ring finger and slide it onto the pinky. "For now. We can get it sized later."

"Deal." He pulls me close and kisses me. The fireworks he didn't buy explode behind my closed eyelids.

When we come up for air, I look at the beautiful ring. "I want to get you one, too."

"I'll take you to see the jeweler who made this one. He specializes in one-of-a-kind pieces. But I'm sure he can make us a matched set."

"The rings of Grissom," I say with a laugh.

"Exactly." And he seals it with a kiss.

THANKS FOR READING! If you enjoyed this story, you can read more about Triana, O'Neill, and Vanti in *Planetary Spin Cycle*.

AUTHOR'S NOTE

December 2020

It's New Year's Eve eve as I write this. We don't have big plans for tomorrow night, because no one does this year. Plus, we rarely even stay awake until midnight, much less party. How things change as we get older!

If you'd like to know when my next book comes out, sign up for my newsletter at my website: juliahuni.com.

I want to thank everyone who made this book possible, starting with my amazing Kickstarter Backers. I launched a Kickstarter campaign in October to help fund the audiobooks of the Space Janitor series. Nearly a hundred backers chipped in, including:

Alex McGilvery, Alice Bell, Al Lee, Anne K., Annie Jenkins, Barb Collishaw, Brian Chee, Bridget Horn, C.A. Rowland, Carl Kerschner, Christian Meyer, Chrissy Chronert, Colin Jenkins, Craig A. Price Jr., Danny Shaw, David Kidd, Dean Wesley Smith, Deanna Stanley, Diana Rehfield, Duane Eisele, Eidolon, Emma Allen-Goss, Eron Wyngarde, Faith Hakimian, Gary Olsen, Goldeen Ogawa, Ian Bannon aka Joe Cool, Dr. Jim Caplan, James Gotaas, James Parks, Jane, "JustJeff" Omodt, Jennifer Heiden, Jennifer L., Jennifer Fah-Vayhinger, Joel Thorne, Johanna Rothman, John Lagerquist, John Lamar, John Jutoy, Joshua Dean Hackworth, Karl Hakimian, Katherine Gordon, Kelli King, Krystal Bohannan, Lawrence M. Schoen, Lydia T., Mai Miller, Marcel de Jong, Marcus Alexander Hart, Melissa Bernhard, Melissa Cheu, Michele Kinsey Roszell, Paul Hathcox, Paul Parker, Rob Crosby, Robert Battle, Robert Parker, Ross Bernheim, Royd Warren, S. Busby, Sam Backus, Sam Wright, SciFi Cadre, Shadowfall, Spanielhill, Stacy Shuda, Stephen Ballentine, Steve

Huth, Steven Bolbot, Tami Veldura, Ted Young, Thomas Cook, Tricia Babinski, Valerie Fetsch, Vic Tapscott and several anonymous readers.

Without them, this book would literally not have been written.

Thanks to my sprint team: A.M. Scott, Hillary Avis, Paula Lester, Kate Pickford, Alison Kervin, and Tony James Slater. They keep me working when I really don't want to.

Thanks to Paula at Polaris Editing for the editing. Any mistakes you find, I probably added after she was done! And thanks to Les at German Creative for the beautiful cover.

Thank you for reading and enjoying Triana's story. I don't know when she'll be back, but she will be. She keeps popping up when I sit at the keyboard.

I hope you find all the things you're looking for in 2021.

And of course, thanks to the Big Dude for making all things possible.

ALSO BY JULIA HUNI

Colonial Explorer Corps Series:

The Earth Concurrence

The Grissom Contention

The Saha Declination

Colonial Explorer Corps (books 1-3)

Recycled World Series:

Recycled World

Reduced World

Space Janitor Series:

The Vacuum of Space

The Dust of Kaku

The Trouble with Tinsel

Orbital Operations

Glitter in the Stars

Sweeping S'Ride

Triana Moore, Space Janitor (the complete series)

Tales of a Former Space Janitor

The Rings of Grissom

Planetary Spin Cycle

Waxing the Moon of Lewei

The Phoenix and Katie Li

Luna City Limited

Krimson Empire (with Craig Martelle):

Milton Keynes UK
Ingram Content Group UK Ltd.
UKHW010643290424
441924UK00006B/501